Woman of Clay

LINDA CADDICK

You, LORD, are our Father.
We are the clay, you are the potter;
we are all the work of your hand.
ISAIAH 64:8

Copyright © December 2012 Linda Caddick
All rights reserved.
ISBN-13: 978-1481233057

To my husband,
who has granted me
the freedom to be myself.

ACKNOWLEDGMENTS

Thank you to my daughter, Ashleigh,
whose wonderful gift of encouragement
provided the wind in my sails
to see this project through,
and to my son, Raymond,
for lending a discerning ear.

AUTHOR'S NOTE

There is very little evidence other than what we can glean from the Bible, of ancient customs and daily life in the time of Jesus, and enormous differences of opinion on the subject. For example, many sources of information present women as being virtual prisoners of their homes, but the Bible suggests a far freer lifestyle – women travelling, trading, making decisions, interacting socially, and some of them were educated. Mary the mother of Jesus, as a young unmarried girl, travelled of her own volition the considerable distance from Nazareth to the Judean hill country. There is no mention of an escort, though undoubtedly she would have travelled with a caravan. Also, archaeological finds do not support the view that there was a separate partition for women in the synagogues.

Were betrothed couples forbidden to see one another during the year before marriage, as many scholars believe? Perhaps, but it makes more sense that the period of betrothal (especially as an analogy of Christ and his Bride) would have included developing emotional bonds with the spouse-to-be in preparation for marriage.

FACT or FICTION?

The narrative weaves in and out of biblically recorded events, not necessarily in chronological order, and is intended to reflect the essence of what the Bible teaches. Some of the characters are drawn directly from the Bible, and others are entirely fictitious. In order to clarify the difference between fact and fiction, notes are included at the end of the book detailing supporting scriptures for each chapter.

CHAPTER 1

"SHUSHANA, Rafael is here!"

Milcah's delighted voice interrupted Shana's quiet reverie in the back room, where she was absently flicking a broom over the mud floor of their tiny stone-walled home. The girl ducked into the bedchamber to give herself time to recover from the jolt of shock that tingled through her body. Her mother gushed on, hardly giving Rafael a chance to speak.

"What a wonderful surprise! It's been such a long time. You must have completed your training by now."

"Yes, I can qualify as a leatherworker at last," came the resonant voice, "though I do still need a lot of practice."

"Come in, come in, my boy –er you look so . . . so grown up, I suppose I really can't call you a boy any longer."

Hearing Rafael's familiar laugh triggered a rush of gladness. Shana came out of the bed chamber, still holding onto the broom to steady her nerves, and gaped at his tall figure filling the doorframe. He certainly had changed in the two years he'd been away in Jerusalem; his shoulders strained at the seams of his robe and a dense beard had replaced the soft fluff she used to tease him about.

He smiled at her, inclining his head in a slight bow. "Shalom."

Shana was speechless. Who was this man?

"I've brought you all some gifts," he said, reaching into a bag. He drew out a leather article which he held out to Shana's mother with abashed pride. "Milcah, this is for you and Hassin, my first attempt at crafting a wineskin. It took a while to get the stitching right."

Milcah took the gift and stroked the soft leather with a crooked finger, her face alight with pleasure.

"Here, Shana, I made this for you. Don't look too closely at the handiwork." It was a drawstring bag with a delicate pattern carved around the edge.

"It's beautiful," breathed Shana. "Thank you so—"

"And for Beth, there is a little purse. Where is she?"

A young girl came tearing in from outside, a deluge of titian hair swamping her small figure. She flung her arms around Rafael's waist, panting and spilling over with excited exclamations.

"Well, I'm not the only one who has grown up," said Rafael, extricating himself and patting Beth's cheek fondly.

"Tell us all about Jerusalem," said Beth, tugging on his sleeve. Shana and Milcah spoke at the same time, "How—how was your apprenticeship?" Milcah motioned him towards a stool. "Do come and sit down, my er—"

"Boy will do," said Rafael, and they all laughed.

His voice was deeper too, and there was something else

which Shana couldn't quite define, a new assurance in his manner. While Beth was engaging most of his attention, Shana observed him discreetly. Now and again, he smiled across at her as if to say he would catch up with her later, once Beth's effervescence had subsided. She hoped her ridiculous shyness did not show.

"Well, I'd better be going; I need to help my father with the sheep," said Rafael eventually, unfolding his lithe body and standing up, tall and gracious. "I'll come and greet Hassin tomorrow evening."

"And stay for supper?" asked Milcah.

"I would be honoured."

It was hard to believe, seeing him like this, that he was the same person Shana had known so well as a lad in the days when they used to skip to synagogue together, with their parents following in cheery conversation. He was the only son of her father's friend, the sheep farmer, and they had been like brother and sister. Beth had been too young for their games, and they would chase one another through the fields of wheat and hide among the fragrant stalks. She could still remember when Rafael picked off an ear of wheat to present to her with a mock bow, and she had tickled him under his chin with its spiky fronds, breaking into torrents of excited giggles, until he snatched it from her and pushed it down the back of her tunic. He had been her closest friend for many years.

Then almost overnight, Rafael had withdrawn and begun to seek the company of a crowd of boys from the village. Shana had been puzzled and hurt, but before long she too had joined a group of leggy, reed-like girls, awkwardly graceful in their sashed robes and beautiful sandaled feet. The girls would converse in secretive tones interspersed with muffled giggles, throwing quick glances over their shoulders in a constant vigil of the effect they might be having on the boys, who barely noticed them at all. But, one by one, it was as though the boys' eyes began to open and they found themselves drawn magnetically to these mysterious creatures who flitted across their paths with slender swaying hips – more demure now, and taking their turn to apparently ignore the boys.

After that, Sabbath visits to the synagogue were anticipated with an undercurrent of excitement. The small, simple room with benches on either side became charged with a tangible energy, and the rabbi's wise words fell largely unheeded into the gap separating the two opposite rows of worshippers. The boys stared blatantly across the chasm, seeking out the objects of their affection, and the girls peeked from beneath their lashes with heads lowered and the folds of their head-dresses concealing their blushing cheeks. If their mothers were aware of this silent communication, they did not show it. These flirtations were generally quite harmless since most of them would eventually settle down with a spouse of their parents' choice.

With a stab of private embarrassment, Shana recalled the moment when, deep in a daydream and staring blankly across the synagogue hall, she had unexpectedly caught Rafael's eyes upon her. They had both looked away hurriedly, and she had felt vaguely disturbed, but dismissed it from her mind.

Their fathers often used to meet to discuss business propositions, and Shana's father made it clear from the start that it was his intention she marry Rafael and thereby cement the business partnership. Shana always balked at the idea, negating any allusion to it as pointedly as she dared, which her father ignored with a warning frown. She was glad when Rafael went away to Jerusalem to train as a leatherworker, for she had no intention of complying with her father's wishes.

But now that he was back again, she realised she had missed him and hoped they could resume their friendship, never suspecting that his return was about to precipitate a head-on conflict with her father.

Once she had adjusted to the changes in him and returned to the easy familiarity they had always shared, Shana began to look forward to his frequent visits to the family. Other than her best friend Kyla, she did not have many friends in the small community, partly because she enjoyed much solitude, but also because she had never quite fitted in with the village girls. During her childhood she had preferred the company of boys, priding herself on being included in their rough games, so it was perfectly natural for her to maintain this friendship with Rafael.

He spoiled everything one day, when he paid a visit to her father to request his permission to marry her, and her father confronted her with his wish for her acceptance.

"I could never marry him, Father, we're like brother and sister," she protested, knowing she was treading close to the line of disobedience. A purple stain rose slowly up Hassin's neck, and Shana felt the flow of sweat down her sides.

"Don't be silly, child," her mother scolded. "Rafael is a fine young man and will make a wonderful husband for you, and father for your children."

Shana's stomach contracted; it was unthinkable! She stamped her foot. "No, no, I cannot, I will not! I do not love him and I do not want to be married yet. I haven't even lived–"

Her father's face darkened, swelling like a cobra as he

fixed a cold reptilian gaze upon her. Her eyes remained steady on his, though her body quaked beneath her robe, for she was daring for the first time to challenge his authority. She knew he had the power either to insist on her agreement or to cast her out of the family, but either way his rage would strike.

Her mother saw the danger and quickly intervened. "Go outside now, girl. Go to the well and fetch some water for the cooking, and search your heart on the way, for you need to repent of your behaviour. In time you will grow used to the idea and come to see that your father is absolutely right in his wise choice of a husband for you."

Shana fled, thankful to be granted a reprieve while her father assimilated the shock of her defiance. She sprinted down the road between the two fields belonging to the family and took the track that edged the hillside, her bare feet impervious to the hard stones. At a safe distance from the village, she stumbled onto the dust beside the path, forcing breath into her constricted lungs. Everything within her shouted "No!" She could not bear to throw her life away before it had yet begun, and the thought of staying forever trapped in the diminutive little village of Halhul, high up in the Judean mountains so far from where real life happened, brought on a sense of panic. She loved Rafael well enough, but not in that way. To her, he was merely a grown-up boy, she knew him too well. In her dreams she wanted to marry a man – someone like . . . like her older cousin, Haziel, whom she had admired since she was a little girl.

She remained exiled till the soft night fell, bringing with it a deep yearning that issued from her centre and reached out longingly towards the stars. She knew she had reached a crossroad, and without any doubt it was the path leading to the unknown that called the loudest.

After a while, the insistent screech of crickets urged her homewards; she could not defer her father's wrath forever. At the corner of the house, her steps froze. She listened for her father's voice but heard only her mother's desultory comments to Beth above the rattle of dishes. Creeping closer, she could see him sitting cross-legged on a cushion at the low table, leaning back against the wall, with his short fingers clasped together on his protruding belly. Yellow light from a small oil lamp on a shelf pooled on the glistening bulges of his cheeks and lower lip, blacking out his eyes and outlining the ugly twist of his mouth. Thankfully he had already eaten, for his bowl was pushed aside.

Trembling, she crept into the room, staying near the door in case his temper erupted in violence. He neither looked at her nor acknowledged her. She glanced at her mother for guidance, and Milcah motioned her to sit down in the small alcove that led off the main room, where she and Beth shared a mattress. She placed a bowl in her lap. "Here, eat your food, my girl, and get to bed. We've much to discuss in the morning."

Later, when it seemed that the immediate danger had passed, Shana prepared for bed and lay rigid next to Beth, staring up at the reed ceiling.

"Why, why don't you want to marry Rafael?" Beth kept asking, finding it incomprehensible that her older sister would turn down the opportunity for a dream wedding. Rafael was Beth's hero, and she had always been entranced with the idea of marriage.

"It's not that simple. You wouldn't understand," Shana replied.

"Please, marry him, please. Then I will have the big

brother I've always wanted. It will be so—"

"Go to sleep, Beth. It's bad enough Father trying to make me."

In the morning, Hassin had already gone out to the fields when Shana arose. Her mother said nothing as she set about preparing breakfast, except to instruct Shana about the usual chores. After they had eaten, she sent Beth out to play with her friends and took Shana to the bench at the back of the house.

"Your strange attitude about this matter is a deep disappointment to your father, not to mention how that poor boy would feel. I understand you might have been a little startled at first, but no doubt you have had a chance to think it over by now."

"Yes, Mother, I have thought about it very carefully."

Milcah looked at her expectantly.

"I will not marry Rafael."

Milcah let out her breath in a deep sigh and looked away. "Do you have someone else in mind?"

"No."

She searched Shana's face incredulously. "Then why?"

"Please don't let Father make me."

"I don't understand."

"I'm sorry, Mama." Shana stared down at her clenched fists in her lap, her mouth set. How could she explain to her mother the strong desires that boiled inside her, the urgent questing for something she herself did not understand, something more than the life she knew.

After a long silence, Milcah said, "Rafael is going to be heart-broken."

"There are plenty of other girls in the village, and he can

still have me as his friend."

Milcah sighed vocally and laid her hand heavily over Shana's, and then rose and retied the strings of her apron around her plump waist as though girding herself up for a difficult task. "I will have to explain the best I can to your father. He'll not try to force you, though it won't improve matters between you. Anyone would have thought you'd be glad to get away and start your own home. Nor would Rafael take you against your will. Oh, I am so sorry; I love that boy." A little sob escaped her as she quickly walked away, and Shana's frigid heart sorrowed for her.

After that, there was a hostile silence in the house when her father was around. Whatever her mother had said to him had held off any immediate repercussions to her resisting his will, but Shana felt constantly on edge, knowing his resentment towards her was continually fermenting and terribly afraid of its eruption.

Rafael stopped coming around. Shana was angry with him; he should not allow such a thing to destroy their friendship. Then one day he came to the house to say goodbye. He was going away for another year to study the Torah under the Pharisees in a remote place where his uncle lived.

At first it was a relief, but after he had left, Shana felt unexpectedly bereft. The insidious restlessness that had already asserted itself, now crept into her bones. She went about her daily duties – fetching water, grinding grain for bread, laying wood for the fire, tending the small flock of sheep – but the days became ever more mundane and meaningless. The atmosphere in the house remained heavy and threatening. She knew her father had cut her out of his heart, however small a part of it she had previously been apportioned. She had defied him, and he would not forgive her.

"What was it like, Mama, to marry a man you hardly knew?" asked Shana one day while they were scrubbing clothes at the stream.

"What do you mean?"

"Well – you know – weren't you afraid that you would not like him?"

Milcah put down the dripping linen and sat down on a rock. "It was never a question of whether you liked your husband or not," she said. "Your duty was to love him, that was all. And this you learned to do in time."

"But–but were you happy?"

Milcah smiled fondly at her daughter. "Happy? Of course I was happy, especially when you came along."

Shana was often left puzzling about whether women in those days experienced things differently, or whether her mother was just not telling. Great gulfs seemed to separate them when it came to sharing matters of the heart.

Shana's general dissatisfaction manifested as extreme irritation over every little thing. If a piece of wood dropped out of the bundle she had collected, or the bucket tipped over while she was milking the goat, rage would rip through her, out of all proportion to the incident that provoked it. The noise of her father's snoring at night in the adjacent room wound her up so tightly she thought she would explode; even her sister's incessant questioning drove her mad. She felt like a caged bird desperate for the open skies.

One day, Shana's frustration ignited a spark of her father's anger, which erupted with frightening intensity. She had dared to defend herself against an unjust accusation, and he became apoplectic, bellowing like an enraged bull and throwing furniture at the walls. Before she knew it, he had her arm in a painful grip and hurled her out of the house, telling her to go to the devil. He refused to let her return for three days. She slept outside at the back of the house like a dog, with only her cloak for cover and the food Beth smuggled her to eat. She could hear her mother and sister inside, pleading on her behalf, and her father's hateful responses, which hurt even more than her humiliation. It was only when she sacrificed her dignity and begged his forgiveness that she was permitted, begrudgingly, to re-join the family.

After a few more uneasy weeks, Milcah, with judicious insight, came to her rescue in an unexpected way. "Shushana, your Aunt Ada has sent word that she would like you to go and help your cousin Haziel and his wife with their textile business. The market has opened up in Damascus, which is a good opportunity for them but Judith is struggling to keep up with the weaving and needs help with dying the wool and household chores. Ada is getting too old to do the heavy work now."

Shana's heart fluttered wildly against its cage; how exciting it would be to live near Jerusalem, the city she loved more than any other, and what a relief to be able to escape from her father.

"When can I go, Mama?" she cried, the colour already returning to her cheeks. "Does . . . does Father know?"

"Of course he does. He thinks it a good idea. He's still hoping that you just need some time to grow up a bit and then you will change your mind about Rafael. Perhaps you will amend your wilful ways under your aunt's watchful eye. You must go as soon as the next caravan leaves tomorrow morning. I'll go down to the marketplace to arrange for a donkey. You can start getting ready."

As soon as her mother left, Shana ran out of the house in a fit of euphoria. She raced down the track through the forest and out into the meadows beyond, her feet as light and swift as a filly's. The long grass parted before her, and the wind rushing through her hair seemed to lift her into the sky until she flew like a bird released. When she could run no more, she flung herself down on her back and let the months of pent up emotion flood out on her panting breath, until she felt herself floating upwards into the blue expanse and dancing amid the clouds.

Her father's farewell was cold, briefly quenching her excitement. Beth clung to her beloved sister and cried, begging her to come back soon. Her mother held her for a long time and then, dabbing the corner of her eye with her sleeve, she helped her daughter onto the little hired donkey with her bag already tethered to its side.

The caravan was fairly large, having started off earlier from Hebron. Most of the women and children travelled behind the men, and another group of older men took up the rear. It was Shana's first adventure by herself; how eager she was to grasp every moment of it and make it her own. Sixteen and still unmarried by her own defiant choice, it was none too soon to leave her father's house and set out to discover whatever the world had to offer.

The mountains shone in the morning sunlight with a vibrancy she had never seen before. After passing the barley fields and travelling through some rocky pastureland, the village disappeared from view, and then the landscape became increasingly dry as they made the long winding descent into the valley. The heat intensified as the day progressed, and Shana drank sparingly from her skin of water to make it last. Too distracted to join in the chatter around her, she became mesmerised by the rhythmic swaying of the donkey and the road moving beneath until eventually her eyelids grew heavy and she drifted into short spells of sleep, waking with a start each time she felt herself slipping.

At midday, they stopped in the shade of some bushes to rest the animals and eat lunch. The leather pouch Rafael had given her contained a ration of bread and fruit, which she ate with enjoyment. Afterwards the children slept on the sand while their mothers dozed, and the men sat around in groups, the drone of their conversation pleasantly reassuring.

Towards nightfall, a sense of anticipation rippled through the travellers and their voices grew animated. This was the moment Shana had been waiting for – the first glimpse of the city. A majestic mass of buildings rose up on a hill, shining gold in the low rays of the setting sun. Jerusalem! The very name stirred every one of Shana's senses. Jerusalem – the beautiful city of David, the ultimate prize of warring kings, the joy of the whole earth.

Her tired little donkey stumbled, almost tipping her onto the stony road, so she dismounted to lead him awhile. They passed through a ravine, with the walled city looming above them like a fortress. A final ascent, and then through the arched gate and they were instantly transported into another world – noisy, bustling crowds quickened by a mutual energy, towering buildings, a confusion of narrow streets. Voices shouted across the moving throng and a child began to cry.

They halted at the main market square. An uncomfortable nervousness quivered in Shana's belly. Everyone around her seemed so purposeful, so confidently familiar with the procedures as they tethered their donkeys and began to untie their bags, calling out cheerful comments to one another over the heaps of luggage, while their children gaped through veils of sleep.

"When you arrive," Mama had told her, "ask for the house of Phineas ben Jacobs. He is well known around there. He will take care of you and get you to your aunt's home."

And with those hesitating words, she took the first step of her transition out of girlhood and passed through a gateway into her new life. Promises of a bright new future hung like ripe plums ready for picking. She would bite into each one until the sweet juices burst forth. She would taste and savour and swallow, and still there would be more for the plucking.

CHAPTER 2

S HANA TORE OFF her head-covering and flung it across
the courtyard with a defiant flourish, unleashing a tumble
of dark curls that reached almost to the slender curve of her
waist. Rabbinical law was far too restrictive for her youthful
exuberance. A quick sideways glance from beneath her lashes
confirmed that she had Haziel's attention.

"What a beautiful morning!" she sang out as she skipped
over the cobbles to throw open the slatted gate, which led
from the enclosed courtyard onto the road.

Haziel was lounging on a bench in the sun, watching her
performance with obvious amusement. "So it is, sweet
cousin. And what have you in mind to do with it?" he
drawled, accommodating her with a hint of mockery, which
delighted Shana nonetheless because he was so often given to
melancholy, his brooding disposition denying her access to
his mysterious private thoughts.

"I have a day off; I can do whatever I please." She
stretched out her arms and twirled around, bathed in the

warmth of his affection and her pleasurable anticipation of the new day. "Judith doesn't need me here this morning and I don't have to mind the neighbour's boys this afternoon. It's time I had a break from them; it's hard work trying to restrain their perfectly natural energy. When I have children, I shall set them free!"

"Free to be brats," said Haziel drily.

"Those children are brats anyway. As much as I love them, I don't think I could manage them more than five afternoons a week. Now, what shall I do today?"

She caught Haziel's fond smile and saw she still had his attention. She had been in awe of him since she was a little girl and him already a handsome young man – ever so handsome she thought. Her family used to stay with his during their regular pilgrimages to Jerusalem for the Passover. He had treated her with superior disdain in those days, but now he surely noticed she had become a woman and took her more seriously.

"I could walk on the hills and collect lilies." She paused to savour the possibility, staring for a moment over the sun-sparkled olive groves framed in the gateway. "Or I could come with you to the city," she checked for his response and picked up his quick frown, "or perhaps visit the old lady. Yes, I'll do that, but first I'll bake some date cakes to take her. She hardly goes out anymore because of her legs. I miss her help with the children; she used to keep them amused for hours telling them stories."

Haziel's wife emerged from the house, her arms loaded with linen, which she plunged into the stone tub that doubled as a water trough for the livestock.

"You, bake? Heaven help us!" she said, intercepting Shana's outspoken thoughts. She bustled past Haziel and dropped a kiss on top of his shaggy head. "Good morning, my husband. Shall I cook some barley porridge for your breakfast?"

Haziel got up and embraced her, as prodigious as a bear beside her. Shana always associated Judith with words from the book of Proverbs: 'He who has a wife has a good thing.' Five years of marriage had proved that, and Haziel seemed content, the innate restlessness of his nature for the most part subdued. But Shana suspected that he took advantage of his extended trips as a cloth merchant to satisfy his wanderlust.

"Where is Ada?" asked Judith.

"Putting the goats out to graze," said Haziel. "I came to do it, but you know my mother, she always gets there first." Ada shared her small wattle-and-clay home with them, her husband having died when Haziel was still a boy. She was a pleasant, steady woman, content to observe life flowing past without asserting her opinions or preferences, and as such, was easy to live with and contributed an agreeable stability to the family. Shana would have missed her mother a lot more if it were not for her aunt's devotion to her.

"Perhaps Aunt Ada will help me make the cakes. If I can improve my baking, perhaps it will improve my father's opinion of me when I get back home," said Shana. She rolled her eyes. "That's if he ever allows me back."

"Of course he will," said Haziel, "just as soon as you decide to comply with his wishes."

"Never! Why should he decide my future? I—"

A swift look from Judith checked her outburst. Judith had a way of making her reproofs clear without words. She pushed a basket towards Shana. "Before you vanish, could you give me a hand with hanging out this washing?"

Ada had returned from the field and was busy stoking up

the embers of the courtyard fire. "I'll do it," she said. "Let Shana have her day off." She indulged her niece at every opportunity.

"Not at all, Aunt, it's my favourite job!" Shana thrust her nose into the basket, gulping in the clean fragrance of the wet linen with exaggerated pleasure, and hauled it up the steps onto the sunny rooftop terrace, singing in a clear lilting voice.

From the terrace, she could see Haziel watching his wife as she stirred the pot at the fire, his fond expression apparent even from here. An unpleasant twinge in her stomach caused her song to falter and fade. Judith was everything she was not. Her sweet, quiet spirit and level-headed manner was so opposite to her own untamed vivacity. Judith was wise, sensible, unselfish . . . except that she was not particularly comely, though her features were regular and there was an attractive wholesomeness about her.

Shana ran her fingertips over the smooth contours of her raised cheekbones and shapely lips, recalling again with relish what Haziel had said to her when she arrived six months ago, having not seen her since she was twelve. Looking her over appraisingly as she stood before him, dishevelled from her journey, he had commented, "I always thought you'd become a beauty; I see I was not wrong." She had turned crimson, furious with herself for displaying her immaturity, but had sailed on the clouds with his compliment ever since.

She smiled to herself and began to hum again as her dampened spirits revived. She shook out a dripping robe and threw it over the parapet. Judith was laughing at something Haziel had said, and he smiled back at her, his teeth showing through his bush of black whiskers.

Poor Judith, thought Shana, her heart going out to her, she longed so much for a child, and what a disappointment it must be for Haziel. Their happy anticipation in the early years of marriage had become for Judith a desolate yearning. She once confided in Shana that the endless cycle of hope and hope dashed, proved more painful than laying the hope down, and she had not mentioned it since. But one night, Shana had awakened in the outside room she shared with Aunt Ada and heard Judith slip out into the olive groves, where she wept privately in the moonlight until her heart could be emptied again of its grief.

There was still time, she was yet young, but each year robbed her ruthlessly of the limited storehouse of her youth. She bore her sorrow with patient endurance, but her bridal glow had dimmed and barrenness clothed her cruelly in a mantle of shame.

Shana smoothed her hands over her own flat stomach and tried to imagine it swelling with new life. If her father had his way, she would be married and carrying her first child by now. But unlike most girls her age, who just lived for motherhood, she was certain life had more to offer than that. And hopefully by now Rafael would have got over her turning him down.

She went down to the courtyard, still humming, and Judith gave her a quick hug.

"You uplift us so with your high spirits," she said, "doesn't she, Haziel?"

"When she's in a good mood. Which does make up for when she's annoying."

Shana pulled a face at him. She enjoyed his teasing; it was better than being treated as though she was invisible, which was more usual.

"She's never annoying," said Aunt Ada, always quick to defend her. But Shana had to admit that she did bring a measure of chaos into the settled routines of her aunt's household. She had always been flighty and whimsical, a dreamer who floated through life quite oblivious to much of reality. Her father told her she was headstrong and recklessly impulsive – she liked the sound of the latter – and Judith often got exasperated with her because of her inability to live in the same time frame as everyone else. She would so easily become obsessive about whatever she was doing and give it her full focus, to the exclusion of all else, and then when she tried to regain control of all the tasks left undone, there would be upheaval in the household, storms of haste and frustration while she raged at time for not accommodating her. She was guiltily aware that she often left the other women with more than their fair share of the chores as she rushed out to catch up on her errands. Haziel would look on with undisguised amusement. Perhaps it gave expression to his own turbulent nature.

Judith took Haziel's bowl, and he got up and stretched. In his sleeveless tunic, his muscle-bound arms and broad chest made him look more like a stone mason than a cloth merchant.

"I'm off to the city," he said. "We're getting behind with the orders, my dear. See what you can do."

Haziel's textile shop was in the market area of Jerusalem. He had acquired a number of looms for producing fabrics in both wool and linen and employed a small team of weavers, but his finest work came from his wife. Judith worked diligently on a loom set up under the reed-covered awning in the courtyard. The high quality of her work attracted an ever increasing clientele, and the pressure to keep up with the demand was often overwhelming. She was training Shana in the mornings to give her a hand with the weaving.

On Shana's free days, Haziel sometimes allowed her to accompany him to the city, a short two-mile walk, to help him in his shop. She loved the vibrancy of Jerusalem, where she could be swept along with the crowds and become one with people from every culture and nation who continually flocked to the holy city. Anonymous among strangers, she would peer into their faces and wonder what stories lay behind their composed expressions. What hopes, what fears, what sorrows and joys did they share of her own? What secrets of wisdom or quiet despair, and what was the reason for it all? Life, to her, was one big question. Was she the only one asking it?

In her efforts to please Haziel, she often made mistakes, and suspected that he really only tolerated her help in his shop. Regretfully, she had not been permitted that privilege today, otherwise she would gladly have forsaken all her other plans. She watched him stride away, wishing she could have gone with him.

Ada, having tried unsuccessfully to instruct her in the necessity to have patience when baking, sat down in the gateway to mend Haziel's cloak, and Shana set off with her slightly burnt date cakes.

"See you later, Aunt," she called. "Thanks for the help. I'm taking the long way round the edge of the village, I feel like a walk."

The sun had soared into a clear sky and Shana filled her lungs with warm, meadow-scented air, taking pleasure in being able to dawdle along and let the day unfold without agenda. She savoured every moment of her freedom. How pleasant not to have her father breathing down her neck with his constant disapproval, controlling her every move. If it were not for her mother and younger sister, she could happily

23

live here forever. She thought of Beth with a pang and wondered how she was managing without her. It consoled her to think that at least her absence would have fostered a more harmonious atmosphere at home.

The goat track meandered along a lower slope below the village, allowing Shana precious solitude to give rein to her wandering thoughts. Her mind drifted to Rafael. Since coming here, she had barely brought him to mind, discarded him along with all the other paraphernalia of her past, yet he remained always steadfast on the outskirts, waiting to be admitted.

CHAPTER 3

THAT EVENING the family gathered indoors to dine as the night temperatures were still a sharp contrast to the warmth of the days. They sat around the table in the lamplight, dipping chunks of bread into a pot of lentil stew and sharing the details of their day.

"How did the old lady like your cakes?" asked Ada.

"You didn't really force those blackened rocks on her, did you?" said Haziel through a mouthful.

Shana flashed him a look. "They were only a little burnt around the edges. Anyway, she wasn't home, so I brought them back for you." She gave him an arch smile and turned back to her aunt. "I bumped into the old man who used to teach at the synagogue and spent most of the day chatting to him. It was fascinating. He told me he had recently returned from a journey to Cana and had himself been among the crowds of people who are following that mysterious new prophet everyone's talking about. He actually saw him and heard him speak! Apparently he teaches using all kinds of stories, so a lot of the time people can't figure out what he's talking about, but they follow him anyway because he has supernatural healing powers."

"Oh Shana, do you really believe that?" said Judith.

"Well, old What's-his-name wouldn't have spent a whole morning telling me about something that wasn't true," Shana protested, and Haziel laughed. He was always amused at what he called her simple logic, and it peeved her that he was entertained by it.

"People believe what they want to believe," said Judith sensibly. "They take a truth and build it into whatever they want."

"Why ever would they?" demanded Shana.

"Perhaps they need some excitement in their lives," replied Judith, unruffled.

"What do you think?" said Shana, turning to Haziel for support. How she hated having her enthusiasm dampened by rationalism.

"I'll make up my mind when I see for myself."

"When will that ever be?" she said sarcastically.

"Well, as a matter of fact I'm going to Galilee next week to take some fabric samples to Tiberias. The palace has ordered them, so it stands to be a very profitable trip. And you never know who I might bump into."

"Really?" Shana sat up straight on her stool, eyes wide and eager. "Oh please, do let me come with you?"

"Don't be absurd," said Judith. "You can't just jump up and disappear; what about those children?"

Shana kept looking at Haziel, waiting.

"It's a rough four-day journey; I doubt you'd manage it. Two of my workers are coming with me, and we're taking the three pack-donkeys to deliver woollens to Scythopolis on the way. Afterwards I intend to spend a week at Uncle Ethan's house."

"Uncle Ethan!" Shana cried. "I've never been to Galilee and I've longed for an opportunity to see my other cousins again. I haven't seen them since I was a child when we all got together here, do you remember, Haziel? It was quite a crowd. And I still haven't met the youngest ones. It will be so wonderful to see Aunt Deborah again. I can give them news of my family."

"Yes, of your disobedience to your father," said Haziel, his whiskers parting in a wry grin. "They'll be most interested, I'm sure."

"Haziel said no," said Judith matter-of-factly, casting a fleeting shadow over Shana's excitement. But this new possibility had taken root so swiftly that she was already in love with the idea, and everything else in her life faded into grey insignificance in a moment.

"The children's mother said I could take a couple of weeks off whenever I want to visit my family. Well, I certainly won't be going home just yet, but it is still family. She has her sister staying with her right now, who can help her. It's perfect timing!"

"Haziel said no," reminded Judith gently.

But Shana knew he hadn't.

At dawn in the middle of the following week, they departed.

"Wait! Wait for me!" yelled Shana as Haziel eventually marched out of the house without her. She frantically stuffed her extra tunic and other things into a linen bag and tore after him, veil askew. The household had been a fluster of preparation and high-pitched excitement for days, but somehow she had still not managed to finish packing. At the gate, she skidded to a halt and ran back. "I almost forgot to say goodbye," she said, hastily hugging her aunt and kissing Judith's cheek.

"Enjoy every moment," said Judith. "I wish I could come too."

Shana hesitated. "Oh Judith, I'm so sorry, I didn't realise. Do you mind very much Haziel being away?"

"Not at all, I'm used to it, as long as it's not for too long, although I always miss him. I don't think he misses me as much," she added with a short laugh, "but I know how much he needs a change of scenery and time on his own now and again, or he gets fidgety."

Shana started walking backwards, throwing anxious glances over her shoulder at Haziel's receding figure. "I hope he doesn't mind me going with him," she said.

Judith laughed. "He would have said so, loud and clear, if that was the case. He's very fond of you. Now you'd better get going or you'll be left behind. Take care, dearest."

They were meeting the caravan about a mile out of the village at the intersection to the main route, where Haziel's colleagues would be waiting with the loaded donkeys. These caravans travelled to Galilee twice a week, taking safety in numbers when traversing the perilous terrain, which was notorious for attack by robbers, and occasionally wild animals too.

They fell in step with the company of about fifty travellers and began the steep descent to Jericho just as the sun sparked between the battalions of hills that bordered the wilderness. It was a cold morning but would soon reach temperatures that would make the journey increasingly strenuous and uncomfortable. However, now spirits and energy levels were high, and a pleasant repartee circulated among the travellers. Shana thrilled at each light step of her winged feet, enjoying the sting of cold air moving across her skin and the sense of purpose and transition. Every few yards, she had to make little runs to match Haziel's long strides. Filled with giddy euphoria, her bright chit-chat breathlessly pursued Haziel's attention, until he said, "I can't tell whether it's you or the birds chirping," and she took it to mean he'd had enough.

As the sun climbed into a cloudless sky, the road took them down towards the Jordan River valley through a bizarre landscape of barren, crumpled hills, stripped of greenery and possessed of a mystical silence that hushed the flow of conversation. By midday, pools of heat had collected in the valley, and the verdant shores of the Jordan River offered welcoming shade. They stopped to rest awhile, but before Shana could recover her strength, the caravan pressed on again, crossing the river at a wide, shallow place and beginning the long climb into the hills where the road connected with the Roman highway.

Ten hours into the journey, Shana was wearier than she could ever remember being. Stones kept finding their way into her leather shoes and bruising her feet, and dust coated her throat until her voice rasped, finally rendering her silent. She struggled to keep up with the group's more practised pace without complaint and maintain a pretence of stamina. Haziel remained deep in his own thoughts and seemed oblivious to her, or even to his colleagues, who chatted among themselves.

After a while, Shana began to resent his indifference towards her. She felt like a small child, mincing along beside his burly frame, with the top of her head just reaching the height of his shoulder. It reminded her of the times she would accompany her father to the synagogue when she was only knee height and had to run to keep up with him. She would look longingly at the other little girls riding royally on their fathers' arms, and notice the tender pride softening the men's faces. Even at that age, she could see that it was different to the almost reverent regard they held for their sons. She would trot along beside her father crying, "Papa! Papa!" holding up her arms for him to pick her up, but he would brush her off irritably, and she would not understand.

The more tired she became, the lower her emotions sank and she longed to stop and rest a while. As the light faded, an ochre shroud settled over the parched hills and the bushes beside the road turned into black shapes which seemed to move threateningly towards her, like wild creatures singling her out for attack. Beside her, the little donkey carrying their packs kept up its regular rhythm of hoof against stone; she envied its trance-like patience. She stumbled, catching hold of Haziel's arm, which apparently reminded him of her presence.

"Are you getting tired, little cousin?" he asked, his unexpected gentleness bringing quick tears to her eyes.

"A little," she said.

"See, there are the lights of a village. It's not far to go, and we'll be stopping at the caravan shelter for the night."

She took a deep breath and fixed her eyes grimly on the tiny sparkles in the distance, willing them to draw her towards them.

The group spent an uncomfortable night huddled together in an open shelter, which failed to protect them from the keen wind that kept up a shrill, hostile whining till dawn, and then stopped abruptly as if scared away by the onset of light.

The second day Shana managed to endure with dogged

determination, jaded as she was from lack of sleep, but the third day was the worst, though shorter in distance. Her muscles ached from the unfamiliar strain, and the road rose and fell repeatedly, offering little relief. She fought to hide her weakness from Haziel. It was plain that he would not indulge her, or take any responsibility for her decision to tag along, and she began to regret her impulsive action. Painful blisters had formed on her feet, making every step an agony, and devoid of any support from Haziel, she had to fight continually to keep her tears at bay.

His lack of communication disappointed her. She had been looking forward to this uninterrupted time with him, to enjoy some good discussion. Normally she could converse so easily with him – when he was in the mood – and she enjoyed debating his unconventional views. How much quicker the journey would go if she could be distracted by some absorbing conversation. But he remained disengaged and preoccupied, leaving her feeling negated and alone, and she did not want to join the other women.

How she hated being ignored! She thrived on being noticed, and her natural vivaciousness drew its energy from the attention she so easily attracted. But now in the absence of this stimulant, she floundered, haunted by the ghosts of her inadequacies and secret fears. She often felt painfully vulnerable, afraid of the power each person had to hurt her, captive to their expectations and judgements. It was a private suffering, of which she was very much ashamed.

Eventually a numbing dejection settled upon her. She treated Haziel with what she hoped was detached disregard, but in fact she was conscious of his every move.

The overnight stop in the lively town of Scythopolis did much to restore her flagging spirits. There were comfortable beds and a hot meal at the inn, for which she was profoundly grateful. In the women's quarters, she tentatively integrated with the others, drawing strength from their united feminine resilience. Finally she could surrender to the sweet sleep of exhaustion.

The last day was easier. Haziel left his colleagues in Scythopolis with the cargo of cloth, which freed up one of the donkeys for Shana to ride the rest of the way. What a relief to rest her blistered feet and be able to lift her eyes off the path and take in the wild beauty of the Jordan Valley, snaking through the landscape below. In the distance, the green hills of Galilee came into view, garlanded with forests of oak and juniper and ringed with terraces of vines.

Galilee itself was a taste of paradise, the whole land appeared to have been planted as a country garden, so profuse were the flowers of every colour and kind. Somewhere in this vista of peaceful hills and valleys, the Prophet was working his miracles. She had to find him. The old man's stories had kindled a flame in her heart that drew her with an alluring power she did not understand, but which could not be ignored.

Haziel and Shana separated from the others now, turning off onto a footpath that wound along the edge of a succession of hills. They needed to reach their destination before nightfall for the start of the Sabbath and so redoubled their pace. Haziel returned at last from his remote frame of mind and invited some conversation, which dissolved Shana's resentful coolness in a moment.

"Look, Haziel," she exclaimed, beginning to enjoy herself. "Those clouds with the sun behind them look like phantom eagles in flight. See their wings of blazing gold. And look over there at that field catching the wind as though a herd of invisible horses was stampeding through it. Isn't it perfectly beautiful?" She babbled on delightedly, and Haziel patiently kept agreeing, pausing occasionally to enjoy the scenes she picked out.

Then unexpectedly he gave her a startling peek into a private chamber of his mind. Looking out over the landscape, he spoke with a strange wistfulness, "If only I could view the world through your innocent eyes, with vision less dulled and tarnished by bitter perception, I might be a kinder man."

He walked on, his brows pulled down over his eyes, leaving her nonplussed but exhilarated – she had something he wanted. Oh, how she longed for him to say more, but he had a way of delivering a statement and then discarding it for the baffled interpretation of his hearers.

He turned frivolous again and joked about the Galileans' slack attitude to life, and they went on to chat about the crops that grew in the valleys.

"I wonder where he is," said Shana.

"Where who is?"

"The Prophet, of course. Isn't that one of the reasons we've come?"

"Speak for yourself, my lamb, I've got business to attend to. I hope you're not planning to go out chasing rainbows. My mother will expect me to return you home."

"I can't look for him on my own," cried Shana in alarm.

"Perhaps you can find another willing cousin at Uncle Ethan's house to escort you," said Haziel, "though I doubt you'll track the man down, the way he keeps moving about."

Shana turned on him with a vehemence that sounded childish. "I must find him. I will find him! He has to be here somewhere."

"It scares me when you get that determined look on your

face," said Haziel. "It makes me think you're about to do something stupid."

"It's my only chance to get to see someone this famous. I'm not going to pass it by."

"Infamous you mean."

"That depends whose side you're on, I suppose."

Below them stretched a plain, chequered with red tilled fields and plantations of green and yellow. The road ribboned up to a town on a hill beyond, where a smattering of houses shone in the late afternoon sun. Shana halted the donkey and gazed at the idyllic scene. A ripple of excitement bubbled up from an inner spring, but even as her spirit began to soar, she was aware that something held captive the full release of her joy. Beneath the daily ups and downs of her happiness, a deep place inside her silently grieved. She felt like a bird created to fly but tethered with a chain to the ground.

She sighed as a powerful yearning took hold of her, a yearning for something she could not identify.

"Is this going to take long?" said Haziel, leaning back against a tree trunk and crossing his arms. She had to laugh; he was so blunt.

When they reached the village, they made their way to their uncle's house, Shana aflutter with nerves. Haziel knocked on a shabby door, set in a stone wall. A woman opened it. Her plump, creased face remained blank for a moment, and then she squealed with delight as she recognised Haziel. She pulled him into her keen fleshy arms, exclaiming, "My favourite nephew; how good to see you. It's been far too long!"

"All your nephews are favourites, Aunt Deborah," laughed Haziel, disentangling himself. "Look, I've brought Shushana with me."

The woman stepped back and studied Shana's face with an expression of wonderment. "My child," she said, "is this really you, all grown up? How lovely you are. You have the same wide, dark eyes as your mother." She gathered Shana to her bosom, an extravagance of maternal softness. "This is a pleasure indeed! Come in, come in. Ethan, look who's here."

They were immediately swamped by a crowd of adoring cousins, the younger ones staring in awe, shyly nudging one another closer, while Deborah and Ethan hovered nearby with eager hospitality.

"You must be weary. Here Dania, take Shushana's cloak and bring a bowl of water for her poor tired feet. Ivan, you see to the donkeys – unpack them and take them to the stables. Are you hungry?" Deborah flustered around like an excited hen, asking a dozen questions, while Ethan drew Haziel aside for a less effusive enquiry about his affairs.

Later that evening, seated on cushions around a long table for the Sabbath meal, the family connected again with their Jewish heritage through the ancient traditions of their forefathers. Deborah lit the candles, and Ethan blessed each member of the family and pronounced a short prayer, after which the wine and bread were passed around. The ceremony was pious, yet accommodating to the giggles of the two youngest when they spilt the wine, and the good-natured jibes of the siblings. Together they sang the well-loved hymns. Shana sang from her heart as the warm red wine infused her hot red blood, enlivening every nerve of her body until she felt she would burst with elation. There was a bounteous feast of fish and vegetable dishes flavoured with aromatic herbs, followed by dates, figs and puddings, and afterwards a final blessing. Through these rituals they were bonded in their corporate identity as God's chosen people, deeply rooted in their beloved nation that centuries of past conflict had only served to strengthen.

Shana was the centre of attention. The little ones gazed at her admiringly, and the older cousins jostled for a chance to ask her questions. Permeated with the warmth of their focus, she felt her cheeks glow with youthful radiance and beauty. Her hair, curling around her face, was fiery in the candlelight, and she glittered with happiness, displaying her dazzling smile, which showed her dimples, for the benefit of all. Uncle Ethan watched her with a fond expression, and Ivan, Ethan's eldest son, couldn't take his eyes off her. Intoxicated with the pleasing effect she was having on the men, she blazed like a fanned flame, until Haziel rose from the table and commented, "It's late and our cousin is keeping us captive with her charm," and she wasn't at all sure whether it was a compliment.

When the family had fed their guests as much as they could eat and questioned them dry, the older cousins drifted off to put the little ones to bed while the men went for a stroll, and Shana was left alone with her aunt.

"How is dear Judith?" asked Deborah. "No news, I suppose, or Haziel would have mentioned it. Oh how my heart aches for her, and here I am blessed with such a brood, it's hard to imagine what it must be like for her. I'm fearful that Haziel might consider a divorce."

"There's no chance of that, Aunt, he loves her dearly."

Deborah looked at her imploringly. "Do you really think so?"

"Without any doubt. I've stayed with them long enough."

"It's a great consolation to hear that, my dear. I don't like to bring up the subject with Haziel, but I have worried so much about it and have had no one else to ask."

Shana longed to enquire about the Prophet but was afraid to appear too eager, as if it was the only reason she had come. "Aunt," she said nonchalantly, "have you heard of the travelling rabbi who has been around here? Do you know anything about him?"

"Oh yes," Deborah replied immediately. "He caused a huge commotion in our quiet little town. People behaved most irresponsibly, even leaving their jobs to follow him around. Some say he has healing powers and has even raised someone's daughter from the dead!"

"Have you seen him? Is he still here?" interrupted Shana, forgetting her restraint.

"I haven't seen him myself. A woman in the town says her two sons – fishermen you know – have taken off after him, leaving their poor father to do all the work. She's very upset and doesn't have much good to say about him, and I've heard many other stories, though I can't say I believe them all."

"Where is he now?"

"People say that he's gone out into the hills yonder, next to the lake, taking a huge crowd with him. Most had to come back, as there is no place to get food out there unless you can fish, but people keep setting out to find him. He can be quite elusive, I believe, slipping away without warning into the mountains or to the other side of the lake."

"I would so love to see him," Shana burst out. "I may never get another chance. Do you think it might be possible?"

"Dear girl," said Deborah, "is that why you've come all this way? Perhaps Ivan can accompany you if you can find a group to go with, but don't get your hopes up, it's quite far out, and you could get there and find he's already left."

It was difficult to sleep much that night, though the sleeping mat was comfortable and the little house quiet. A sense of mission had taken hold of Shana like never before, and she could not rest until it was accomplished. A pale moon hesitated in the high window; she felt a kinship with its mystical light. It spoke of things beyond the confines of earth, of mysteries untold and life transcended. She sensed that this wandering prophet had answers to the big questions about life, about God, questions she had carried with her since her first painful realisation that the world was not the perfect place it was surely designed to be.

She just had to find him!

CHAPTER 4

A WAKENED FROM her scant sleep by the bustling vigour of the crowded household, Shana went upstairs to the little rooftop shelter to wash the dust from her hair and bathe in the icy water brought from the well. She dressed in a clean tunic, her favourite one with the pale blue striped border and girdle, and feeling wonderfully rejuvenated, joined the family for the short walk to the synagogue.

The meeting was less formal than she was accustomed to, the relaxed attitude of the Galileans being evident. She listened while a passage from the Torah was read and discussed, but heard nothing as her thoughts were fully occupied with her quest.

Back at the house, the family shared a pre-prepared meal of bread, olives, goat's cheese, and a selection of regional fruit, which they took outside into the open courtyard. They sat around cross-legged while they ate, and chatted idly about their plans for the coming week.

"I'll be leaving at first light tomorrow to see the flax

merchants but will be back in the evening," said Haziel. "The meeting at the palace is the day after."

"I have to do some washing," said Shana. "Haziel will need clean clothes for his meeting." She liked claiming ownership of him.

"Be sure to bring me back some fresh fish from the lake, Haziel," said Deborah.

"Only if you promise to prepare it the way I like it, Aunt," he replied, causing Deborah to twinkle with fondness.

"Uncle Ethan has given Ivan the day off work tomorrow to take you around, Shana," she said.

Ivan leapt to his feet to hide his embarrassment and stumbled into the house with his empty bowl, his neck blazing.

"I'm looking forward to it," Shana called after him.

Ivan was a gangling youth of about fifteen – vigorous, intense, and somewhat uncoordinated as though his limbs were attached too loosely to his body. The faint imprint of manhood was evident in the shadow above his upper lip, and his voice had lowered an octave, which he took down further for added effect. His soft, brown eyes fixed themselves adoringly onto Shana. He had fallen unashamedly in love with her the moment he saw her, and she could not deny that she was enjoying being treated like a princess.

"Where are you taking me this morning?" asked Shana brightly.

"I can take you to Father's shop and show you some of my carpentry, if–if you'd like," replied Ivan, already flushing with pleasure.

On the way, Ivan proudly introduced her to everyone they passed, displaying her as though she was his personal asset.

She played her part with intuitive grace, establishing a sisterly rapport with him, in which he could safely indulge his infatuation, and she could playfully express her affection without fear of inviting too ardent a response.

At Uncle Ethan's shop, a small crowd had gathered to inspect the furniture displayed outside. Shana watched happily, observing the absorbed interest of the women as they stroked the polished wood with gnarled, work-worn hands, their minds summing up the possibilities – or perhaps impossibilities – of ownership. For the men it was clearly an opportunity for a social occasion, and the rumble of voices rose and fell pleasantly. The slow pace of the town was reflected in the leisurely trading, with occasional notes of excitement as bargaining for an item began. Here, Uncle Ethan was in his element. Years of practice had taught him how to weigh up the value of a piece of furniture against the means of the buyer. Aunt Ada had spoken of his trading techniques, saying her sister had married a true tradesman: so many shekels of silver, delivered each new moon for six months, plus half a dozen sheep may well clinch the deal for a young farmer and his new wife for a strong table that would see their grandchildren gathered around it. Whereas if his old friend, the harness-maker, wanted a storage chest for his daughter, it would be paid for handsomely with several skins of his home-made wine plus a few shekels owing when he sold his next harness.

Ivan proudly showed Shana the pieces he had worked on, rubbing them over with a cloth until the wood glowed. Suddenly Shana's ears caught a word among the general hum of conversation. She stepped closer, pretending to examine a carved bed frame. Some men were discussing the Prophet, and a disagreement had arisen between them.

"I have personally heard him speak," a young ginger-haired man asserted. "He is definitely not a fake. His very words will tell you that. He has a powerful charisma and—"

"That does not mean he speaks the truth," interrupted an older man. "The problem is that his charisma is exactly what is drawing the crowds! He's a trouble-maker who is stirring up all kinds of conflict by discrediting our guardians of the law, even publicly denouncing them."

"On the contrary, he is a peacemaker, and the extraordinary peace he radiates substantiates his teaching."

"It would be better if he would leave us in peace!" said the old man crossly. "He sent an entire herd of pigs on the other side of the lake to their death and didn't offer to pay a single denarius of compensation."

"Nonsense!" put in a defender. "They took flight themselves. That madman must have frightened them over the edge of the cliff into the sea."

"That madman – the demoniac – was healed," a woman said quietly, but the men were too intent on arguing their case to acknowledge her.

Shana was bursting to ask questions, but strict protocol prohibited young women from speaking out in public, so she had to bite her lip in frustration. Just then she saw Ivan wave a greeting to the ginger-haired man, diverting his attention from the argument, and found her opportunity. She clutched his arm and said urgently, "Ivan! Go and ask that man if he knows where the Prophet is."

Ivan moved off, eager to please, and returned with his friend in tow. "Shushana, this is David. Perhaps you'd like to ask him about the man everyone's talking about."

David was a tall man, a little older than Ivan. His thin high-bridged nose and earnest deep-set eyes suggested a refined intelligence, which Shana found both attractive and intimidating.

"Tell me everything!" she said eager emphasis.

David's eyes lit up with matching enthusiasm. "I went with some friends. We heard he was in a nearby place and were just curious – as were quite a few thousand others, it turned out."

"W–what did he look like?" asked Shana.

David looked vague. "He didn't make much of an impression on me, rather ordinary actually, but it was his voice – no not even that . . . no, it was his words which were so captivating."

"What did he say?" she asked, hungrily drawing out the information.

"Well, that's the point. He said a lot of things which didn't make sense at first, but . . . but you had to listen with your heart as well as your ears, and only then it became meaningful." David tugged at his beard thoughtfully while Shana waited with bated breath. "For example, he kept talking about the kingdom of God, using different situations to describe it . . . I can't really explain. All I can say is that you wanted to hear more, to follow after him and keep on listening, even if it didn't always make sense."

At last Shana released her burning question. "Where is he now?"

"The last I heard he was in Capernaum. He was teaching in the synagogue there, but he never stays long in one place. I can find out from someone I know, who travels that way a lot. Are you hoping to see him?"

"Oh yes! I have to return to Jerusalem in a week, so I don't have long. If there are others setting out to look for him, perhaps Ivan and I could go along with them." She caught Ivan's quizzical look.

"I'll find out for you," David promised.

Haziel returned from Tiberius and then left again for the palace. Precious days passed with no sign of David. Ivan had unsuccessfully made enquiries about the Prophet's whereabouts, but Shana knew he didn't care whether they found him or not, as long as he could be with her every possible moment. He hovered about her like a shadow, alert as a sheepdog for the slightest indication of her wanting his company. His self-effacing devotion held no expectations and demanded no response; he treated her like a priceless work of art that can be admired but never owned. Shana was amused and not uncomfortable. She warmed to him, understanding his immature emotions.

When Ivan wasn't around, Aunt Deborah, in a well-meaning effort to keep her entertained, regimented every hour of her days. There were organised visits to meet the neighbours and trips to one or another interesting site in the village, and Shana had to obligingly tidy herself up and accompany her aunt on each tedious outing, which she would not have found tiresome at all, had she not had a more pressing ambition.

One morning, with only two days left of the visit, Shana was gloomily preparing to accompany her aunt to the market when Ivan burst in, beaming triumphantly, with David panting behind him.

"I've found out where he is," said David, wasting no time on formalities. "He has drawn a crowd by the lake just beyond Tiberias, about a four-hour walk from here. The rabbinical college has given me time off to investigate his teachings, and my mother has agreed to accompany you.

We're ready to leave immediately. Can you come? We'll have to stay overnight."

"Definitely!" Shana exclaimed. "I'll just go and tell my aunt. You are coming too, aren't you Ivan?"

"My father has sent me to escort you," he said with pride and began to collect his things together. Deborah came back inside with Shana and filled a bag with a few loaves, some dried fish, olives, and a skin of goat's milk. "Don't forget to take your cloaks and a rug," she said. "It gets very cold out of doors at night."

Shana stuffed whatever she could find into her bag, her heart racing with excitement. She hugged her aunt hurriedly, and the three of them went to meet David's mother, who Shana liked immediately for her youthful sense of adventure and ready laughter. They set off at a bracing pace, David and his mother settling easily into a swinging stride, Shana almost running ahead, and Ivan following with his lumbering gait.

The hot miles stretched out before and behind, and Shana maintained her urgent pace with untiring strength and determination, afraid that the Prophet might move on before they got there. Even stopping at midday for a bite to eat made her impatient. Her dainty feet, now dusty and dirty, were on fire, but she pressed on as though her life depended on it. And she felt, somehow, that it did.

"What is it that makes you so keen to find this rabbi you call the Prophet?" David asked.

Shana slowed down and considered a while, asking herself that question for the first time. "I'm just following my heart," she said at last. "Now tell me all you know about him."

David needed no encouragement. "Many people believe he is the Messiah."

"Why is that?"

"Because he fulfils so many of the prophecies about the one who God was to send to Israel. They're very specific: it is written that a leader or a ruler would come from the royal line of David – he is a descendant of David – who will shepherd and deliver the people of Israel; that he would be born in Bethlehem in Judea, which he was, and that he would be called out of Egypt, where indeed he lived for a while as a child."

"Isn't he the one who was said to be born of a virgin?"

"Yes, that was also prophesied. There has of course been a lot of controversy about that, but the story has been passed down as true, and it is unlikely it would have survived otherwise, especially here among people who know Mary, his mother, personally."

"It sounds extraordinary!" Shana burst out.

"The more I study it, the more I believe it," said David, enjoying himself. "Seven hundred years ago the prophet Isaiah wrote of a saviour who would heal the lame, blind, deaf and dumb. Isaiah also mentioned another strange man who would announce his coming – this turned out to be the Rabbi's cousin John, that crazy character who lived in the desert and was beheaded by Herod. So if you put everything together, there can be little doubt that this man is someone exceptional."

Shana wished she too could have gone to school and studied the scrolls herself. The readings she heard discussed in synagogue, usually about Moses and the law, were all she knew about God, and to her he sounded as harsh as her father.

The little group paused on the crest of the last hill, awed by the scene before them. Down in the valley, the famous Sea of Galilee sparkled like a turquoise jewel in an emerald setting, cupped on the far side by a bank of russet cliffs. Below where they stood, terraces of fruit trees flowed down to the shores, and a row of fishing boats swayed lazily on the smooth waters. From their elevated position, they caught sight of movement below. It was multitudes of people swarming among the trees on a lower slope. Shana's heart leapt in her chest. Without waiting for the others, she raced down the steep uneven path, skidding on the loose stones, heedless of cuts and grazes. Panting heavily, she ran to the edge of the crowd but found it impossible to penetrate the wall of people blocking the view ahead. Even standing on tiptoe, she was dwarfed by the men in front of her, who were roughly elbowing each other out of the way. She could have cried with frustration – to have got this close and still not be able to see him!

A strong, clear voice could be heard above the jostling mob. Shana strained to hear but could only catch a few words here and there.

"Truly I tell you, anyone who will not receive the kingdom of God like a little child will never enter . . . secrets of the kingdom . . . given to men . . . but hearts have become calloused."

Now and again when a gap opened up, she slipped under the maze of elbows to get another inch closer. Turning to locate Ivan, she spotted him standing some way back with a rather comical, horrified look on his face at finding himself separated from her. He frantically shoved his way through, receiving a couple of sharp blows to his chest as he did so, and reached out to catch Shana's wrist in an iron grip. "Stay with me!" he hissed with uncharacteristic forcefulness. "How will I ever find you again if you disappear?"

"We have to get closer," Shana protested, but he remained resolutely rooted to the spot, so she was forced to try to catch whatever she could of the speech.

As darkness fell, many people began to drift away, which loosened up the tightly packed crowd. Some made their way back up the path, separating into groups, and soon small fires sprang up all over the hillside. The Rabbi had disappeared, and Shana's disappointment was acute, but she still held hope for the next day.

It was a pleasant evening with warm drifts of air displacing the chill that fell with sundown. David and Ivan found a level spot and collected some twigs to make a fire. They were all weary and subdued as they ate their meagre portions, and soon snuggled into their cloaks and fell asleep around the flickering embers, with the stars blinking above in the vast open heaven.

Awakened by a heavy dewfall just before dawn, dark figures rose up from the ground to coax reluctant embers into a blaze. Shana, thick with sleep, sat up and stretched, remembering where she was with a rush of elation. David was all action, snapping twigs to add to the fire and rubbing his hands together energetically. A magical morning rose through the thin mist, laying shafts of shimmering gold upon the water. Never had a meal of salted fish and toasted bread tasted so good.

Presently there was a stirring all over the hillside as people sprang to their feet, mumbling excitedly. Of one accord they began to surge down towards the shore. Shana's group gathered their things hastily and ran to keep near the front. As they reached the shore, Shana scanned the gathering crowd eagerly – peasants, officials, scribes, rich and poor pressed together, side by side. A small party of Pharisees stood a little distance away in their flamboyant robes, like a row of vigilant raptors.

And then she saw him!

He was standing a few feet from the water's edge with the sun blazing into his face so she could not see his features. He was not speaking, but the quiet authority of his bearing was immediately evident. Behind him, some fishermen were busy launching a boat, while people streamed from every direction, collecting in a massive throng before him. As the crowd pressed closer and closer, he turned around and waded out to the boat. Shana's heart plunged. He was making a getaway! But instead he climbed into the boat and stood facing the crowd, smiling warmly.

He waited until the crowd quietened and then began to speak. "If anyone has ears to hear, let him hear. My sheep listen to my voice and they follow me. I am the good shepherd and I lay down my life for the sheep. I give them eternal life, and they shall never perish."

He paused to allow time for this astonishing statement to sink in and then went on, "The thief comes only to steal, kill and destroy. I have come that you might have life, and have it to the full."

Life to the full! Shana's soul strained against its fetters.

"I did not come to condemn the world, but to save it," he continued. "Whoever believes in the Son has eternal life."

There was a murmuring among the people as each reacted in a different way. Some were saying he had a demon! Others said his miracles proved that he was from God.

"Do not worry about your life, what you will eat or drink, or what you will wear. Your heavenly Father knows you need these things, and who of you by worrying can add a single hour to his life? But first seek the kingdom of God and his righteousness, and all these things will be given to you as well." His voice rose and fell with light emphasis on the words. "So don't worry about tomorrow; it will worry about itself." He laughed. "Each day has enough trouble of its own."

Just then, some of the Pharisees moved forwards. The crowds parted in honour of their status, and they stood on the edge of the shore in front of the boat. Shana had always disliked their holier-than-thou attitude and air of self-importance and was curious to see how the Rabbi would respond to them, especially as David told her they were always trying to trap him with their questions.

"Tell us," said one of them, "when will this, er, kingdom of God come?"

The Rabbi's reply came clearly across the water. "People will not say, 'Here it is,' or 'There it is,' because the kingdom of God is within you."

And then to Shana's amazement, he began to denounce the Pharisees, warning people not to do as they did, because they did not practice what they preached. He addressed them directly saying, "Woe to you, you blind guides, you hypocrites! On the outside you appear to people as righteous, but on the inside you are full of wickedness, greed and self-indulgence."

A shocked silence fell upon the crowd. It was inconceivable that this mild-mannered man would use such cutting words and willingly stir up opposition against himself like this.

"Why is he doing that?" Shana whispered to David in alarm.

"I think he wants to expose their religious pride. He doesn't want people to equate the kingdom of God with the way they carry on. He has said worse things than this to them! It's surprising they keep coming back for more, but it's only because they're trying to uncover error in him, which they cannot find."

"Is he always this harsh with them?"

"No. He knows which of them are teachable and genuinely seeking the truth. The last time I saw him, one of the Pharisees asked him a similar question, and he explained to him at length that no one can see the kingdom of God unless he is born again, in other words, born of water and the Spirit – a physical as well as a spiritual birth."

The fishermen on the boat with him pulled up the anchor, and without another word the Rabbi simply sailed away across the lake, leaving the enraged Pharisees to deal with their humiliation. Shana watched as the little boat grew smaller and smaller until it disappeared. She was disappointed that she had not been able to see him perform a miracle but filled with gratitude for having had this opportunity to hear such awe-inspiring words from the Prophet's own lips – words which glowed inside her like treasures of indescribable value.

The crowds, finding themselves suddenly stranded, milled around aimlessly and then began to disperse. David said that they too would have to set off in order to arrive back home before nightfall.

This time David and his mother took the lead, engaged in a long animated discussion with Ivan, while Shana lagged behind, hugging her thoughts to herself. She was wondering what the Rabbi meant by saying, "Whoever wants to save his life will lose it, but whoever loses his life for me will find it. What good will it be to gain the whole world, yet forfeit your soul?

CHAPTER 5

AFTER ALL THE upheaval of the trip to Galilee, Shana was more than ready to return to Aunt Ada's home again. A bewildering shift seemed to have taken place in the subterranean levels of her being, which unsettled her and made her feel uncomfortable in her own skin. It was good to be back in the safe place of familiar streets and predictable rhythms of daily life in the village, where the frayed edges of her identity could be re-hemmed. She did not speak much about her experiences of the past couple of weeks, or even think about them consciously, but for a time drifted through the pleasant ebb and flow of the days. When she was no longer needed to mind the neighbour's children in the mornings, she was able to give her full attention to helping Judith with the weaving, a task she very much enjoyed.

But underneath her contentment, something continued to niggle at her.

She had first noticed it on the trip back from Galilee, when four days in Haziel's company had been charged with a new awareness of him, perhaps not so much of him, as of herself – her delicate femininity alongside his maleness, her prettiness radiating towards him when he looked at her, the supple fluidity of her shapely body as she moved. She began to experience a taut self-consciousness whenever he was around.

It was a relief when he went away on his trips because his presence had become disturbing. She found herself always striving to please him, seeing herself constantly through his eyes and placing his perceived judgment on her every word – either good or bad. It was like looking into the mirror of his mind, seeing herself reflected back, and then critically examining the insinuations of his every response. At the same time, not knowing how much of it was conceived in her own thoughts, she could never be sure of the accuracy of her interpretation. It became a relentless obsession that caused her to become contrived – an actor playing a part to an audience of one, who quite possibly wasn't even watching. She was happy when he noticed her, and wilted with dejection when he did not. Why, she wondered, had it become so important to win his approval?

Though his absence gave her a measure of relief, she missed him when he was gone and waited eagerly for his return. One evening, when he had arrived back from a particularly long trip, the family were gathered around the table after dinner. Three clay lamps flickered pleasantly between them, making little puffing sounds. Shana sat across from Haziel, twisting some strands of thread together and watching him sort through fabric samples he had brought back with him. Judith sat next to him mending a tunic, and Aunt Ada was threading beads for a headband. No one spoke, each absorbed in their work. Haziel's powerful presence filled the small room, which had been devoid of masculine company for some weeks. His hair had grown too long, and black wiry curls crowded his face, reaching into his overgrown beard so that only his eyes showed in the dim light. His hands, burnt brown by the sun, seemed huge against the dainty, pale hands of the women. He looked as undomesticated as a wild animal.

Presently Shana put down her thread, stretched drowsily and yawned, drawing a long full breath into her breast. Suddenly an almost imperceptible tremor stirred deep inside her. She opened her eyes and caught Haziel's gaze upon her. Before she could look away, their eyes locked together and held, just a second too long. With lightning speed, a potent spark leapt between them, connecting them, propelling them towards one another with a powerful magnetism. Shana quickly looked down at her hands but her pulse throbbed in her neck, and heat rose to her face. She dared not look up, but could feel his eyes still upon her and knew he had registered her response. Her heart lurched with an exhilarating mixture of joy and fear, for in that brief thrilling instant – that single pulsating moment, held suspended between them – she knew that he desired her.

Silent shockwaves charged the atmosphere with a forewarning of danger. Judith, oblivious to the undercurrents flooding the room, sat with her head bent demurely over her work. The soft curves of her neck and cheek conveyed her gentleness, and there was a trusting, docile sweetness about her that reminded Shana of a calf.

Immediately a flood of conscience exposed Shana's self-deception, and with deep shame she understood her recent behaviour. In her hunger for Haziel's admiration, she had been attracting him, luring him, using the only power she had

– the power of being a woman, and now she held her prize in her hand. The full comprehension of what she had unwittingly brought about sent an icy shiver through her, even as she revelled in it.

After an age, Judith broke the tension by putting down her handwork and announcing that she was going to bed. Shana hurriedly got to her feet, stumbling over her stool, and went outside to wash. Haziel remained at the table, a dark ominous figure in the flickering light.

Shana waited until Aunt Ada shuffled through to her room, and slipped in behind her. Quietly she prepared for bed, her heart jerking unevenly in her chest. When at last the house was still, she lay rigid on her mattress, her mind flitting disjointedly between the implications of what had just happened, and re-living that wonderful, terrible moment – Haziel's burning eyes upon her. She knew, in a sane part of herself, that she had to run from this temptation – not the temptation to respond to Haziel, she knew she would never do that – but the temptation to continue as normal, under cover of innocence, and savour the secret victorious knowledge of her power over the great icon of her existence.

That single instant had changed everything, and the sinking realisation grew heavier and heavier that her time in the home of these dearly loved people had come to an end. She could not risk staying a moment longer than necessary.

Sleep was intermittent. Sometime during the night she devised her plan. She would have to pretend she had received a message from her sister in the morning when she went to the market, saying she was needed at home as soon as possible to help with the harvesting, and announce that she intended to leave the following day. Having made up her mind about what she had to do, she wanted to act fast before she weakened.

Morning came. Numb and miserable, she went out to the market to receive the fabricated news. She would not allow herself to think of Haziel, but his eyes stayed constantly before her. How meaningless life would be without him. On her way back, she wavered, telling herself that now that she understood what she was doing, she could change her behaviour and everything would return to normal. But when she entered the house and saw Haziel sitting on his stool with his back to her, his bull-neck so mighty on his muscular shoulders, her stomach wrung with a forbidden hunger, and she quickly dispatched the news of her intended departure.

"Oh, I can't bear you to go," cried Judith, dropping what she was doing and coming over to embrace Shana. "I know you must, but promise you'll be back as soon as you can!"

"Of course," Shana replied, without conviction.

Haziel's eyes flickered, but he said nothing.

That evening, while Ada chatted and fussed, preparing food for Shana's journey, he sat broodingly, his brows drawn together in a frown, expression closed. There was a coldness in his manner, a brittleness, as though bracing himself. It chilled Shana to the core and she began to wonder if she could have been mistaken about what happened. She felt herself crumbling inside, reduced to a child again in his presence, and every moment became an ordeal of forced cheerfulness.

The next morning she left amid hugs, tears, and loving words from the women who had grown so dear to her, and a rough and hasty embrace from Haziel.

She dared not look back.

CHAPTER 6

THE STRING OF donkeys carrying the luggage for the small caravan picked their way carefully over the rocky terrain. The constant ascents and descents of the Judean mountains made the journey home slow and arduous. Having travelled this way with her parents several times during her childhood, Shana remembered how, in order to overcome the fatigue of the last steep incline, she would imagine that she was climbing up into heaven, step by step, and the first sight of their village in its sublime setting was always reward enough for the effort.

The familiar stone houses came into view, lodging on a rounded peak among cypress and oak forests. They seemed afloat in a vast choppy sea of hills encircled with contours of fruit and olive trees, with neatly cultivated fields curving gracefully into the valleys.

Anticipation and dread wrestled uncomfortably in Shana's stomach as the well-known sights of her childhood came into view. How would her father react? What was her future now? It was a comfort at least to know that her mother would receive her gladly and that Beth would be overjoyed. Somehow she had to shake off the crushing sense of loss that weighed her down.

She unloaded her bags from the donkey and walked to the outskirts of the village, where her father's small farm merged with the open pasturelands. In a field behind the house, Milcah was hoeing the vegetable patch, her dear figure bent to the task.

Shana broke into a run. "Mama!" she shouted, overwhelmed with emotion.

The woman threw up her hoe in surprise and started towards her daughter with sobs of joy. "My child, you've come home at last. Oh, how I've longed to see you!"

Shana plunged into her all-protecting embrace with enormous relief. This was her home right here, in the safety of her mother's arms, not the little peasant house in which they dwelt.

"Beth has pined so much for you, and here you are at last. You're here at last," she repeated as if trying to convince herself it was true.

"How is Father? Is he still angry?"

"Disappointed more than angry, but you know how he expresses it as anger. I think he has missed you more than he will admit."

They went towards the house, arm-in-arm, Milcah releasing a flood of questions, which she hardly noticed remained unanswered. There would be time enough later.

In the large open courtyard shared by several homes, a group of girls were playing a hopping game. One long-legged redhead with the skirt of her tunic tucked into her sash, disengaged from the group and sprinted towards them, shouting wildly. "*Achuti*, my sister! I thought you would never come!" She flung her arms around Shana's neck, almost knocking her off her feet. "I'm so happy! I can't believe you're here." The girl jumped up and down with uninhibited delight. "I have so much to tell you, I've nearly burst with waiting. Tell me all your news, and then I can tell you all mine."

"Perhaps it should be the other way round, it seems you might have more to tell," laughed Shana. "We'll have time tonight for a long chat, I'm sure."

The house. Shana didn't remember it being so small. She stooped through the low door into the dim room, breathing in the familiar scent of burnt oil and damp mud floors. There was pleasure in its familiarity but also a strong aversion. Too many unpleasant associations lurked in its dark unswept corners. She had left them behind, but they clung to her still, attached to her bones like sinews.

Before she had a chance to settle in, the squat figure of her father, Hassin, filled the doorway, shutting out the last of the daylight. Shana stiffened, the forgotten fear pinching at her spine.

"Well, daughter," he said, "What brings you this way?"

A chill went through her. What did his question imply? Was he being sarcastic or simply enquiring?

"Just a visit, Father," she faltered. "I . . . I've missed you all."

"Welcome," he said offhandedly and began the ritual of washing the mud off his feet before dinner.

Shana wondered if he still resented her for challenging his authority and wished they could just go on as though it had never happened, impersonal as their relationship had always been. She was prepared to forgive him for throwing her out of the house, knowing it had more to do with her refusal to marry Rafael than the incident itself, but it would not help if he continued to blame her.

There was an awkward silence, which her mother quickly filled with cheerful chit-chat. A weight hung below Shana's heart, and she longed to crawl into her bed and sob it away; it was such a strain to keep her face smiling.

"You're tired from your journey, my dear," said Milcah, touching her daughter's brow with a soothing hand, her empathy almost unleashing the tears pressing against Shana's eyelids. "You must rest just as soon as you've had something to eat and drink. Here you are now, sit down. I'll go and prepare a bed for you." She bustled into the adjoining room, leaving a faint smell of laundered clothes and bread dough behind her, and Shana sank down gratefully onto a cushion, only half listening to Beth's excited babble. Later she could sort through the jumble in her mind. Right now it was necessary only to keep focused on one moment at a time.

Lying down at last on the old lumpy mattress, with her nose pressed into a clean-smelling blanket and Beth snuggled up beside her, Shana was a child again in her Mama's home. The cacophonous braying of the donkey in the yard and flutter and squawk of surprised chickens, the lonely howl of a distant wolf, even her father's snoring, were the music of her childhood, and sleep came quickly.

Sometime in the night, she awoke with the moonlight shining into her eyes. Her first thought was of Haziel and the distance between them. With the veil of pretence lifted, she was now fully conscious of her love for him. In truth, she had loved him since she was a girl and had always thought that he belonged to her in a special way as her cousin. But this kind of love was different. He had become her frame of reference, the pivotal point of her life. She wanted so much for him to love her too. And somehow Judith was in the way.

She could picture him clearly, his dark intense eyes, always guarded so she could never be certain of his mood. At times he could be so tender, taking a small child onto his lap and letting him play with his strong fingers, or thoughtfully doing things for his wife and his mother to lighten their work. At other times she would feel acutely uncomfortable in his presence, as though she were the cause of his scathing irritability. Then he would refuse to enter into conversation, and her own chatter would fall discordantly into the silence – frivolous words which were merely a means of connecting with him, but which sounded foolishly inane without a response.

Haziel – imposing, perplexing, inscrutable; a complex fusion of power and sensitivity.

Shana gave full rein to her exploding heart and allowed herself to yearn for him with thrilling tenderness. She knew it was a dangerous indulgence, but it so effectively overcame her misery that she pushed aside the warnings of her conscience. Again and again she saw his face flash before her as it was on that fateful evening, frozen in that brief powerful glance, and she let the safe distance between them allow her freedom now to respond, melting, yielding, overflowing with love.

Abruptly the delirious pleasure of her fantasy was replaced by the cold ashes of reality: Haziel did not belong to her! Heartbroken, she began to cry silently into her pillow, grieving the renunciation of her forbidden passion. The future stretched out before her, a succession of days without him – no longer listening for his step or hearing his clever ambiguous quips and contemptuous laugh, no longer being charmed or exasperated by his enigmatic, unpredictable disposition or experiencing the bitter-sweet pining for him in his absence. A vast emptiness swamped her like a desert without horizons.

Unexpectedly she slept again, and now the sounds and smells of morning roused her. Milcah was energetically kneading bread with her strong capable arms. A light rain was falling, so the little oven had been brought indoors and the house was filled with smoke. Beth was sitting on the mattress, watching for the first flutter of Shana's eyelids, at which she gleefully exclaimed, "At last! Now you can come and eat breakfast with me and tell me all about your time with Aunt Ada. You went straight to sleep last night and wouldn't answer me." She jumped to her feet, did a little skip and spun around, and Shana saw she was in that delightful stage of girlish self-expression – coquettish, a little cheeky, every move deliberate, every gesture on display. It was uplifting to watch, and Shana smiled as she quickly dressed and followed her sister to the table.

Hassin had gone out at first light as usual but would be back shortly for breakfast. The table was already laid with a basket for the fresh baked bread, and bowls of olives, fruit, cheese, and cucumbers. How comforting it was to be in the haven of her mother's care that not even her father could intrude upon. Milcah's quiet strength had laid down invisible boundaries, which he dared not cross when she was around, though he remained unaware of the power she held over him. She never argued with her husband, but often it was what she left unsaid that built a fortress around things she considered sacred. She was adept at keeping him on the peripherals of many family activities, lest his blundering insensitivity destroy what she had built up for her daughters.

However, he was always head of every family meal in true Jewish tradition, and the traditions were carefully respected. He assumed this role with imperious ceremony, which irked

Shana intensely, but Milcah accepted it with loving patience.

He came in now, casting a shadow over the room. Shana tensed and waited uncertainly to gauge his mood. He seemed preoccupied but even-tempered as he said good morning and settled himself at the table. Beth, always oblivious to the intimations of his temper, danced around him, leaning in towards his face and saying, "Hello, my father, and how are you today?" and then skipping away. She never failed to soften his humour.

"Come sit down, you little bear," he growled, with a half-smile. She made two big hops and landed on the reed mat beside him. Milcah tipped the hot bread into the basket and joined the family at the table.

"For all these blessings we thank the Lord our God with praise," Hassin began in a solemn voice, and before the words were out, his fat hand was already reaching for the bread. He tore off a large chunk, scooped up a generous portion of goat's cheese, and began to chomp rapidly like a dog with a bone, breathing noisily, eyes darting from side to side. The urgency in the way he ate made mealtimes a tense affair, and Shana deliberately ate slowly to compensate for his haste and tried not to look at him.

With his mouth half full, he addressed her, "So, my girl, what news of Judith and Haziel?"

The unexpected mention of his name brought a swift flame to her cheeks, which she feared would give away her secret. "They're very well, Father. Aunt Ada is suffering rather badly with her legs and can only walk with a stick now."

"Have you been a help to them?" he asked with an accusing undertone.

"Y–yes, of course, Father, I have done whatever I could,"

she replied, noting how their communication slipped back into the usual pattern of attack and defence. Every word was in danger of being misinterpreted, and it was never clear whether what was said was distorted by the speaker or the hearer.

Her father grunted, disapprovingly it seemed, and went on eating, his eyebrows drawn together in a disagreeable way.

Shana looked around. Nothing much had changed. The remaining clay pitcher still stood on the shelf next to the oil lamp, the worn farming tools leaned against the flaking wall outside the door, and she was experiencing the same discomfit at the table with her father, the same feeling of wanting to escape and never come back, if it were not for her mother and Beth.

She studied her sister, really seeing her for the first time since her arrival. She was not a little girl anymore. Eight months had brought noticeable changes. She was taller than Shana now, tall for her thirteen years, and her chest displayed a hint of her approaching womanhood. There was a pretty bloom on her freckled cheeks, which still retained their chubby childishness, and her hair was curly like Shana's but the colour of sun-dried apricots. What she lacked in Shana's own striking looks, her effervescent personality made up for.

"Let's go find Kyla," said Beth. "She will be so happy to have you back. She hasn't found another friend as much fun as you. She says most of those other girls just want to stay home and talk about boys. Or about each other!"

"There is work to be done before you two go flitting off," their father cut in. "Plenty of it!"

Shana always felt edgy around her father whenever he saw her idle. If she took a break from her daily chores, she would go out of her way to avoid him. He expected her to labour long and hard in the fields, like the son she should have been.

She realised with dismay that she had come right back to the life she had hoped to leave behind forever, only now it was all the more bitter for having tasted the succulent fruit of freedom.

CHAPTER 7

THE SWEET FRAGRANCE of cut barley warmed in spring sunshine, and the rattle of sheaves heavy with grain nourished Shana's wilting soul, just as the harvest would provide rich nutrients for the body. It was a back-breaking job, but one she always enjoyed. Beth came to glean the rows behind her, and sometimes Milcah too, and their songs would rise together in the field while they worked. Hassin, no longer able to bend to the task, would occasionally waddle up from the shed and stand watching them, with his legs planted apart and one hand shading his eyes.

The sheaves were tied and loaded onto the donkey to be taken to the threshing floor, where the women beat out the grain in a rhythmic dance while they sang. How thankful Shana was to have this work that involved both body and soul, to help break her obsession with Haziel.

After a couple of months of hard labour, most of the early season work was done, and Haziel had, for the most part, been banished from her mind. Except when his image showed up unexpectedly before her eyes, grinning impishly after an obtuse remark or looking endearingly crestfallen in a moment of vulnerability.

Mid-summer now smouldered down upon the village, sapping the vitality from every living thing. The colourless landscape echoed the dryness of Shana's heart, and a deep lassitude assailed her as though her limbs were weighted down like clay. The routines of village life had resumed and with them a return of discontent. It was the same, day in and day out: trudging to the well, braced with polite enquiries and a thin smile; sweeping the mud-floored house; grinding, grinding, grinding corn; attending synagogue every Sabbath, going back home, and starting all over again. The days limped by. Oh, how life lacked spice without Haziel.

Shana envied the other young women in her village, who so willingly accepted their lot, many of them already proudly carrying babies on their hips. But the nagging hankering for something more never left her, something that would fill the void inside her, which her brief taste of life, love and adventure had only deepened. Often she pondered the Rabbi's words, which held such fascinating promises of abundant life, but without him being around, it remained out of reach.

Milcah went out of her way to offer little comforts, helpful suggestions, and encouragements. Her quick anxious glances told Shana that she sensed something was wrong but knew Shana would not speak of it to her. She did whatever she could to make things easier for her daughter by giving her the more pleasant of the chores.

"Would you go to the market today?" she said one morning. "You look so pale, it will do you good to get out of the house. You are bound to meet your friends there; perhaps you would like to bring someone home with you to share our dinner."

Shana sighed and took up her basket listlessly. She pulled her faded blue shawl over her head and dawdled along the path, scraping her sandals over the stones and watching the dust fly up around her feet. Crocuses blazed violet in the dry grass, and a startled kingfisher flashed turquoise against the brown monochrome, but she hardly noticed. She dragged the basket along the ground and kicked crossly at a clod of earth. It was her own stupid fault that she had ended up here again when she could have been enjoying her freedom. But now for Judith's sake, she could never go back.

Just then, a shadow fell beside her own, jolting her out of her sullen mindset. She looked up, dazzled by the sun for a moment, and saw a vaguely familiar face smiling down at her.

"Rafael!"

"Yes, home at last. It's been a long year."

Shana blinked. He came gradually into focus. Another year had sculpted his face into a more angular shape, which was emphasised by his trimmed beard and closely cropped hair. The furrows in his cheeks had deepened and his brows were heavier, giving his face a masculine strength that was pleasingly attractive. She felt suddenly shy.

"How have you been?" he asked, his eyes spiked with happiness.

"Oh, um . . . alright, I suppose. How about you?"

"Well, not only am I a fully qualified leather-worker but I now know the Torah backwards," he said with a laugh. "I heard you've also been away."

Shana flushed. "Yes, I went to help my cousin, er cousin's wife with their weaving business near Jerusalem."

"So you've also learnt a craft. Well, I'm sure you must be

glad to be back home too. The city can be tiring after our wonderfully simple lifestyle here, don't you think?"

"I–I love Jerusalem. I miss it a lot. I find it rather too quiet here after– after . . ." She shrugged as her words tailed off and bent to pick a dried head of grass, which she crushed between her fingers.

They walked on, side by side, as Rafael recounted his experiences brightly with frequent interjections of laughter. His happy chatter flowed over Shana like a refreshing stream. She hadn't felt this way in a long time – revitalised, almost gay. It was good to have him back.

"Are you here to stay?" she asked.

"For a time, yes," he said. "I hope to sell my leatherware on the trade route, perhaps take on a couple of students, and set up my own home near my father's house. Father needs help with the sheep; he has aged a lot recently. What about you?"

"I don't know. I don't–don't really have many choices."

He stopped and searched her face. She looked away, still crushing the grass seeds in her palm.

"You don't seem happy. What is it?"

She avoided his eyes. "N-nothing in particular. I'm restless, a little bored I suppose. I don't really know."

"Most of your friends are married now and busy with their babies. Perhaps you feel a little excluded?"

"It's certainly not that!" Shana retorted, flinging away the grass seeds and dusting her hands on her skirt. She turned to walk on, but Rafael caught her hand. "Wait, I have something to say."

She looked at him in surprise and withdrew her hand awkwardly.

"Shushana, listen. I have missed you more than I can tell

you," he said in a breathless rush of words. "You know, of course, that before I went away, I asked your father for you as my wife, and you know it is his will that we marry. I understood that you were not ready then, so I have waited. I want you to be my wife, Shana. We would go well together. Tell me how you feel. Tell me truthfully."

Shana's legs almost gave way. She took a step backwards and stared at him. His gentle intelligent eyes were so familiar to her, yet different now. He was so very dear to her – but to marry? She froze, as cornered as a field mouse, knowing she would have to reply.

"Raf. Oh, Raf, I'm so confused right now." Tears glistened in her eyes. "I have felt so lost recently, I scarcely know who I am, much less what I want. I would hardly make a fit wife for you the way I am now."

His face darkened. "If you settled down in a home of your own with me, you would soon feel steadier. I would help you." He reached for her hand again. "I love you, Shana. I have always loved you."

"Please," she pleaded in a small desperate voice, putting her hands behind her back. "Please, not now. Can we . . . can't we be friends again like we've always been, can't we . . ."

"As my wife, you and I will always be friends."

"For a while, Raf, can you just be my friend. I have missed you and I'm so happy that you're back, but please understand, I'm not ready to take such a huge step. It's just so . . . so permanent."

"You're afraid, aren't you?" he said. "I shouldn't have sprung it on you like this."

She said nothing but stood twisting the end of her shawl around her finger, and he watched her with an expression of aching tenderness. "Will you think about it?" he said.

She nodded slightly and they continued along the path again. He made an effort to resume his chatter, but it had become contrived. It was a relief when they parted at the crossroads.

"Would you like to join us for dinner later?" she asked, suddenly uncertain whether it was the right thing to do.

"I would love to very much. I'm looking forward to seeing your parents and finding out how much Beth has grown up."

"See you later then," she called, plunging down the track with unnecessary haste.

Dinner was strained. Rafael valiantly tried to reclaim his former levity, but his disappointment weighed him down, and Shana tried too eagerly to coax him into a brighter mood. Thankfully, Beth's undisguised show of affection distracted him, and her girlish humour cheered him up.

A week passed and Shana did not see Rafael. She absorbed herself in each of her chores with studied concentration. On the surface, her mind remained free of any thoughts except such things as, "This grain needs soaking. Where is that jar? I must put the wood on the fire and fetch water. I've left it a bit late, I'd better hurry." But on a deeper level her thoughts had a life of their own, never still for a moment, day or night, see-sawing, questioning, conflicting, turning round and round; many voices argued within her, telling her things and then disagreeing, ceaselessly trying to work out the answer to a problem she had not properly defined. It was like an army of dissidents wrestling in the dark, uncertain of who was the opponent. She worked furiously at her tasks, and when her mother spoke to her, she sometimes did not even hear.

One afternoon, Shana was sitting on the bench behind the house, busy stripping corn for the evening meal, when Rafael appeared. Her heart lifted spontaneously. He held out a pair of thonged leather sandals with the straps tied loosely at the back. "Look what I made for you," he said, grinning self-consciously.

Shana took them with candid delight. "For m–me?" she stammered. She slipped one onto her bare foot, and Rafael squatted in front of her to tie the thongs. His touch on her ankle was like a caress and she felt an involuntary response in her body.

"How pretty your feet are," he murmured. "These little square toes look so . . . vulnerable." He pinched one of them between his fingers, and she snatched her foot away, giggling, leaving the sandal in his hand.

"Give your foot back, or you won't get your sandal," he said, laughing up at her. "Give it to me; I want to kiss those toes one by one."

"No!" she squealed, still giggling. He had never been this intimate with her before, and she didn't know how to react to his teasing. She placed her foot gingerly into the sandal again, ready to retract it if necessary, and watched his shapely artistic fingers tie the thongs, so skilfully nimble with the leather. He tied on the other sandal and then drew back to view his work.

"They fit perfectly," said Shana.

"Yes, perfectly," said Rafael.

Bathed in a moment of shared happiness, Rafael lifted his eyes to meet hers, searching for the answer to his question. She blinked nervously a few times and looked away.

All the warmth and levity of the moment was gone. A grave expression clouded his features. He drew a breath and hesitated for a long time, tracing patterns in the sand with his finger. Then he got to his feet, preparing to leave.

"I release you, Shana," he said softly, without animosity.

An uncertain smile played on her lips. She wanted to say thank you, but no words would come. He smiled and patted her shoulder as he left.

"Friends always," he said.

Shana stared down the road after him, feeling a shiver of cold in spite of the afternoon heat. It was what she wanted, but she felt suddenly abandoned.

He did not visit often after that. She could see that he was trying to maintain their friendship, but that it cost him. Eventually he stopped coming and when their paths crossed he was polite but restrained. She missed him more than she ever thought she would. Life had been much easier before his return.

CHAPTER 8

ARLY RAINS HAD FALLEN. Shana's father ordered her to
begin the ploughing work, which was always the most
taxing of the agricultural tasks – usually a job left to men, in
particular the sons of the family. Since Hassin had no son and
his back had become painful, he drove his daughter to the
fields, saying with bitter pride that at least he had bred a
strong descendant, in spite of her being a girl. And strong she
was, for a steel resilience resided within her slight frame.
Nevertheless, the work pushed her to the limits of her
capability.

The first ploughing was the toughest, the stony ground
having formed an unyielding crust during the long dry
months. Shana slipped the yoke over the ox's leathery neck
and anchored the iron point of the plough deep into the soil.
Then she prodded the animal with a goad to get him moving.
The powerful scent of turned earth excited her senses, and
she loved seeing the ridges form in neat lines behind her.
Every now and again, the plough would hit a rock below the

surface, and she would have to prod the heaving animal until the ground gave way and they were both drenched with sweat.

The day's work had to be completed before the sun reached its zenith in order to avoid the worst of the heat. They had got almost to the end of the final furrow when something suddenly snagged the plough and jerked the ox hard onto his knees. As the animal struggled to get up, the end of the yoke dug into the soil and snapped. Shana felt as though she'd been kicked in the gut. Her father's precious plough was broken, and she would get the blame!

With trembling hands, she unhitched the ropes, released the ox and turned for home, dragging the ruined implement behind her. Hassin had been so proud of it, it was the first new farming device he had bought himself as a young man, and the curved wood of the bars had been smoothed to a burnished gloss with years of use. The hole in one tapered end had worn down with the friction of the ropes, and it was in this weakened area that the wood had fractured.

Her father would only be back that evening from Hebron, by which time he would be tired and ill-humoured. Shana could picture his face when she showed it to him.

"It wasn't your fault," Beth kept telling her, but Shana knew it would make no difference. The hours passed slowly and miserably, and she recoiled each time she heard a sound outside. When finally she heard the crunch of her father's boots crossing the courtyard, she went out to meet him, holding the broken implement out in front of her, her head hanging in shame and fear.

Like a beast with a cornered victim, his wrath was slow and dangerous, welling up until the eyes bulged in his head, and then striking, using cruel words as his weapon. "Is it not enough to deny me your bride price and cost me an extra mouth to feed?" he snarled. "Now you prevent me from earning a living too!" He grabbed the yoke out of her hands and flung it across the courtyard. It looked as though he would strike her, though he had never done so before, and Shana instinctively threw her arms up over her head. But the caustic verbal thrashing that followed was as crushing as if it had been blows of his fists.

Afterwards, he turned and walked into the house, shoulders sagging, as deflated as a burst wine skin, and Shana felt an involuntary pang of pity. She went to sit down behind the house. The worst was over; now it was just a matter of waiting for the ache in her throat and crushing sense of shame to subside.

She sat listening to the night sounds, longing for Haziel's huge protective bulk, and then unexpectedly she thought of Rafael's reassuring gentleness and began to cry.

A memory surfaced, and pain tightened around her chest, squeezing the breath out of her. She was about seven years old – a whimsical child, who irritated her father constantly with her vague inability to understand his instructions. One day, Milcah was at home with little Beth, and Hassin had taken Shana to the fields with him so that she could watch their small flock of sheep while he harvested olives on the mountain slopes nearby.

"Take care not to let the sheep stray close to the edge of the cliff," he ordered, "and call me if you need me."

Shana swelled with pride at being given such responsibility. She could see her father working among the trees and she delighted in watching the shaggy, soft-eyed sheep with their bouncing lambs, grazing between the rocks. Suddenly the urgent bleating of a lamb interrupted her happy reverie. She ran in the direction of the sound and, with rising dismay, traced it to a place just below the edge of the cliff. She ran as fast as her little legs could go to fetch her father, with the pitiful screams of the lamb ringing in her ears. He stomped back with her, red in the face and sweating, and peered over the edge of the cliff. Catching her by the arm, he yanked her to the edge and pointed to a gap between the rocks, where the bleating lamb was standing on a ledge a few feet down the cliff side.

"You will have to climb down and fetch it," he growled. "You are small enough to fit between these rocks. Get down there, and pass the lamb up to me."

Shana began to shake. The ledge was quite wide, but all she could see was the yawning valley far below. "I'm afraid, Papa," she whimpered, clinging to the rock.

"Don't be silly!" he snarled. "Go on, do as you are told before I toss you over."

She took a step towards the edge, dizzy with fear as the cavernous space opened up before her. She could see the desperate yellow eyes of the shivering lamb, and its pathetic cries urged her forward even more than her father's wrath. Quaking convulsively, she lowered her thin little body between the two jutting rocks, supporting herself with her elbows. For a ghastly moment her legs swung in mid-air, thrashing about wildly to find a footing.

"Be careful, you'll knock the lamb right off!" shouted her father from above. Her elbows gave way and she fell the last few inches onto the ledge, but it felt as though she was plunging down towards the jagged rocks below. She was trembling so much she could barely keep hold of the frantic wriggling little creature, but with a monumental effort she managed to hold it up until her father could grab it and lift it to safety. He disappeared for a minute while he went to return the lamb to its mother, and terror gripped her with talons as sharp and deadly as an eagle's. She could not climb up unaided, and the dreadful depths seemed to be pulling her towards the edge, claiming her. Her piercing screams echoed through the valley.

Her father's face appeared again. "Don't be such a baby!" he sneered. "If you don't stop crying, I'll leave you there."

"No, Papa, please! Please don't leave me," she begged, sobbing hysterically. "I will stop crying. I will, I promise! Please!"

"It was only a joke," he said and began to laugh – a harsh, terrible, mocking laugh – and then jerked her up by her arm, bumping her knee against the jagged rock. Never would she forget the shame and misery she experienced as she walked back home behind him, while he herded the sheep to the pen. Her little soul sickened within her, and she never called him Papa again.

There had been a son, born a year after Shana. Her mother only spoke of him once when Shana was ten, after a particularly ugly scene between her and her father. Shana understood even then that her mother offered the information to explain her father's harshness, and it did help to soften her judgment of him a little. The long-awaited baby son had been Hassin's pride and joy, the crown of his youth, and when the baby died a few short months later, Hassin had never been the same again. He was glad, her mother told her, when Beth turned out to be a daughter, because he never wanted to risk suffering that kind of loss again. In the incomprehensible reasoning of children, Shana somehow felt she was to blame for her little brother's death, and this explained perfectly why her father despised her so.

And now, even as a young woman, he still had the power to reduce her to a cringing good-for-nothing who could not please him, no matter how hard she tried. She crawled into her bed without supper, just wanting the day to end.

The courtyard was already astir with women up and about, tackling their work with robust, early morning energy and haste before the heat of the day could rob them of their strength. Children ran and skipped between them, celebrating the sunshine and the new day, overjoyed at the sight of their friends. Their laughter cascaded through the streets as they chased each other around the houses. Shana stumbled out, tying her apron around her waist, with her hair in a tangled mess and her eyes swollen from her midnight tears. She took up a sack of corn and knelt down with the hand mill.

"Shana!" called Kyla, coming over to her. "There you are. You look terrible. Where have you been the last few days?" She sank down opposite her friend and pulled the handle of the mill forward to activate the mechanical motion – round and round it hummed and scraped. Shana shook a handful of corn into the centre and yawned, trying to fashion a reply that would not invite further enquiry. The truth was that she had been avoiding company. Her fluctuating emotions and unpredictable plunges into gloom were bewildering enough without having to try to explain them.

"Oh, just helping my mother, the usual. I'm teaching my sister to spin; she's growing up now and–"

"Have you heard about that awful Juan divorcing his wife? No loss to her, I shouldn't think, and thankfully she had no children to part with. You have to be so careful who you marry these days, or you'll be cast out for burning the breakfast!"

Kyla chatted on and on, skimming seamlessly from one subject to another. Shana half listened, while her thoughts tumbled on like the background noise of a running river.

"There's talk of Rafael considering a betrothal," said Kyla.

Shana let go of the handle and looked up, shocked. She saw Kyla watching her closely to catch her reaction. This would certainly be news of general interest since it had always been expected in the community that he would marry Shana.

"To whom?" Shana asked in a small voice, feeling the blood drain from her face.

"Zippora," said Kyla triumphantly, relishing the moment. She had been outraged when she learned of Shana refusing Rafael a second time. Having been recently betrothed to a good friend of Rafael's, she wanted nothing more than to have her own best friend share married life with her, especially with that nice Rafael, who was such a perfect match for Shana, as she kept telling her.

Shana felt sick. "Why her, of all people?" she blurted out. "She . . . she just won't suit him at all!"

"Well, he needs a wife, and I guess she'll be as good as any. Obviously their parents have found reason enough for the alliance."

"It's all wrong!" exclaimed Shana angrily. "Why should parents decide who will be happy or not and treat their children like prize market goats!"

"Shana!" A look of wicked glee flitted across Kyla's face at her friend's bold impertinence. "Well, they're not always wrong you know. Hey, watch what you're throwing in here! There'll be stones in the bread!"

Shana got abruptly to her feet. "I'm going to fetch water," she said. "See you later."

She swung the water jar onto her shoulder and left before

Kyla could try to accompany her. The stream of her thoughts had rushed in a new direction, running hot and loud in her ears. "Zippora! Anyone but her! I must warn Rafael; I cannot let him make this mistake." Shana knew only too well how Zippora was always boasting about finding herself a match who would keep her in luxury, a man of good standing in the village.

Rafael would be busy at his work in the little shop he had built facing the street in front of his home. If she took the long way round to the well, she would pass his shop and hopefully get a chance to speak to him. It was still early, perhaps there would not be many people around.

The path led up a slope, where a scattering of houses, with washing flapping on the rooftop terraces, tumbled haphazardly. The sun was already hot, and Shana panted excessively as she climbed, her heart pounding more than the exertion required. Rafael was her friend, she reasoned to herself, it would only be right to warn him.

She could see his tall figure bent over the workbench with his back towards her as she approached. People passing by called out greetings to him, but thankfully no one stopped. She hurried on with needless haste, so that by the time she reached him she was quite out of breath.

"What's the matter?" asked Rafael, alarmed. "Is something wrong?"

"Oh, no," said Shana breathlessly, adding a foolish laugh. "Nothing at all . . . Well actually, yes, there is something a . . . a bit wrong. I need to speak to you." She glanced around nervously. Rafael put down his paring knife and gave her his attention, his brows drawn together with concern.

"Raf," she began hesitantly, not at all sure of herself and beginning to wish she hadn't come. She noted again the quiet confidence he exuded. He was a man now, no longer her pudgy friend, and she was suddenly afraid. It was none of her business what he did, and she had no right to interfere.

"What is it?" he insisted. It was too late to back out.

"It's about Zippora," she blundered on. He blanched slightly. "Is it true that you are going to marry her?"

His mouth twitched; he looked annoyed. "A man needs a wife," he said, echoing Kyla's words.

"But you don't know her, you . . . you don't know what she's like . . ."

Shana felt her mouth tugging down at the corners the way it did when she was about to cry. Her hand trembled on his arm, "Listen to me, she's not what you think. She'll make you unhappy. She—"

"Enough said!" His tone was unusually harsh. He turned back to his work, cutting savagely into the leather with his knife. Shana flicked the quickly pooling tears from her eyes. Someone was approaching. She straightened up and walked away, with her head held high and her fingers tightly gripping the water jar. A trembling uncertainty consumed her and cast her adrift.

CHAPTER 9

THE OLIVE FESTIVAL was always one of the merriest festivals in the highlands because the country's choicest olives came from this region. An air of celebration bubbled through the village, and everyday chores were done with a new lightness of spirit. Preparations for the occasion united the community in a spirit of thankfulness for their beloved land. The young men sang as they brought in some of the early harvest and placed it in heaped baskets in the village square, together with jugs of newly pressed oil. There were stalls overflowing with fruit in colourful symphonies of greens, yellows, and rosy pinks to delight the eye, and tall jars of wine banked up ready for the tasting. The finest robes were brought out of storage chests, and bright embroidered shawls arranged stylishly over heads and shoulders and pinned with treasured brooches. Clusters of tittering young girls collected on street corners, alight with excitement.

"Praise be to God," the women called out as they passed one another on their hurried ways.

As night fell, people began to gather in the square. The musicians struck up a few hesitant bars of a song, faltered to a discordant halt, and then started again until the music began to liberate itself in lilting melodies, underscored by the clash of tambourines, which never failed to rouse the limbs to movement. As the wine flowed, the dancing began, self-consciously at first but soon inviting young and old to join the lively jig, which so aptly gave expression to their rejoicing hearts. Even Shana cheered up as she united with the joyful throng, and she abandoned herself to the festivities with some of the former spontaneity of her girlhood. She saw Rafael watching her from across the square but gave no indication that she noticed him.

Zippora was there, of course, looking very becoming in a fashionable dress of fine linen wound closely around her body in soft pleats, her large round eyes further emphasised with kohl. She had grown up to be a real beauty, Shana noted regretfully, but brushed the thought aside and focused on the dancing. Soon the aroma of roasting lamb enticed the dancers to tables laden with the seasonal bounty of their fertile region, and the feasting began amidst a robust clamour of voices and laughter. The night was warm, and the winking of a million stars seemed to shower down approval from above.

After the banquet, the dancing resumed, first the women, weaving sinuously in and out of the crowd, and then the men, leaping and clapping. Rafael joined a line of dancers opposite Shana. He wore an embroidered sleeveless tunic Shana had not seen before, which set off his fine physique. She caught his eye as she bounced to and fro, laughing with exhilaration.

Zippora took note. She pushed through the dancers and took up a position directly in front of Rafael, edging Shana out of the way. She began to sway her shapely body sensuously, exquisitely, in time to the music. No man could fail to notice her – she was mesmerising – and all the time her eyes never left Rafael's face. Shana could see that he was captivated by her, she held a power over him, he was bewitched and elated by her charms, which mingled alluringly with the wine in his veins.

It was only half way through the evening but Shana felt suddenly deflated. She backed away into the crowd and found somewhere to sit down. She caught brief glimpses of their beaming faces flickering among the dancers, lit up and glistening in the blaze of the fires and torches, immersed in one another, already united. Never had she felt so cut out, so rejected and alone. The pain of it burned through the core of her being and lodged in her throat in a hot, throbbing lump. Only once was she aware that Rafael noticed her, but she did not know then that the picture of her white suffering face had etched onto his mind, and for the rest of the evening his heart was heavy.

However, he appeared to be merry and jovial, right up until the noise died down and the crowds eventually faded away, yawning contentedly and stumbling with fatigue as the first glimmer of dawn betrayed the coming day.

Another month passed. Shana did not see Rafael, nor hear anything more about his plans for the future. His association with Zippora did not seem widely known, since no one else had mentioned it, and Shana began to wonder if Kyla had made a premature assumption. She missed Rafael terribly, but the passing of days took the edge off that first raw emotion, and she hoped that in time she would grow accustomed to the idea of his eventual marriage.

One afternoon, when it was too hot to go on with the

ploughing, Shana turned the ox out to rest and sought refuge in the cool of the forest. Since that first early flush of rain, the clouds had fled and the sun again shrivelled the surface of the earth. Hot suffocating air, heavy as a blanket, pressed down on man and beast as they moved in a languid daze towards shelter. She dropped down in the shade of a large carob tree at the edge of an open field and leant limply against its trunk. The ground shimmered in the heat, desperate to draw down the fleeting clouds and suck out their life-giving moisture, but they sped by, indifferent. Dust flew up, swirled, and advanced across the dry field, and then vanished like a series of spiralling apparitions.

Presently a keen wind whipped up, summoning banks of cloud from the west horizon, which mounted up layer upon layer and crowded the sky, extinguishing the sun. A tremulous hush fell upon the parched earth. Suddenly, a jagged tongue of brilliant light flickered in the distance, sending a powerful thrill through Shana.

Nothing breathed.

Then the reverent silence was broken by a long, deep-throated rumble, which quivered through the earth in waves. Shana sat up alert, not wanting to miss a moment of the drama on display for her audience alone. A second flash of lightning ripped the sky, followed more quickly by another growl of thunder. Gusts of wind stirred up the crisp leaves at her feet. Once again the heavens clawed at the earth with bewitched, electric fingers, and a final mighty climactic explosion slit the sky. A single drop of rain plummeted into the dust, and then another and another, falling faster and faster.

Shana came out from under the tree and, discarding her shawl, turned her face upward to receive the stabbing droplets into her eyes and her mouth, which soaked through her hair and ran in cold rivulets down her neck, cascading down her body like a waterfall, and between her toes into the ecstatic soil. It was like bathing in a heavenly stream, where water and light infused every cell of her being, penetrating right into her shimmering soul, and she felt her essence completely in perfect wordless interaction with her Creator.

After a long while, she turned for home, still suspended in a trance-like state and unwilling to break the spell as she knew she must, knowing that the first person to cross her path would invade her shining realm, capture her and drag her back to the world of normalcy. Worse still, they would scold her for getting wet, tell her she would be ill, and hurry her home, oblivious to the glory she had experienced. She smiled to herself and sighed, surrendering herself to the inevitable.

The rain settled into a steady shower, refreshing the earth and washing away the grime and thirst of the long hot summer. Shana came through the dripping trees at the edge of the forest and saw a figure hurrying towards her. With a surge of delight, she recognised Rafael.

He stopped in astonishment when he saw her. "I came to look for you," he began. "Beth said you had gone out for a walk, and I was concerned about you in this storm."

Shana laughed gaily. "Oh Raf, it was glorious. I wish you could have been there."

Her robe clung to her body, puckering at her waist and hips, and her hair stuck to her cheeks. Rafael gazed at her with an expression of overwhelming tenderness.

"You have diamonds all along your lashes," he said softly, and then turned brisk. "You should get some dry clothes on. The wind is starting up and—"

"Don't fuss so. Don't you know I am made of clay and

raindrops?" she said, smiling coyly. "But thanks for the concern. Were you visiting?"

"Just delivering a bag of seed to your father. I must get back home to finish digging the ditches before dark or we'll be flooded. I'm glad you're alright."

She felt his departure with a twinge of regret and continued on her way, sodden and suddenly crestfallen.

Not long after that, Rafael appeared unexpectedly outside her house, where Shana was threshing grain. He looked extremely apprehensive. "I want to speak to you. Can you meet me at the Big Tree? I'll wait for you there after lunch."

Shana's heart sank. She knew what it was he was going to tell her and hated the way it made her feel. She spent the morning preparing herself so that she could appear happy about his news. She practised her words in her mind, but none of them sounded right. She was grateful at least for his consideration in letting her be the first to know.

Midday came too soon. She wasn't hungry but swallowed some bread and milk to give her strength and set off, weak with trepidation, along the track through the forest that led to the Big Tree.

They had named this tree together when they used to meet here as children to hide away from the others. They used a secret sign: one of them would toss a white stone and shout, "Catch!" It had to be a white one. If the stone was thrown back, it signalled agreement, and then whoever made the sign would go first. The Big Tree was a towering oak with low spreading branches into which they would climb and hide among the leaves. Shana enjoyed the game thoroughly until one day, after Rafael had been going to synagogue school for a while, he announced that he could not meet her there anymore because it was wrong before God to deceive people. She had felt ashamed and perplexed by his new concern for righteousness.

Now they would never meet here again.

She dragged her feet as she drew near. She could see Rafael leaning against the tree, one arm resting on a low branch. A great sadness filled the empty space in her heart. She drew a deep breath, braced her shoulders, and went to him.

Rafael shifted from one foot to the other, uncharacteristically nervous. Shana stood in front of him with her hands behind her back, twisting her fingers together, dreading his words. He seemed reluctant to speak. He swallowed, rubbed his hand over his beard and began, low and serious.

"Shana, I can only ever say this to you one last time . . ." He hesitated, looked deep into her eyes, and his words came slow and clear. "I want you, and you only, to be my wife."

She sucked in her breath sharply and began to tremble. Blood pounded in her ears as one predominant thought separated from her confusion and registered on her brain. He still loved her!

And . . . and yes, she loved him too. It had been unbearable to be without him, to think of him belonging to someone else. How could there ever be anyone else for her? She looked at his face, so clean, so kind, so dearly familiar. She saw the love in his eyes, the timorous hope mingled with the courageous preparing for pain. He was strong and he was steady, and he would be her husband and her friend.

"Yes," she said weakly.

"D–do you mean, yes?"

"Yes," she said.

He stood still for a moment trying to assimilate her response, and then relief flooded his face, followed by an exploding gladness that recaptured the boy in him Shana knew so well.

"I'll go right now to speak to your father," he said, and departed hastily, leaving her stunned, slumped against the tree.

In one instant her whole life had changed. She was a different person now, though she did not yet know who that person was. She was going to be a wife, go and live in Rafael's house with him, cook his meals, lay down in his bed, eventually to have children . . . It was an exhilarating, wonderful, terrifying thought.

It was a good thing that the usual term of betrothal was a year. She would have plenty of time to get used to the idea.

The betrothal celebrations were a blur through which Shana drifted like an Elysian princess. All around her people dressed her, fussed over her, rejoiced and made plans. It all seemed to be happening to somebody else.

Then she was led to Rafael's house to be promised to him before the rabbi. Rafael was aglow with love and happiness, handsome in a new white tunic. He gave her a beautiful gold ring, which he hung on a leather thong around her neck. "I will put this on your finger the day of our wedding," he told her.

The people danced and clapped, Zippora too, as she had set her sights on a wealthy man, new to the district. Shana's father looked pleased and important, even acknowledged her with a generous smile. Her mother's joy overflowed enough for both of them, and all was well. Beth was so enamoured with the whole affair that anyone would have thought it was she who was going to get married.

Shana was quietly serene. Something had settled down within her. She hardly ever thought about Haziel anymore and was glad she had grown out of her childhood infatuation. Best of all, she had her friend back, and it was so good to have him back.

In the days that followed, Rafael visited almost every day. There was a greater leniency now on their spending time together, although they could not be found alone after dark. They walked to synagogue together on the Sabbaths, and in the late afternoons would often stroll on the hills, rejoicing in the autumn magnificence of the mountains. They marvelled together at how each day presented such a unique rendering of the same landscape, altered by changes of light and weather and season.

One evening towards the end of autumn, Rafael came to visit Shana later than usual, but it was such a fine evening that they were reluctant to miss their walk. They climbed up out of the village and strolled in comfortable silence, in mutual appreciation of the beauty around them. The sinking sun cut furrows through the ploughed hillside fields, and a fallen tree, silhouetted on the horizon, raised its bare branches to the heavens in pleading defiance of death. They crossed a field, surprising an army of crows, which launched clumsily into the air with rasping shrieks and dived to the ground with wings like witches capes. Presently, a cold wind whipped up from the earth, filling their nostrils with the tangy smell of moist loam. They hurried back down the hill as the sun plunged behind a bank of clouds, reappearing briefly in streaks of fiery gold before day surrendered to night, pulling down behind it a curtain of gradually thickening darkness.

Down in the valley, the hot earth breathed warm draughts through their hair, enticing them to linger. Rafael stopped and took Shana in his arms, lifting her chin as he bent to kiss her. She gave her lips to him, uncertain at the strangeness of it. He held her close against his chest, his breath hot on her cheek. "My love, my beautiful one," he murmured and began to kiss her neck, but his fervour disturbed her, and she could not respond. If only he would just hold her and be still.

"It's almost dark," she said, pulling away. "We must hurry back."

They walked in silence to the crossroad. Shana felt troubled and did not know why.

As they parted, Rafael squeezed her hand briefly. "I'm sorry," he said.

CHAPTER 10

THE WINTER WAS HARSH but brief, with one heavy snowfall obliterating all that was familiar, transforming the high places into an enchanted realm, which froze time in its icy grip. But now the white world had been replaced by a land of brilliant green, and the sheep gorged themselves on the rich new grass in preparation for lambing.

"Shushana, Shushana!" Milcah called out as she approached the house carrying baskets laden with fresh vegetables from the market. She walked with stiff laboured steps, which rocked her plump body from side to side. Shana ran to help her.

"What is it, Mama?"

"I've just had news that your Aunt Ada is not at all well," she panted, her forehead pleated with alarm. "Judith has asked me to come. I wish I could go but I cannot leave your father right now. I passed him at the threshing floor, and he said he wants me to stay and help him with the lambing. We're hoping for a good birth rate this year." She set down the baskets and straightened up wearily. "I will go when the season is over, but you could go right away. Beth can take over most of your jobs now. It will help them so much."

Milcah had no idea of the effect of her words on her daughter. The thought of having to face Haziel again had instantly kindled a terrible mixture of dread and excitement. Her reaction scared her. Whatever was the matter with her? Was she still a silly child who could not take command of herself? She had always known she would have to face Haziel someday but imagined it would be when she was safely established as a married woman.

"How good to see you again," she would say, brushing his cheek lightly with her lips, and he would notice the dignified maturity of her wifely status, and their brief secret attraction would be forgotten, just as though it had never happened. They would both consider it so. And then she told herself he would probably not remember anyway – men were surely like that, able to desire a woman momentarily and then forget she even existed.

Shana was suddenly aware that she was staring intently into her mother's face without seeing her, and her mother was anxiously awaiting a response.

"Of course I will go, Mama," she said, squeezing her shoulder reassuringly. "Otherwise, I could take over the lambing work and let you go instead?" But even as she suggested it she realised guiltily that as much as she dreaded the thought of going, she desired it even more. Change and adventure were powerful magnets.

"No, my dear, your father does not want me to go. Beth is old enough to help me now, and anyway, soon you will be attending to your own husband's affairs," she said, smiling at the remembrance. "Come now, we must make preparations

94

for you to leave tomorrow, and let Rafael know."

"How long should I stay?" asked Shana.

"If Ada recovers quickly, come back as soon as Judith can manage without you. If . . ." She broke off and looked away.

When Shana kissed her mother goodbye, Milcah took the necklace she always wore around her neck and pressed it into Shana's hand. "Give this to Ada from me and tell her to wait for me. I will come as soon as I can. And be sure to send news at every opportunity."

Approaching her aunt's home after almost a year, Shana experienced an immediate sense of belonging, as one does when returning to a place one has once laid claim to. There was the little shepherd's hut standing alone on top of the hill, keeping watch, it seemed, over all the earth, and here the crooked tree that leaned sideways, forever held in the tension of imbalance. The winter rains had transformed the landscape into a soft green that awaited the spring sunshine to fully develop its colour. She crossed the stream and took the overgrown track that her own frequent steps had once formed, which led up a slope, across a field and through an olive grove to the little home which had offered her such a place of belonging when she most needed it.

The courtyard door was open, lamps already lit sending out a weak glow from inside the house. She could see Judith's dark figure moving back and forth across the room, busy no doubt preparing the evening meal. She wondered if Haziel was sitting at the table. She hoped he would be at home so that their first meeting might take place among the general distraction of her arrival.

She hesitated a moment outside the door to compose herself. In a few moments it would be over, and her nerves could settle down again. She knocked and was instantly engulfed in Judith's tearful embrace. Over Judith's shoulder, she saw Haziel get up from his stool and come forward to greet her.

"Hello, cousin," he said, politely restrained. "Welcome back."

"How is Aunt Ada?" she said, looking around anxiously.

"She's in her room," said Judith. "We're keeping her quiet, her fever is very high."

"Can I see her?" asked Shana.

"She will be glad to see you but don't excite her. Here, take this cup of water in with you. She needs to drink as much as possible."

The room was dark except for a small lamp, which caught the perspiration glistening on Ada's pale forehead. Shana recoiled from the unpleasant smell of illness but tiptoed forward and knelt beside her mattress. "Aunt, it's me – Shushana," she whispered. "I've come to bring you greetings from my mother and to help you get better."

The old woman opened her eyes and tried to raise her head. "My precious one," she said, smiling weakly, "how blessed I am. Tell me all your news." Her head dropped back onto the pillow, her breath rasping from the exertion. "I hear you are betrothed at last. I am very happy." She forced the words out with great effort, and Shana leaned forward to lift her head to the cup of water.

"Drink a little, Aunt. There will be time to hear all my news. I want you to get strong first. Rest now, and I'll be here in the morning with my special porridge for you."

She kissed the burning forehead and quietly left the room. How she hated illness. It was such an imposition, such an interruption and inconvenience to life. She was afraid of the power it held, and the way it rendered its victims so impotent. She hated the way it attacked ageing people, as if they didn't have troubles enough with their failing bodies. She felt suddenly angry at God but hastily smothered her irreverence and went back into the house.

The cosiness of the familiar home cheered Shana considerably. She tugged off her shawl and went to sit down at the table. Judith added a log to the fire burning on a small raised hearth at the back of the room and came to join her. Haziel stood in the shadows with his hands clasped behind his back, rocking on his heels and watching the women.

"Tell me all about the celebrations for your betrothal. I want to know every detail," said Judith. "And about Rafael too of course. We are so much looking forward to meeting him."

Shana chatted on and on, answering all Judith's eager questions, while Judith beamed with the special happiness such matters seem to bring upon all women, as though each of them shares in the joy of the heavenly union. The oftentimes harsh facts about their own marriages never seemed to deter them in the least. This marriage would be perfect in every way!

Shana attempted to draw Haziel into the conversation. "What news of you, cousin?" she asked. "Is business good?"

"Quite good," he said curtly. He was never one for small talk but made an effort. "How is your father? He must be well pleased with your betrothal."

"Yes, it will benefit him nicely with his business associations."

Judith put a steaming pot onto the table. Haziel passed around a cup of wine and they all relaxed as the warm food filled their stomachs. Judith looked tired. Shana knew how hard the weaving work was on her; Haziel expected a lot from her, and it would have been an added burden to take care of her mother-in-law. She was glad to be here to help.

"Have you heard the latest news about the Healer?" asked Judith, once they had caught up on the family news.

"The Healer?"

"The man you told us about, who you went to see in Galilee. He has become known by that name around here because he has healed so many people. He was near here quite recently, in the next village – Bethany that is – staying at Martha's house. Do you remember her – the widow who came here a few times to visit Aunt Ada? She lives on the outskirts of the village with her sister, Mary, and this rabbi is friends with them and their brother, Lazarus."

Shana leaned forward with full interest.

"Well, Lazarus was very ill. The sisters called for their friend, the Healer, to come but their brother died before he got there." Judith sounded unsympathetic, and Haziel was frowning.

"The Healer arrived a few days later and, you'll never believe this, he raised Lazarus from the dead!"

"He did what?" exclaimed Shana. "How certain is it he was really dead to begin with?"

Haziel grunted, and Judith put her hand soothingly on his arm but he got up and moved away from the table.

"He was dead for sure," said Judith. "It was known all over the village; he had already been in the tomb for four days. You can't get much more dead than that! It was truly a miracle, Shana. That rabbi has amazing powers. You must have heard about all the hundreds of people he has healed?"

"News doesn't reach our part of the world much," said Shana. "Perhaps our village rabbi makes sure of that. He has already warned our community that the man's a heretic. Oh, Judith, this is wonderful news. How can he be anything bad if he does so much good?"

"People will do anything as a means to an end," said Haziel gruffly, poking at the fire. "What better way to get the masses on his side. He clearly plans to take over completely."

"Well, you can hardly fake a miracle like that," said Shana, knowing she was taking a chance when Haziel was so touchy.

"He's not the only one who has strange powers. It's the way he uses his power that is causing problems. He's very unpopular with the chief priests and the law for the way he flaunts it and doesn't care what they think. Who does he think he is, upsetting the way things have always been done? Well, he won't get very far."

"Hush, my dear," said his wife quietly. "Aren't you happy for dear Martha and Mary?"

"I certainly am," admitted Haziel more agreeably, and the subject would have been closed had Shana not pressed Judith for more.

"Where is he now?" she asked. "Can't we ask him to come and make Aunt Ada better?"

"It's not right to interfere with God's will," said Haziel in a way that did not invite argument.

"He's left now but often comes to Jerusalem," Judith told her. "There is a lot of trouble brewing concerning him."

Shana wanted to find out more but considered it unwise to aggravate Haziel any further on her first night back. An uncomfortable silence fell between them as Judith went outside to fetch some water, so she said good night and went to attend to Aunt Ada, after which she settled down in a corner of her room for the night. She lay awake for a long time, pondering the impossible facts of the miracle Judith had described. Even knowing that it must surely be true – it would be impossible to counterfeit a thing like that under the scrutiny of an entire village – she still felt curiously disassociated from it, as though her mind refused to accept it. If she, who was more than willing to believe, still doubted even when there was no doubt, it was no wonder that so many others simply refused to believe!

She slept. In her dream, Rafael had died and was lying waiting for her in a tomb, and for some reason that the dream did not explain, it was her fault.

Having to sit still for hours day after day in the darkened room at Ada's bedside tested Shana to the limit. Her aunt shifted about restlessly from side to side, first too hot and then too cold, showing no signs of improvement. At least she was no worse.

Shana placed yet another damp towel on her yellowed forehead and gently stroked her hair. She was so very fond of her but sometimes it seemed like this lifeless old body was not really her aunt anymore, instead some stranger who she didn't want anything to do with. She had to keep reminding herself that she was doing this for her mother and for Judith, and for Haziel of course, who often put his head around the door looking awkwardly helpless.

To pass the time, she often sang the psalms Rafael had taught her. Her clear, melodious voice had a soothing effect on Ada, who would close her eyes and grow still until she eventually fell asleep. One afternoon, Shana was warming herself in a shaft of sunlight slanting through the open door, her face turned upwards and eyes closed, singing a wistful melody over and over again. So enraptured she was in the song and the sunlight that she lost consciousness of herself and her surroundings. A slight movement outside caught her attention, and she glimpsed a shape against the light through her half-closed eyes. It was Haziel standing watching her. She pretended not to see him but her song had lost its winged cadence, so she broke off to attend to Ada. The next time she looked, he had gone, and a sense of disquiet stole into her heart.

She needed to take a walk to clear her mind. The day was bright after spending so long in the gloomy room and she walked briskly, breathing in the spicy resonance of the damp, sun-warmed earth. The countryside was alive with creatures: butterflies dived haphazardly among the grasses, birds darted between the trees, calling merrily, grasshoppers and bumble bees clicked and buzzed, and her spirits lifted. The world was good.

She went to the place she loved most, down beside the stream where she often used to bathe, where a clump of reeds massed at the water's edge, providing privacy. The winter rains had quickened the stream to full flow, and she sat on a rock and watched the sun-sparks fly off the water as it bubbled over the stones with a hollow echoing sound. The warmth made her drowsy, and she lay back with her hands behind her head and gazed up into the sky, watching the clouds form pictures and erase them again, losing herself in the immeasurable blue.

She returned home at dusk and, as usual, gloom settled upon her with the retiring day as if her fleeting spells of happiness were never meant to last. At such times, life seemed so purposeless. What was the point of it all – to live and to die? It seemed such a waste of energy, going through all the motions of the days, over and over through the years as the body grew tired, stiff and sore until the end became a welcome release. And then what? To live on and on, a soul without even a body? Or just sleep and never wake up, so that one may as well not have existed at all.

Coming back here had destabilised her again, brought back the fluctuating emotions she thought had been laid to rest when she decided to settle down with Rafael. His steadfast certainty about life had anchored her for a time as she yielded to his leadership. He would not understand these strange confusing moods that afflicted her for no apparent reason.

For six long weeks, Ada lay feebly inching her way towards recovery. She was out of danger, thankfully, as Milcah had sent word that she was unable to come just yet, and it meant that Shana could now help Judith with the back-breaking job of washing and dyeing the wool while they took turns nursing Ada.

One evening at nightfall, Shana was particularly weary. The all too familiar feeling of desolation began to descend upon her again, together with a deep inexplicable loneliness. It felt as though the ground beneath her feet was pulling her down, down, down into its murky depths to imprison her in a dark place from which there was no escape. She went out into the olive grove to try and get a grip on herself so that her oddness would not show, but in her struggle, tears started flowing.

"Where are you, God? Who are you?" she whispered.

No answer came back – it never did. She did not doubt that there was a God, but whoever he was, he remained uninvolved and disinterested in her. She stared into the sky, fighting to stifle the frightening irrational sense of despair.

A figure was moving through the trees. She hurriedly

dabbed at her face with her shawl and began to walk on but heard the footfalls quicken to catch up with her. Startled, she swung around.

Haziel!

He came to her, enfolded her in his arms and held her against his chest. "What is it, Dove? What ails you so?"

Haziel's strong arms were around her! Haziel, a solid tower of strength. His tenderness touched a deep well of anguish, and she sobbed against him, unable to give a reason for her outburst. He held her until her tears subsided, and she pressed her face into the folds of his robe, growing peaceful, so peaceful, in the haven of his embrace. She never wanted to leave the custody of these strong affirming arms. It was the safe place she had always longed for, always sought after with a hunger that had never been satisfied until now.

"Come," said Haziel, releasing her abruptly and turning towards the house, "we must go. Judith will have the meal prepared and wonder where we are."

Shana floated dreamily behind him, still enveloped in the warmth of his presence. She hardly spoke during the meal, but Haziel chatted freely, apparently unaffected by their encounter. Shana took a bowl of stew to Ada, who was now able to sit up in bed, and stayed with her while she picked at it, grateful for the chance to sit quietly and soak in the memory of that wonderful, nourishing embrace. Somehow it had fulfilled some incomprehensible craving for something only Haziel could give. It was no longer the hot attraction between a man and a woman, which had briefly flared on that previous occasion. This was comfort, empathy, and caring – the purest form of love.

CHAPTER 11

Spring burst almost overnight in a full palette of brilliant colour, transforming the world into one which barely resembled the one Shana had inhabited just a week or two before. The days dispensed one by one in a glorious succession, each a personal gift from the Creator. Weaned lambs bounced over daisy spangled meadows on stiff, bulbous legs, and pink-tipped buds waited, poised in anticipation, for the touch of the morning sun before exploding into flower. Shana felt the budding in herself like something awakening, reaching out, ripening.

Ada was up and about again, shaky and slow on her feet, but able to shuffle into the main room to share company with the others. The little home was filled with happiness, as though a dark cloud had parted to let the sun through. Shana loved being able to give her time to the weaving, working outside in the corner of the courtyard, which was now flooded with sunshine. The rhythm of the shuttle flashing to and fro, to and fro between the threads connected her somehow to the creative rhythm of life, and it was deeply satisfying to watch the colourful fabric extend magically from her fingers. A comfortable warmth had developed between her and Haziel. She was content now, whether he was around or not.

As Ada grew stronger day by day, Shana realised that she would soon have to return home. She did not want to leave – not yet. She hardly ever thought of home. Here, she lived a different life in a different world, quite unrelated to her other life, which she was happy to put on hold for a while, especially as her days as an unmarried woman were numbered. She brushed away a momentary twinge of guilt that she did not miss Rafael as much as she should, unwilling to let anything interfere with the pleasant day-to-day existence she was enjoying.

Beyond the immediate arena of their lives, a rumbling unrest was disturbing the peace in Jerusalem, caused by a division between the Pharisees and teachers of the law, and a growing number of people who were giving their allegiance to the rabbi Yeshua. Whenever Shana went to the village market, she would hear angry voices raised in hot disagreement. Even those she knew to be firm friends were in conflict. She listened in at the stalls, trying to catch the gist of the arguments.

"It's an abomination!" a man said angrily. "No one has ever challenged the Law like this before. It cannot be permitted."

"The people love him. They flock to him like sheep being offered greener pastures. One can't blame them. Who wants to stay in a dead, dry desert?"

"Are you suggesting that the Law is dead?" another man reared up threateningly.

"The Rabbi himself says he upholds every letter of the Law. It just seems he has a new interpretation of it."

"Deliberately doing a work on the Sabbath can hardly be called an interpretation! He clearly intends to stir up trouble. He could easily have performed his 'miracle' a few hours later when Shabbat was over, but he wanted to show himself off and unsettle the masses from their traditional religious observances."

"Exactly!" remonstrated another. "That's exactly the point he's trying to make. Don't you see? Tradition has sucked the life out of our Jewish faith. It's hardly about God anymore!"

A thin man in a brown robe hobbled over, leaning on a bent stick. "It is said that the chief priests are out to trap him, flush him out and show him up for whom he truly is," he said in a shrill voice, his eyes sparking in anticipation of a good argument. Shana was forced to move on before her eavesdropping became obvious, but she did not have to go far to catch another dispute on the subject. Everyone was talking about it.

When Shana came home that evening, she mentioned the subject to Haziel, who had his own outspoken views on the matter, which he needed no encouragement to voice.

"Be calm, my husband," said Judith. "Your hot temper has already got you into trouble with the law and made you some confirmed enemies. I worry about you. They will be looking for an opportunity to punish you for your radical views."

"Radical views! Just because I disagreed with the legal council about certain petty laws no longer being appropriate, they assume I am siding with that Nazarene. The only thing I agree with him about is calling those Pharisees a brood of vipers. No wonder he's so unpopular with them." He threw his head back and roared with laughter. He had always had a fiery contempt for the religious men 'who minced about with their books under their arms, thinking they were God's gift to mankind', as he put it.

He wiped his beard on his sleeve and grew serious. "I admire his courage, but that certainly doesn't mean I condone the way he is challenging our religion. That is a very different matter."

It was nearing the time of the Passover and it was expected that this rabbi would soon be in Jerusalem again for the Feast. Shana was filled with anticipation at the possibility of seeing him once more, especially as she had decided that immediately after Passover she would return home and may never have another chance.

"We're taking all this to the city. Would you like to come along?" asked Judith as she rolled up the lengths of woven cloth resulting from their last two weeks of labour.

"I'd love to," Shana replied. "Shall I fetch the donkey?"

"Haziel has already gone to get her. Here, help me tie the cord around this roll. We can also buy what we need for Passover. My sister's family will be with us as usual."

"All seven of them?"

"Yes, as well as Haziel's brother and wife. That will make twelve of us. We've still got two weeks to prepare. I'm so grateful to have your help." Judith squeezed Shana's arm affectionately and Shana smiled back, though inwardly she retracted with a twinge of irritation. As much as she loved her, Judith was so very different from her in every way that Shana often felt as though they were two unrelated species. Judith was entirely practical; her whole world consisted of such things as whether there was enough oil left for the lamps, if the rugs should be washed before or after Shabbat, and how much flour would be needed for tomorrow's bread. She did not question things, or fret, or consider it necessary to concern herself with deep issues, and Shana could never share with her the ups and downs of her own emotional, ever-questing nature. And so the two women lived side by side, yet did not know one another intimately.

"Ah, here is Haziel. Shall we go? We must get back before nightfall so I can see to the stew," said Judith briskly.

They stacked the rolls of fabric onto the donkey and set off together. As they passed the village synagogue, three members of the local ruling council came out, deep in conversation.

"Shalom," said Haziel.

The men stopped briefly to return the greeting, their sharp eyes quickly assessing the donkey's load for any violation of the law and then darting across to Shana.

"We are not acquainted with this young woman," said one of them.

Shana pulled her veil across her face, disliking their scrutiny.

"She is the betrothed daughter of my mother's sister. She is staying with us," Haziel replied flatly and walked on.

When they were out of earshot, Shana said crossly, "What business is it of theirs?"

"They make everything their business, always on the look-out for any transgression of the law, especially now that they consider me a radical," said Haziel with a snort of laughter.

"Be careful, my love," said Judith. "You know they can impose restrictions on your trading if they decide to."

"A man is entitled to his opinion, and anyway I am entirely

above reproach," he said, slapping his chest and brushing away her concerns with a roguish grin.

Jerusalem was beginning to fill up ahead of the Festival. For many it was an excellent commercial opportunity, and tradesmen streamed in from miles around to secure a spot to sell their wares. Colourful stalls had sprung up along the edges of the already crowded streets. Shana recognised a few traders from her own village and wondered whether Rafael would make the journey too.

She eagerly scrutinised the crowds in the hope of spotting the Rabbi. She had never forgotten his words but had been left with more questions than answers, and no one to ask. David was the only person she had met who would be able to give her meaningful answers, but there was little chance of seeing him again. When she had tried to discuss her questions with Rafael, he had quoted long passages he had learnt from the Torah and been clearly reluctant to stray from the confines of the written Law.

The Rabbi's teachings had stirred up in her a strong desire to unlock the great mystery of the Most High God, and she sensed that it was this rabbi who held the key.

CHAPTER 12

THE MIDNIGHT AIR was warm. The moon had not yet risen, and the sky glittered with stars. Shana moved silently between the dark shapes of the olive trees along the track to her favourite spot near the stream. An inner urge compelled her, though she was a little afraid. She had woken in the night, as she often did, with oppressive thoughts jangling in her mind, and the little room with its low beams and thick, close walls was too small to contain them, so she had risen quietly and crept out. She needed to think, to let the open heavens bring her some clarity.

She tiptoed along the path, hugging her cloak around herself, her bare feet knowing instinctively where each stone lay. Her thoughts turned to Rafael. She held him always in a special place in her heart, like a lamp that never went out, warm and constant in its comforting light. He anchored her, and she loved him dearly.

Yet she was drawn to Haziel with such a powerful magnetism that she couldn't bear the thought of leaving him.

Not that she wanted him to be her own – she would never dare to think like that – he belonged to Judith and no one else – but she wanted to be near him. His heartbeat was her own heartbeat. He was the missing part of herself that completed her, gave full meaning to her existence. His wild and rugged strength echoed her own, but which she could not express in her feminine form. He embodied something of immense value to her; she would be content just to live in his shadow, not requiring anything of him other than to please him. How could she be Rafael's wife knowing that her soul belonged to someone else, even though her body never could?

A light wind stirred through the silvered leaves as though the trees whispered her secret meditation among themselves. The night pulsated with the ceaseless serenade of cicadas, accompanied by distant frog-song thrumming in a lower key. Hidden creatures all around were watching her.

She came out onto the field beyond the olive grove, pursued by her creeping shadow. Feeling suddenly exposed, reduced to a tiny speck beneath the mighty firmament, she walked faster to cross the open space and took shelter among the trees by the stream. She stood uncertainly, senses acute, suddenly feeling she should go back. The sound of the trickling water was too loud, too urgent. The wooded knoll, so friendly and welcoming in daylight, now seemed unpleasantly hostile. Dark shadows crept through the grass and flickered on the ground beneath the trees. She thought she heard a step and whirled around, her heart thumping. Blood rushed in her ears as she strained to hear. It was only the leaves slapping together.

Then another sound. Someone was approaching! She stood rooted to the ground, shivering, not knowing whether to take flight or stroll out casually.

"Shana," a man's voice called softly.

Relief rushed through her, leaving her faint and breathless. It was Haziel. He must have seen her go out and followed her.

He strode up to her, close and towering above her, and took her face in his big rough hands. The whites of his eyes flashed before her. She could smell the feral tang of him. His mouth crushed down upon hers, igniting a quick, hot flame in her body. His breath was urgent against her ear, her throat, his hands forceful on her back. She melted into him; the world spun dizzily above her. There was no longer anyone else on earth except her and Haziel. She wanted to give him whatever he wanted of her. His passion, so long held in check, was rough and hungry as he covered her with his body, there beneath the trees. She gave herself to him as a gift. She sacrificed herself to him, laid her body on the altar for him, recklessly mindless of the consequences.

Later, she lay against his chest, breathing him in as he slept and, still wrapped in the shroud of her delusion, she felt complete. This was what she had always longed for: to be loved by him, wanted by him, close, oh so close to him. She nuzzled into his shoulder and stared up into his shadowed sleeping face, the bristled outline of his jaw glinting darkly in the moonlight. His lips, slightly parted, were a soft contrast to the rock-like mass of his body. Most of all, it was those strong arms, encircling and containing her, that filled Shana with delirious happiness such as she had never known before.

After an enchanted zenith of time, the first bird began to make little noises in the branches above. Shana slipped out from under Haziel's relaxed embrace and tiptoed to the stream to wash in its cold, cleansing rivulets. She returned to him, refreshed, and snuggled back into his arms, knowing they did not have much more time. As the daylight gathered, she knew the spell would soon be broken. They would have to go about their business as though nothing had happened – nor ever would again – in whatever way this had changed their lives, each harbouring their secret forever. They would have to face whatever remorse might ensue. But not now; not yet! They had only a few precious moments left, and they should not be spoiled.

He awakened and drew her to himself, and again that strange, eager urge overtook him. This time it felt all wrong; she wanted him only to hold her and love her, but not this! Rafael's face swam before her and a sick feeling surged through her veins.

Before she had time to question her confusion, the sound of voices shattered their brief paradise. Five men in the flowing garb of the Pharisees appeared through the trees before they had a chance to scramble to their feet. They must have seen her at the stream on their way to the temple and come to investigate! The men stopped in their tracks, each face registering astonishment as they took in the details of the scene before them. Haziel stood up, his face stony pale. Shana struggled to her feet, smoothing down her crumpled gown. Five pairs of eyes fixed themselves on her and narrowed with flint-sharp accusation. Two of the men she recognised from the encounter of the previous week. She clutched her cloak around her, shaking violently.

One of the men took a step towards her and shouted, "Adulteress!" The hideous sound of the word splintered the early morning quiet. He looked around at his companions and cried, "Such a thing should never be seen in Israel. She must be taken to the courts for judgment!"

Two men grabbed her roughly by each arm and thrust her

forward between them. Shana cried out in pain and shock at this unspeakable turn of events. Haziel leapt forward to try to stop them, but the other men stepped in front of him threateningly, repeating rote stanzas of the Law like blows of a hammer. He did not try to follow.

"Please, please," Shana begged, "Please let me go! This won't do any good; it will only cause harm to the family." Her voice rose hysterically. "Please, I beg you, rather send me away. I will leave right now and never come back, I promise, I promise!" She stumbled on a stone and cut her bare toes, pitching forward towards the ground. The men dragged her along until she found her footing again. She continued to plead for mercy, her gasping words strangled in her throat. Their merciless, cold-blooded judgment remained rigid in their righteous upholding of the Law, which she had clearly transgressed. She was scum in their eyes, a rat flushed from its hole, fit only to be squashed underfoot.

"Oh God," she sobbed, "have mercy on me. Have mercy on me."

"Be quiet!" snarled one of the men, spitting at her. "You should have considered your ways before you stole another woman's husband and gave what belongs to your husband to another man."

The ring Rafael had given her still hung on the leather thong around her neck, knocking between her breasts. Blinded by tears, she could hardly see where she was going but staggered onwards, sobbing and pleading in abject desperation. One of the men behind them prodded Shana roughly in the back. She could hear the sounds of the city now on either side as she was pushed up some stone steps and along a paved street. She saw vague outlines of people standing aside to let them pass, staring at her in surprise and curiosity. Some followed them in the hope of witnessing a drama. More steps, a covered passageway, and then the entrance to the temple courts.

A crowd was already gathered around a teacher. The men hustled her forward, pushing through the crowd, and thrust her into the small space in front of the rabbi. Shana stood with her face in her hands, weeping, as the accusation against her was spoken out before the crowd.

"Teacher, this woman was caught in the act of adultery!" said one of the men. "How do you say she should be judged?"

There was a long silence. Shana could hear the onlookers shifting restlessly, tense with expectation. The bottom of her robe was flecked with mud, and her bare feet were bleeding. She pushed back the hair stuck to her face and peered through her fingers.

A current of shock ripped through her as the man's face swam into view. She was standing before the rabbi Yeshua!

His eyes held hers for a moment, and in that moment she felt she could not live. All the breath left her body and a dizzy blackness passed in front of her eyes, then partially cleared so that the crowd around her appeared as a sea of dark, slow-moving shapes. She recognised a familiar face from her home village and cringed at his shocked expression.

The people waited, all eyes fixed on the Rabbi. He squatted down and began to trace on the ground with his finger. Shana shivered uncontrollably. She bowed her head and hugged her arms around herself. Her hair was wild around her, soaked with tears and matted with twigs.

"What does the Law say?" said the Rabbi in a quiet voice.

"That evil should be scourged from Israel," a triumphant voice called out from the back, accompanied by a cheer of agreement. "The woman should be taken outside the city and stoned to death!"

Shana's blood ran cold. She knew this was true, though on some occasions there was leniency, depending on how connected the unfortunate victim was to those in authority. She also knew how easily a volatile crowd such as this could be incited.

A group of Pharisees and teachers of the law had collected nearby, waiting for the Rabbi's answer. They knew he could never publicly deny the Law. In her mind's eye, she saw herself cowering as the blur of that first stone hurtled towards her, its keen edge cutting into the soft flesh of her neck. Then another, striking her on the temple with a head-splitting blow, stones slamming into her from every direction. She experienced the terror of death and heard her own screams inside her head.

"God, have mercy on me," she whimpered over and over into her hands. A belligerent hush fell over the crowd. Some men murmured argumentatively at the back. The Rabbi was still writing on the ground; he seemed in no hurry to pronounce her sentence.

Slowly he straightened up and addressed the group. "Whoever of you is without sin, you cast the first stone."

He looked directly at each man in turn. The murmuring stopped as the implication of his words reached its target. He bent down again and continued to draw on the ground as though dismissing them. They looked from one to another with furtive, sidelong glances, waiting for someone to take the lead, but no one did. Shana stood absolutely still, completely spent of emotion, awaiting her fate. An old man took a step, and the crowd tensed. Scowling heavily, he turned and walked away without looking back. One by one, the others followed, some, no doubt, with relief, some disappointed at the anti-climax, and others seething with rage at the way they had been caught in their own web.

More than anything, Shana longed for her mother, to bury her face in the safe harbour of her bosom and hear her say that everything was going to be alright.

Eventually, there was no one left but herself and the Teacher, with some of his disciples standing back, together with a group of curious onlookers. She stood with her head bowed, hands hanging limply at her sides. In the long minute that followed, it was as though her inner eye was opened and she saw with brutal clarity what she had done. She saw how she had deluded herself into thinking that her love for Haziel was pure, when all the time she had continued to seduce him, only more subtly than before, with just an innocent lowering of eyelashes or slow, cat-like stretch of her body, knowing his eye was upon her. She had done it because it got his attention, which was all she wanted, without being conscious of where it was leading. She had never considered betraying Judith.

She thought of Judith now with a sickening pang of remorse, and a fresh flow of tears coursed down her cheeks – Judith, with her simple trusting ways, who loved her totally.

The Teacher spoke, "Woman, who has condemned you?"

She dared not meet his eye. "No one, sir," she answered, in a wavering childlike voice.

He cupped her chin in his hand and gently lifted her face until she met his eyes. He looked at her long and deep, his gaze penetrating right into her soul. She knew with an overwhelming certainty which defied logic, with an indescribable assurance, that he loved her completely – loved her in a way that no one else ever had, or ever could.

"Then neither do I condemn you," he said, each word winging its way into the core of her fractured humanity. "Go now, and sin no more."

The authority with which he spoke cut her to the quick. He turned and walked away, disappearing into the crowds that were filling the temple courts. As she watched him go, something within her changed forever. With every cell of her being she wanted to follow him, follow after that love, that authority – do anything, anything he might ask of her, because he loved her so completely.

"Come, my dear, come with me." The kindly sound of a woman's voice brought Shana back to her present reality. "Come to my home and get something to eat." The woman took Shana by the hand, and she allowed herself to be led away as one saved from death.

"My name is Abigail. I am one of the Master's followers. I will take care of you for him." There was no judgment whatsoever in her manner.

Shana trailed after her like a dependent child, through the maze of streets until they came to a steep set of steps leading up to a door. Abigail unlocked the door, which opened into a small neat room. It was simply furnished with a table, a bed, and a low couch scattered with embroidered cushions. Another door opened onto a tiny balcony, where there was a wood stove and a few utensils.

"You sit here while I fetch some water," said the woman. Shana dropped onto the couch beneath a small high window. She could hear the hum of people passing by below. The world out there seemed so remote in this quiet little haven. Abigail filled a basin and bathed Shana's blood-stained feet, and then let her wash herself. She lent her a clean robe and gave her a bowl of broth, all the time chatting about the Master and what a hard time he always had in Jerusalem because of all the opposition.

"The people love him in Galilee, so much so that it makes it difficult for him there too. He often goes without food because he is so swamped by crowds. His mother tries her best to get him to take a break, but it doesn't help. Now I want you to lie down on the bed and rest, while I go off to the market to get something for our supper. You are very pale." Abigail plumped up the pillow, and Shana obeyed meekly.

As soon as Abigail had left, she fell into an exhausted timeless sleep in which she ceased to exist. Whoever Shana had been before, she was no longer, and would never be again.

CHAPTER 13

IT WAS LATE IN THE afternoon when Shana awoke. She drifted up slowly from the depths of a dark, dark pit towards the faint light, her brain foggy and sluggish, her limbs heavy – so very heavy. Memories of the morning appeared on the screen of her mind like a recent nightmare. Judith's face floated up, expressionless, white as the dead. She would have heard by now. The men who had exposed Shana were well-known in the village and would not have missed the opportunity to make a public example of her shame. Shana began to sink into the blackness again. Another face came into view and remained steady before her. It was that of the Rabbi. He gazed into her soul, repeating, "Neither do I condemn you. Neither do I condemn you. Neither do I condemn you."

The recollection of his words imparted a kind of substance into her, and she sat up. Abigail was sitting beneath the window, busy with some handcraft. She was a plump middle-aged woman with a soft, lined face and matronly figure, dressed in a loose, brown tunic. She immediately got up and came over to sit beside Shana, and took her hand in her own. Her kind, maternal manner was like ointment applied to the great, gaping wound in Shana's soul.

"Tell me all about it, my child, and I will see what I can do."

Shana searched back into the jumbled contents of her mind, not knowing where to begin, not even quite knowing where it did begin. What words could express what had really happened? Abigail reached forward to stroke a lock of hair off Shana's forehead, and that simple motherly gesture gave her the reassurance she needed.

"It was my cousin," she began miserably. "I have always loved him since I was a little girl. But–but . . . not in that way!" She felt suddenly confused, unsure now of whether what she had just said was true or not. Abigail watched the struggle going on inside her.

"I just wanted him to care about me, to love me . . ." She began to cry.

A grey city light leaked through the window, giving the room a cloistered stillness. Outside, the street sounds went on as though nothing had happened. Abigail waited until Shana was quiet enough to blunder through her story, letting her pour it out, together with all the contradictions and confusion. When the story faltered to an end, Abigail asked the question Shana was not ready to face up to. "What are you going to do?"

Confronted with the prospect of her future, Shana's breath quickened in frightened gasps as rising panic threatened to overwhelm her. She pressed her hands against her scalp to relieve her aching head and control the stampeding thoughts.

"I will have to leave here," she stammered at last. "I will

have to return home. I have nowhere else to go. I will have to, I . . . O God help me," she groaned, burying her face in her hands. "I will have to tell Rafael."

"Rafael?"

"My fiancé."

Abigail stiffened and looked up at the window, saddened by everything this meant. Shana, too, saw what lay ahead, in a rapid succession of scenes: Judith's sorrow, her mother's sadness, her father's rage, and worst of all, Rafael! She saw the betrayed look on his face, his terrible disappointment, and the shame that would pursue her wherever she went. Death by stoning seemed a far preferable alternative.

And Haziel? What of Haziel? She never wanted to see him again. It was all wrong now. She had wronged him and Judith, and Judith would have to bear the consequences.

She got unsteadily to her feet, cocooned in a strange numbness that disassociated her from what was happening on the outside.

"I will have to collect my things from my cousin's house and leave tomorrow morning," she said.

"Go now and face who you must," said Abigail. "I will accompany you to the edge of the city and wait for you at the city gate, and then you can come back with me to spend the night. You do not have to leave until you are ready to go and tell your family."

Shana looked at Abigail. "Why are you doing this?" she asked.

A gentle smile deepened the lines around Abigail's mouth. "Because you are God's child," she said.

At the Sheep's Gate, Abigail stopped and Shana walked on alone, completely stripped of any reserves. She felt numb and empty, her body performing the necessary motions as if she herself were not present. It was almost dusk. A chilly wind blew, sending leaves scuttling along the road. Most of the villagers had already gone indoors. As she neared the beloved home, she heard the sound of weeping. She found Judith huddled in the corner of the donkey stall, with her head on her knees.

She looked up as Shana approached, and mopped her face with her sleeve. "Oh, Shana, I've been so worried about you. I didn't know what they had done to you. Thank God you're safe." Behind her concern was evidence of her greater suffering. She pulled herself to her feet, holding tightly onto the hitching rail for support.

"I'm really sorry, Judith," said Shana in an expressionless tone. It was so inadequate, almost a mockery. The two women stared across at one another, both drained of emotion.

"They've taken Haziel away," said Judith at last, "those men from the synagogue. They came to tell me what happened and said I was not to tell anyone. They said they had some business to finish with Haziel and that he would not be back for a while. I'm so afraid for him." She twisted her fingers in her robe, her eyes huge in her smudged face.

Shana's hand flew up to her mouth as she staggered backwards. She knew the men had seized the opportunity to use her as a pawn to try to force the Rabbi into a situation which would give them legal power over him. In view of their public humiliation, it was understandable that they would want to keep the whole thing as quiet as possible, but what would they do to Haziel? They were ruthless, radical men, capable of wielding the law to suit their own purposes, and were known to punish transgressors severely.

"What–what will happen to him?" whispered Shana, swallowing hard.

"I don't know. He was not popular to begin with. Usually it's the woman who is punished." Judith struggled to quell the sob that broke in her throat but her tears fell unchecked. Shana watched them splash one after another onto the front of her tunic.

"I am so very sorry," she said again, screwing up her face desperately. "What happened should never have happened. I did not ever mean to hurt you like this. I . . ." There was nothing she could do. Her presence could not ease Judith's pain, nor bring Haziel back.

"I have to leave," she said quietly, and Judith did not try to stop her. She waited outside while Shana gathered her things. Shana embraced her aunt without explanation, knowing by the way she held her long and tight that she knew everything and still loved her.

Just before she left, she turned once more to Judith. "Haziel loves you very much. It–it was my fault."

Then for a second time, she left her cousin's home and everything he had meant in her life and walked out alone into her dark, uncertain future.

Back at the city lodgings, Abigail tended Shana like a sick child while she passed through her deepest valley, allowing her time to grieve as she lay on the mattress in the corner of the room. She brought her bowls of soup, sponged her hot face after a bout of tears, and stroked her forehead with soothing fingers while Shana came to terms with the fact that by her own actions she had lost everything – the love of a good man and her chance of marriage and children, her family home, as well as the friendship and acceptance of her second home, and her own self-respect.

Sometimes she wondered how it would have been had they not been discovered. Would they have fostered a clandestine relationship, meeting secretly under cover of night? The idea was repugnant to her, far worse even than having been exposed. It seemed unlikely too that they could ever have reverted to their former relationship as though nothing had happened. No, she would have had to leave anyway and cherish the love they had shared, in the silence of her heart forever. But in the cold light of day, it did not seem anymore that it was love they had shared at all, and perhaps Haziel despised her now, as she despised herself.

After she had mourned the loss of Haziel, the flagrant fact of her shattered relationship with Rafael crashed into her consciousness. She hunched over her knees in an involuntary posture of penitence and despair, beyond tears. A flame seared through her centre and up her throat, burning mercilessly with every breath, hollowing out a huge space inside her. She longed for him – her Raf – to come and comfort her and fill that empty space, the place he had always been but would never be again. She would give anything to go back to what was before; if only this great pressure of longing inside her could somehow take away what she had done and let her start over and never make the same mistakes again.

But nothing could halt the relentless sequence of events she had set in motion by her delusional desires.

In the end, it was the thought of how it would affect Rafael that grieved her the most. She rocked on her knees and wept till her heart wrung out – for him, for his pain, for so cruelly destroying his eager happiness. Abigail knelt beside her and cradled her in her arms. For a long time she held her like this, until eventually Shana leaned surrendered against her breast. The room grew still and filled with peace, and Shana rested in its quietness.

After a time, she rose and rinsed her face in the basin. The crushing weight had lifted; she felt strangely light. It was time to prepare for the journey back home where she must confess her transgression to those who loved her, before the story reached them on the cruel tongues of gossip. And after that . . . Her mind could not conceive anything beyond that at all.

"Shana, come and sit down, I want to talk to you," said Abigail, setting a cushion beside the couch. She leaned forward with her elbows on her knees, her wise old face softly framed with grey curls. "I am a widow and–"

"A widow?" interrupted Shana. "Why is it you do not wear the widow's garb?".

"The Master has set me free from my mourning," said Abigail mysteriously. "I had a son too but he died when he was not quite a man. I have no other children. My husband was quite well-off and he left me with the means to support myself, with some to spare, so I have joined the group of women who travel with the Master and his disciples to help take care of their needs. It's tiring work for them out on the roads, especially in Galilee, because they can never escape the crowds and their continual demands. It's our job to find lodging for them wherever possible, to prepare food and attend to such things as washing and mending their clothes."

Shana listened with wide-eyed amazement. For the first time, she turned her attention away from her troubles to this gentle stranger who had come to her rescue like an angel from heaven. Everything about her was soft, kindly, and comforting. Her voice had a melodic timbre suggestive of an inner joy, and the radiance upon her face made her wrinkled features beautiful.

"The Master is probably due to leave again for Galilee next week after the Festival celebrations are over," she continued, "but we have learned to be ready at all times because he never works according to schedules. If you can get back here before then, I would like you to accompany me as my helper. Most of the women are not young, and we could do with someone to help with the heavier work."

Abigail's words were like particles of light in a sea of darkness, offering a faint glimmer of hope and a future, something beyond what seemed like the end of her life. She recalled the way the Rabbi had looked at her with such love in the moment of her greatest degradation, how she had felt so strongly that she wanted to follow him, no matter what it might cost. Now she was being offered that opportunity.

But . . . but he would know who she was. Wouldn't he be ashamed to have her among his followers?

"You're very kind. I do not deserve it," said Shana. "Why should you show me such kindness?"

"God is kind to all of us undeserving," Abigail replied. "Come let us go and buy bread for your journey. You must leave early tomorrow morning."

CHAPTER 14

A T CLOSE OF A very long day, the caravan passed
through a ravine, walled on either side with high, pock-
marked cliffs, and climbed steadily towards the village. Jagged
peaks blotted out the sun prematurely, forming deep shadows
on the creviced slopes. Shana could see the shepherds
gathering in their flocks on the darkening hills. How normal
everything looked. The miniature cubed houses were already
breathing out smoke from fires cooking the evening meal,
and tiny people moved about between them, each absorbed
in his own affairs. As she advanced step by step towards her
loved ones as the bearer of bad news, Shana reflected grimly
upon how her arrival was about to drastically alter their lives.
The last reserves of her courage drained away as her
befuddled brain tried to work out how to go about her
dreaded task – who would she meet when she arrived, who
should she speak to first, and how would she say what she
needed to say?

The question was still unanswered when she handed her

donkey over to the guide at the market square and started towards the house. As she passed the threshing floor, she caught sight of Beth with her friends, sweeping up after the day's work, and stood watching her for a while. She could hear her carefree laughter, an innocent happiness she would soon destroy. When Beth caught sight of her, she dropped her broom and ran up, overjoyed, but her smile faded uncertainly when she saw Shana's strained expression.

"What is it?" she cried. "Is Aunt Ada alright?"

Shana gave her sister a brief, passive hug. "She has recovered very well. It's . . . it's something else. I will tell you about it, but first run to Rafael and ask him to meet me at the Big Tree. Tell him it's important, I will wait for him there. Don't mention to Mother and Father that I'm back yet, I must speak to Rafael first." Shana's tone was flat and resigned. Alarmed, Beth dashed away to deliver the message while Shana turned down a side path before she could be seen.

As she approached the Big Tree, a prickling sense of foreboding ran up her spine. Something was different. Up ahead where the forest had been densely shaded, the evening sun shone through, lighting the path before her. She ran forward and found that the great tree had fallen. It lay with its roots torn from the ground, its massive trunk propped up by the smashed branches. One dry branch lay broken on the ground with the shattered ends worm-eaten and hollow. An acrid smell of decomposing matter emanated from the damp ground, and a mass of ants, crazed by the scent of death, swarmed through the fragments of rotting bark.

Shocked to the core, the memories came rushing back as clear as yesterday of the times she and Rafael had met here over the years – such happy times – such as when he had hidden behind the tree and jumped out at her with a high-pitched, boy version of a roar, and she had screamed and thrown acorns at him and been distrustful ever after when approaching the tree alone. Once, he had hidden himself a little way off behind some rocks and grunted like a wild boar, making scratching sounds on the ground with a twig. Shana had been terrified and made him promise never to do that again.

Then a more recent scene appeared before her in agonising detail: it was the last time they had visited the Tree together – Rafael's enraptured face when she had promised to be his wife, the overwhelming tenderness in his eyes when he looked at her.

"Oh God help me! Help him!"

He was coming towards her now, striding through the bushes, his handsome features clouded with worry. He sat down on the log, and Shana sat beside him so she would not have to look him in the face.

"What's the matter?" he asked, swallowing apprehensively. The whole world held its breath while Shana searched for words to express the devastating truth she must now inflict upon him. Rafael waited, his shoulders squared manfully to receive news he already knew would not be pleasant. He had seen her red-rimmed eyes and the violent trembling of her body.

There was no way to soften the blow.

"I have been with another man," she said, plunging the sword to the hilt.

Rafael turned deathly pale. Nothing could have prepared him for this.

Shana rushed on, her voice rising pitifully, "It should never, never have happened. I would do anything to change what I have done. I did not . . . I did not love him in that way. It was a terrible, terrible mistake."

She turned to face him now, saw the waves of shock slam into him, one after another, each impact reverberating through his being. He tried to swallow, but his throat contracted. The trees stood around them aloof, like silent witnesses to the betrayal.

"Who was it?" asked Rafael eventually, his voice hoarse.

She paused, not wanting to speak the name. It came out in a whisper.

"Haziel."

He gasped and stared at her with an expression wracked with shock and grief, and behind his eyes was something icy cold that scared Shana the most.

"Rafael, I beg you to allow me to explain," Shana pleaded. "If . . . if you can understand, even a little, it may help you to forgive me."

"Forgive you!" he shouted, shaking her hand off his arm and jumping to his feet. He slumped down again, his forehead in his hands, laboured breaths convulsing his shoulders.

Shana sat motionless beside him, calm and defeated, surrendered to the consequences she knew were inevitable. But it was for Rafael's sake that she wanted him to understand – understand that she had confused the meaning of love; that in her rabid lust for acceptance and recognition, her desperate desire for the adoration of a man who represented the ultimate authority on her validity as a human being – as a woman, she had mistaken one kind of love for another; that she had sacrificed herself to please this god she had created for herself and used every innate power she could muster to attract the object of her worship, not realizing what it meant; that it had nothing whatsoever to do with physical desire and was not really about Haziel at all. When she had looked into his eyes, she had only seen herself reflected back like a shimmering queen and fed ravenously on his attention and his desire for her.

She had been in love all the time with herself!

Rafael did not move while she poured out the whole sordid tale. He only flinched once when she told him about her being exposed in the temple courts like a common harlot. He remained silent after she had finished, and Shana knew her task was done. She untied the thong around her neck and held out the ring to him. He stared at it for a long time, as though trying to register the implication of the gesture, and then turned away with a tired wave of his hand.

"Keep it," he said.

She crushed it in her fist, not knowing what he meant by it, and stumbled back down the path. A little way away, she stopped and looked back. She could see Rafael's outline through the trees, still seated on the log, his big shoulders hunched and his head down. She heard him cry out with a deep, agonised howl.

"No!" he shouted, stifling the sound in his hands.

"No!" The awful cry echoed through the forest, followed by a long anguished groan.

It was the sound of a human heart breaking.

She wanted to run back to him, to make it all better, but a great chasm had opened up between them over which she could no longer cross. It hit her with bitter clarity that she was the only one who could comfort him . . . and she was the only one who could not.

She saw him pitch forward and fall prostrate on the

ground and she quickly turned away. It was too private a moment to observe – a broken man crying out to his God.

Both her parents were in the house when Shana stepped through the doorway. Beth was sitting on a rug, leaning against the wall. It was clear from the heavy silence in the room that Beth had forewarned her parents that something was wrong. They did not get up to greet her but waited anxiously for her to speak. The last light of dusk hung suspended in the gloom and a lamp flickered on the table. Shana felt like one condemned to death. Hollow desolation gnawed at her insides; a yawning deep pulled her down into its cold, black depths.

She delivered her message impassively without explanation, simply saying that she had made a terrible mistake and had been caught in adultery. She told them that she had been saved from the death penalty by the rabbi Yeshua, that she was sorrier than they could ever know, and that she would go away immediately to spare them as much shame as possible. Beth burst into tears. Her mother sat still and silent, her face like a pallid moon, shadowed with nameless grief.

Her father exploded to his feet, quivering all over as rage infected his body. "You filthy whore!" he shouted. He seized a clay jar from the table and hurled it against the wall behind Shana. Sharp fragments bit into her ankles as it shattered, and Beth screamed and jumped up, ready to defend her sister. Their father's face was darker than the grave, contorted with a terrifying hatred.

"Get out!" he shouted, spit flying from his mouth and bubbling on his crimson lips. "Get out, and never come back, you slut! I always knew you were no good. You should never have been born to bring such shame on this family!" His voice rose an octave and he took a threatening step towards Shana, who was cowering in the shadows near the door. "Get out!" he yelled, his bloodshot eyes bulging dangerously.

Shana turned and fled, running as fast as she could up her secret path, past the fallow field, and into the forest beyond. It was quite dark now, she could barely see, but knew the track so well that her feet found the way. She passed the fallen Tree, and on the edge of the forest, the pale grey shape of a rocky outcrop materialised. With an overwhelming desire to hide, she squeezed herself into a crevice between two large rocks and crouched there, shivering and panting like a hunted animal, hugging her cloak tightly around her knees. For an endless time, she did not move or think or feel.

The rocks, reserving warmth lent by the sun, offered an element of comfort and safety as the dark hours passed. Then from a great distance, the words of a song she had learnt as a child threaded through her stupefied mind.

"My dove in the clefts of the rock,
in the hiding places on the mountainside,
Show me your face, let me hear your voice;
For your voice is sweet, and your face is lovely."

It was the song of the Almighty reaching out to her, calling to her. She tried to pray but it seemed futile. High above, a strip of stars twinkled remotely, dispassionately, between the rocks, accentuating her utter aloneness.

It was a long, long night. Many times she was terrified by the sound of a wolf howling or the crackle of twigs in the bushes nearby. Once, a curious badger appeared and regarded her with gleaming, coal-black eyes before scurrying off. The dull hunger in her gut was indistinguishable from the ache that had settled there, so long ago it seemed.

In the pre-dawn hour, the falling dew baptised her in its misty vapour, driving the chill of the night deeper into her bones. Night clung interminably, meting out the long hours of her banishment, until finally relinquishing its darkness to the dawn.

Shana went quickly to the meeting place for the daily caravan to Jerusalem where she joined the small crowd of travellers waiting for the pack donkeys to be loaded up and the journey to begin. Her bag containing a stale loaf and a skin of water still hung on her shoulder, and she held the purse Abigail had given her, tightly in her hand. One or two people looked at her curiously but she looked away – the news would be out soon enough. She spotted a friend who had come to say goodbye to her young merchant husband and seized the opportunity to give her a message for Beth and her mother.

"Tell them," she whispered, "that I will be alright. I am going to Galilee with a friend who has invited me to join the group of women who support the rabbi Yeshua and his disciples during their travels. One day I will be back. They must not worry. And tell them . . . tell them all that I love them . . . all of them." Pressure swelled in her chest and stifled her words as she departed from her childhood home, dry-eyed and resolute.

CHAPTER 15

STILL DRESSED IN THE SAME robe she wore when she left Jerusalem, Shana stood outside Abigail's door again. Two days was all it had taken to dispose of her tattered life and leave it behind. She knocked hesitantly and held her breath; her future depended upon whether the door would open. Or had the Master called during her absence??

A scuffle, the sound of a key in the lock, and Abigail stood before her with open arms – immeasurable relief! That night, safe in Abigail's custody, Shana slept properly at last, relinquishing, out of sheer exhaustion, the burden she had been carrying for the last several days.

The two women were up at dawn in order to be present in the temple courts where the Rabbi would be ministering to the ever-increasing crowds that sought him. It was the morning before Passover, and the streets were already teeming with people who had arrived by the thousands for the Festival. Visitors and traders scurried in all directions, each intent on their own private mission, merchants shoved ungainly carts laden with wares around the numerous obstacles, and religious men glided between them like black shadows. Shana pulled her shawl over her face, hoping she would not be recognised as they struggled through the chaos and made their way along the corridor leading to the temple. The courts were already packed with mismatched groups of expectant people, many of them clearly afflicted with one or other disease or disability. The Pharisees and teachers of the law stood apart with stony expressions, striking a discordant note in the general hubbub of excitement. Temple guards were prominent on top of the walls in detachments of five or six.

Abigail led Shana to a group of women who stood in a huddle, chatting excitedly. It was clear from their fine clothing that many of them were wealthy. When Abigail introduced her, they welcomed her warmly but, to Shana's relief, paid little attention to her and continued recounting the previous day's events – story after story of the sick healed.

Presently a hush fell over the courts and every eye turned towards the far entrance. The Rabbi, dressed in a plain cream-coloured robe with a priestly tasselled mantle over his head and shoulders, strolled in unhurriedly, greeting people as he passed. His disciples followed in an untidy cluster, trying to form a barrier between him and the jostling crowds pushing and shoving to get closer. Unperturbed, the Rabbi mounted a few steps onto a raised portico and began to speak. He did not raise his voice but its curious resonance carried as clear as a bell throughout the area.

After a short teaching, he began to move slowly among the people, pausing to lay his hands on those who were sick or disabled. Loud cheers erupted as some who had been unable to stand, now got to their feet. He left behind him a frenzy of rejoicing as here and there extraordinary healings occurred. Shana strained to see what was happening but did not want to separate herself from the company of women who waited quietly in the wings. The crowds were clearly not going to diminish; on the contrary, they were steadily multiplying. How was he ever going to be able to get away from them?

After a while, the Rabbi sat down on a step with his disciples gathered around him and spoke to them privately. Two of the men came over and informed the women that the group would be returning to Galilee after the last day of the Feast and would meet before dawn outside the Dung Gate. A thrill of excitement lifted Shana momentarily out of her misery. How amazing to find herself now numbered among the few privileged above all others to travel with this powerful teacher. Where this would lead to, she did not know, but for now, it was enough that it would take her away from all that had gone before, and for this she was profoundly grateful.

"You will celebrate the Passover with us, won't you?" said one of the women to Shana. "I have family living here in Jerusalem and there is plenty of room for us all. It will be a chance to get to know you."

Shana cringed inwardly; if only she could remain anonymous. How would she be able to answer all the inevitable questions?

"You don't need to explain anything," Abigail told her later. "Simply say you've had troubles with your family and that I asked you to come along with me as my helper."

There was still something Shana had to settle before leaving, something that tugged continually at her conscience, and for which she felt entirely responsible.

"I must go and find out what has happened to Haziel," she told Abigail, aware of the tremble in her voice.

Abigail pressed her lips together and said firmly, "It would be better to make a clean cut with the past."

"But what if –"

"There is nothing you can do. Rather let it go and move forward."

But Shana, finding it unbearable not to know, slipped away to the market to ask the woman who managed Haziel's stall.

"Haziel is in prison. Didn't you know?" said the woman, looking at her curiously. "He is in trouble with the law; his trial will be after Passover. Nobody knows exactly why, but he was unpopular with some of the leaders. No doubt his brother will use his influence to sort everything out. He's visiting now, as you probably know." She turned back to arranging the stacks of folded cloth on a mat.

Haziel in prison! Because of her! Shana flew back to Abigail, distraught. "It's all my fault," she wailed. "He could die because of me."

"He must face the consequences of his choices, whatever they may be. You are responsible for your own misdeeds but are not accountable for another's," said Abigail decisively.

This wise counsel soothed Shana enough to enable her to get through the feast celebrations. She had never been in such a large party before. She counted twenty-four people, including children, around the low tables spread out in the spacious upper room of a well-to-do Jerusalem household. In spite of herself, she began to enjoy the easy-going camaraderie and cheerfulness of the occasion, and above all, the warm affection for one another they so obviously shared.

During the meal, Abigail pointed out the women who would be their travelling companions. There was Joanna, the wife of the man who managed Herod's household, a tall, handsome woman with a proud, regal manner, whose elegant attire distinguished her from the others. Next to her sat Ruth, a thin, insipid looking girl of about Shana's age, dressed in a mourning garment, her small, pinched face forming a blank orb beneath the dark veil. She would have been pretty if her complexion were not so pale and her eyes so dark-ringed.

In bright contrast was Mary, whom Shana warmed to at once. Her colourful, embroidered garments and bangled arms gave her a flamboyant appearance that matched her expressive, exuberant personality. Her deep, husky voice could be heard above all the rest, and she bordered on being raucous with her frequent guffaws of bubbling laughter, but no one seemed to mind. Most of the others were middle-aged women like Abigail – comfortable motherly figures who form the backbone of every society with their steadfast, servant hearts. What circumstances in their lives had brought each of these women to be following the Rabbi? Each one had a story to tell . . . though perhaps some would never be told.

In the crisp twilight of a roseate morning, the group of approximately forty people set off. The Rabbi walked some way ahead together with his twelve personally selected disciples, known as the Twelve, followed by a number of other men, mostly young. The women were towards the rear of the procession, fifteen in all, ranging in age from seventeen to about fifty, Shana being the youngest, and behind them some older men kept a watchful eye over their safety. There were no children and no pack donkeys – they travelled light, keeping up a fairly brisk pace. Shana had a curious sense of being carried along by the communal energy generated by a shared mission and was amazed at how easily distance was covered.

The sun was high and very hot by the time they reached the foothills of the Samarian mountains. They stopped in a wooded area and flopped down onto the grass for a rest and some sustenance. Bread was broken and shared and, one by one, they lay down and slept. Shana gazed up into the leafy boughs that shielded them from the searing heat and listened to the indolent cooing of doves and drowsy chatter of little birds on the branches. The constant ache in her heart was made bearable by this complete change of lifestyle, together with Abigail's comforting support, and she found rest too under the Master's banner. A lethargic breeze caressed her cheeks, and she drifted into a light sleep. Somewhere in another world existed beloved shadowy figures – her mother, darling Beth, Rafael, Judith, Aunt Ada, and yes, Haziel. They dwelt on in a world without her, a world she had left behind and to which she no longer belonged.

After a couple of hours, they all got up, refreshed, and continued down the trodden track that led into the hills. The afternoon heat was stifling, and the steady tempo of their steps became automatic as they marched in unison towards an unknown destination. Just before sundown, when Shana's energy was flagging badly, a cluster of buildings appeared which looked like the outskirts of a small village. The men up front stopped and waited while the women moved ahead to go and seek accommodation in willing households.

They exchanged pleasantries as they passed the men, and the Rabbi acknowledged each one with a friendly nod. Shana shrank back in a paroxysm of nervousness, hoping Abigail would not introduce her – not yet. The Rabbi would surely recognise her from their previous fateful encounter. She lagged behind, using Abigail's plump body as a shield and, peeking out timidly from behind her veil, tried to slip past unnoticed but was compelled to meet his eyes. Blinking in fright, she managed a weak "Shalom". He showed no sign of recalling their previous meeting, yet she felt that he knew her – really knew her, everything about her – and the effects of his smile lingered on for a long time afterwards like warm harvest wine, making her feel giddy and light-headed.

She floated along behind Abigail, hardly noticing that they had split off from the other women and were now approaching one of the houses.

"Shalom," called Abigail at the entrance to a large house, where three women could be seen through the open doorway, busy around a large cooking pot. One of them came forward, wiping her hands on her apron. She was a pleasantly proportioned woman of about thirty-five with a friendly, inquiring face.

"We're on our way to Galilee, travelling with the rabbi Yeshua; you may have heard of him. Would you be able to offer some of us a room for tonight?"

"Certainly," the woman responded without hesitation. "How many will you be?"

"We're a large group, so you tell me how many of us your home can accommodate." Abigail's voice lifted sweetly at the end of the sentence.

The woman considered for a moment and replied, "My sons are on a journey with their father so I have extra room. We will gladly receive five of you as our honoured guests. Dora," she said, turning to a younger woman behind her, "we will need more loaves, and send your sister into the garden to gather more vegetables for the pot. This is a pleasure indeed;

we don't often meet travellers coming this way."

The humble little farming village absorbed all of them into welcoming homes and was immediately propelled into a hive of activity – women scurried here and there, borrowing loaves from friends, men chopped extra wood for the fires, children danced with excitement for having the company of strangers. Guests and villagers worked side by side preparing the evening meal and getting to know one another. Joanna, Ruth, and one of Abigail's friends joined them in the home of their hostess and her two daughters. As they worked, Ruth, the girl in mourning, smiled shyly at Shana, and Shana saw such sadness upon her sweet face. She smiled back, opening the door to a friendship she hoped would develop between them.

After washing, and enjoying a simple, satisfying meal, Abigail invited the family to go with them to meet the Rabbi. They found him in the common courtyard of a block of houses, where a crowd had already gathered. He was sitting on a mat in a relaxed posture with one arm leaning on his knee, and his friends lounging on the steps around him. The villagers stood back a little bashfully, but as he began to speak they moved closer, drawn involuntarily towards him, and eventually sat down in a close huddle at his feet. He was talking about the coming kingdom of God, using illustrations Shana had never heard before, painting pictures before their fascinated eyes of a place that was free of sorrow and oppression – free, then, of Roman control and injustice? He spoke of God as his Father, even using the term 'Papa' to describe the relationship. He spoke of a joyous new world where there was only one law – the law of love. It all sounded too good to be true, and one could be forgiven for thinking him a dreamer, yet he was so certain and confident, and spoke with such authority, that his words were profoundly credible.

"This is my command," he said. "Love each other as I have loved you."

United in the circle of fellowship, with the firelight dancing upon their faces, highlighting first one and then another, they grew drowsy and content, soaking up his message through a soporific haze.

His final statement, delivered conclusively, caused startled reactions among the listeners. "I am the way and the truth and the life. No one comes to the Father except through me."

He gave no further explanation but prayed a blessing over them all and dismissed them, leaving them perplexed but intrigued. However peculiar some of his ideas might be, his words would be pondered for a long time after he had left, and would never be forgotten.

CHAPTER 16

THE MAGIC OF THE PREVIOUS night's get-together faded the next morning when Shana awoke to a grey, sultry day that echoed the desolation of her mood. Weary too from the long hours of walking and the late night, she longed for home, whether it be with her mother or with her aunt Ada, and the painful truth hit her afresh that she did not belong in either of these homes anymore. She rolled up her mat and went outside to wash, fighting down the rising emotion. Ruth, who was sleepily shaking out her mat outside the door, looked up and smiled as she passed. The shadows beneath her eyes were darker still, but her face remained softly surrendered to whatever inner distress she was suffering. Shana's heart went out to her. She looked so fragile, with the bloodless veins on her wrists showing through her transparent skin, and pale wisps of hair against her cheeks.

They went back into the house, which was now alive with activity as the women set about the morning tasks. Ruth touched Shana lightly on the shoulder. "Shall we go and collect wood to get the fire going?" she asked kindly. Shana nodded and followed her out into the woodlands behind the house. Low clouds hung in a brooding sky, and a dreary wind moaned in mournful gusts, threatening rain. As they gathered sticks, Shana asked Ruth how she came to be part of the group and noticed the pinch of pain her question evoked.

"My husband was killed six months ago by Herod's army," she said, pausing to compose herself. "He went to the defence of a friend against an unjust arrest, and the soldiers killed them both."

There was a silence while Shana grappled with how to respond to this shocking statement.

"He was a kind but hot-headed man," Ruth went on. "I loved him with all my heart." She broke off, and Shana laid a hand upon her arm. Her own troubles seemed small in comparison to this.

"How dreadful for you!" she burst out, wishing she could find more meaningful words. "How can you bear it? It must be so . . . so hard!" Tears filled Shana's eyes, and she dropped her bundle of wood and turned all her attention to the small, delicate girl.

"I couldn't bear it," she said. "I was very ill and close to death – my health has never been very strong. The Rabbi was passing through my town at the time, and my father begged him to come and see me. He came and put his hands on my head and prayed for me. He told me that some healing takes time but that I would be strengthened and able to bear the grief. And it is so. I was able to get up immediately, and the dreadful darkness around my heart became much lighter."

"Is that why you are here now?" asked Shana.

"My husband was from a wealthy family in Sepphoris, who saw my amazing recovery, and when they heard about the women helpers travelling with the Rabbi, they asked if I could join them for a while, thinking that work and travelling would help me get over my loss. They also now support the Rabbi financially in his ministry. So here I am." She spread out her hands and smiled her sad smile, and then said, "Now tell me about you."

Shana took Abigail's advice and made only general mention of 'trouble in the family'. Ruth waited for her to elaborate but seeing she was not forthcoming, turned back to the task at hand, giving Shana a look of such concerned empathy that it was like the touch of an angel.

To Shana's relief, heavy rain detained the group in the village for another day. The Rabbi and his twelve friends had been invited to one of the richer houses in the village, so the women were left to help their hostesses with the chores. It was cosy and companionable packed together inside the house, performing the ritual tasks of grinding and kneading, peeling and chopping in the dim light of the oil lamps, with the rain torrenting down outside and the smell of fresh bread baking in the coals. They laughed uproariously as their hostess entertained them with elaborate stories of the village, spiced with humorous anecdotes. The morning's sorrow was forgotten and the girls were cheered by the peculiar bond that womenfolk have when left to themselves. Their hilarity was somewhat dampened in the afternoon when the husband and sons returned from their journey, dripping wet and in sour temper, requiring the whole team of women to pander to their sodden personages. The women attended to them good-humouredly with discreet amusement, sharing their intuitive understanding of menfolk.

The next morning an apologetic sun crept out from behind the retreating clouds to dry off the landscape, so the travellers set off again, escorted some way by the villagers, who had so soon become like family. The road invited them up a long incline that levelled out along the edge of a scant forest, with undulating pastureland on the other side. Refreshed by the sojourn and the vibrant morning air, they were all in high spirits, and outbursts of laughter zigzagged through the disorderly procession. Up front, the Rabbi's disciples clowned around like exuberant school boys, and occasionally the Rabbi, too, turned around and joined in their laughter.

Ruth walked beside Shana, a bond already having formed between them in the brief sharing of their pain. She told Shana that Joanna – the tall, well-dressed one who had shared the accommodation with them – had taken her under her wing. "She watches over me like a mother hen," she laughed. "With her husband being Herod's household manager, she felt personally involved when she heard about the circumstances of my husband's death, and has been very kind."

Even now Joanna glanced around to check on her protégé. She acknowledged Ruth's wave with a smile and then studied Shana for a moment as though assessing the virtues of this new friendship. Shana found her commanding air of superiority intimidating.

"Mary's the one next to Joanna," said Ruth. "Her life changed completely when she met the Rabbi. She had been tormented by evil spirits all her life and had a really dramatic deliverance."

Shana observed the attractive woman with interest, who bounced along with plump swaying hips, her head thrown back with ready laughter, and her long black hair tumbling from beneath her short head-scarf. She remembered her from the Passover supper and had been drawn to her voluptuous personality then, intrigued by her charm and gaiety and the generous warmth she extended towards everyone, as though her heart had an excess of love to give. When Ruth mentioned Mary's former profession, Shana's interest turned to shocked fascination. Could she be using her past earnings to support the Rabbi? It was clear, at any rate, that the Rabbi was not too particular about his followers!

And then she remembered her own reasons for being counted among them and blushed at the impertinence of her judgment.

Ruth's prattle was cut short by the sight of a Samaritan village on a low hill up ahead. Their water supplies were dwindling, and they were all looking forward to a break. Five of the men went into the village while the rest of them waited in the shade. The men returned too soon, looking sorely aggrieved. They had been chased out of the village by some pitchfork-wielding farmers who would have nothing to do with this "trouble-making reactionary". There was no alternative but to continue their journey and seek a more hospitable community.

It was several hour's walk to the next village and the sun was now full strength and merciless. The going was tough because the path had not been trodden since the rains, and a thick tangle of thistles and thorns snagged their steps and scratched their legs. The miles strung out endlessly and drained Shana's last reserves of strength. Her spirits sagged with the sinking sun, which so often pulled her down with its descent into night. The travellers trudged on in silence, submitted to their fatigue, as the great red orb plunged down behind the hills.

Up in front, the Master began to sing a simple well-known

chorus from the Psalms while they marched. Soon more voices joined in until the song began to rise and swell throughout the procession. Mary brought a tambourine out of her bag – who else but Mary would pack such a thing! She began to dance along the path, arms held high as she struck a jaunty rhythm, inspiring those around her until their weariness fell away and, one by one, they all united in worship to the God of Israel. The effect was wonderfully re-energizing as they blended into a glorious oneness, inextricably connected with the one who led them.

"Come to me all you who are weary and burdened," he had told the poor and the sick who mobbed him in Jerusalem, "take my yoke upon you and learn from me, for I am gentle and humble in heart and you will find rest for your souls."

Around a bend, a small cluster of lights beckoned to them from the side of a nearby hill. The sound of bleating sheep and the braying of a donkey could be heard as a few dark buildings came into view.

"You are welcome to use the barn," said the white-haired farmer with his bent wife peering over his shoulder, "but we cannot provide food for so many of you. It's about three hours to the next town."

Shana's heart sank; her stomach churned with hunger and she wondered aloud whether this miracle-working rabbi would multiply their few loaves in the same way she had heard he'd done before.

"I doubt he will do that," said Ruth. "From what I have heard, he will not 'turn stones into bread' for his own convenience like a magician. He does only what his Father commands him."

Other than a few discontented rumblings from some of

the older men, most of the group remained cheerfully uncomplaining as they prepared to settle down for the night with stomachs empty. Apparently, following this rabbi called for an uncompromising acceptance of circumstances, which were not always going to be comfortable. In the half-light, Ruth's face was sweetly composed, the outline of her lips soft in spite of the tired smudges beneath her eyes. Shana squeezed her hand encouragingly, and Ruth returned a shy flicker of a smile. Like sisters, they bedded down together in nests of fragrant, freshly harvested hay and allowed sleep to erase their hunger.

Sometime in the night, Shana was awakened by the unfamiliar sounds around her and lay listening to the restless wind whistling through the eaves, and the distant call of a leopard stalking in the rugged hills – a cry so mournful and repetitive that she imagined it to be a mother calling for her lost cub. She strained to hear an answering cry, but when no sound came back, she ached for the mother's distress, wondering how long it took until forgetfulness obliterated the instinct to nurture and protect. She ached too for Rafael and wondered whether his great, gentle heart was yearning for her as she yearned for him. How desperately she longed for the comforting shelter of his love, to meet him again at the Big Tree and hear his laugh, and her soul bled silent tears into the hay.

"Good morning, my beautiful ones!" sang Mary, swooping upon the two friends and pulling them into a hearty hug. She smelt faintly of some exotic perfume, and there were stalks of hay still stuck in her tangled hair. "You, too, overslept. We'll be right at the back but that's alright; let us walk together so you can tell me all about yourselves. It's time I got to know you better." She hooked her arms through theirs and propelled them forward, adding with a tinkle of laughter, "No doubt you already know all about me." She reminded Shana of a fluffy cat: her rich purring voice, her softness, her feline affinity with human-kind, and unselfconscious expressions of affection – always standing close and touching people as though affirming her bond with one and all.

However, Mary's friendly interest threw Shana into a quandary. Up to now she had only offered a very general sketch of her background. She felt that by not making her story known, she could somehow confine it to the past and put it behind her, and she did not want to be identified by her story the way Mary was. Mary was one of the few people she could perhaps open up to, but not before she had confided in Ruth.

Mary put her arms over the girls' shoulders and bustled along with her bangles jingling in their ears and the exotic layers of her clothing rustling pleasantly. She turned to Ruth and, instead of asking questions, said in a gentle tone, "You have endured a deep sorrow, my dear; you wear it in your eyes, and it hurts my heart too. You are not alone in your suffering. Our Master is the one referred to in the scriptures as 'the man of sorrows who is acquainted with our grief'. He was sent by God to bind up the broken-hearted and comfort those who mourn. He will heal your broken heart, just as he has done for me." Mary spoke with a deep, quivering conviction and her face shone like a woman in love. Her words imparted some of the comfort she spoke about.

Then she addressed Shana in the same candid manner. "I know that you too carry a great unhappiness, my love. The Master says that although we have many troubles, we can take heart because he has overcome the world. His answer to every problem is simply to do what he said, 'Trust in God; trust also in me,' and that is what you need to learn to do."

She cuddled both of them to her sides like a hen gathering her chicks under her wings. Shana yielded momentarily to the tears pressing against her lids, absorbing her message as though it had been given her by the Master himself.

Then abruptly Mary thrust the two girls out again, saying brightly, "Come now, I've made you both cry! Look at this glorious day. Let us all be glad and enjoy the good things we have before us. For it is true what the prophet Isaiah said, 'He has turned my mourning into dancing; he has removed my sackcloth and clothed me with joy!'" She sang out the words and did a little jig in front of them, with her garments flaying out like the wings of a bright butterfly, her feet as light as air. The girls laughed out loud, the tears still wet on their faces, and oh how they loved her.

At that moment Joanna, who was several yards ahead, turned her head and glanced back at them. She turned away and walked on but Shana witnessed the brief narrowing of her eyes, and in them an unmistakable glint of jealousy. The stiff carriage of her head and braced back confirmed this impression. Shana felt shocked and uneasy. She could not tell whether it was herself or Mary, or both, who had evoked the reaction, but she resolved to be cautious in future with her exclusive friendship with Ruth and try to foster a wider field of relationships among the women. She recoiled at the thought. What seemed to come so naturally to others, presented a fearful ordeal to Shana. Her reserved manner was often mistaken for aloofness and resulted in her being left out, which made her feel like an outcast. She was ashamed of being different and often felt alone, even as her arms brushed against her happy companions. How she envied those who could enter so easily into the social group with an innate sense of belonging, confident that the contribution of themselves would enhance the mutual enjoyment of all.

Later in the day, as Shana moved forward to walk beside Abigail, still pondering her secret affliction, she noticed the Rabbi looking back. She was about to turn around to see who he was looking for when his eyes connected with hers, and he smiled at her. She smiled back uncertainly, and he continued on his way but again she experienced the strange conviction that he knew her personally, understood her deepest fears, and was glad she was there. It was as though a river of healing love had streamed from him towards her and altered something within her.

Never again did she experience that sense of separateness. Instead, through the Master's personal acknowledgement of her, she was able to embrace her uniqueness and begin to offer herself more freely to others.

CHAPTER 17

THERE WAS NOW NO CHANCE of finding anything to eat; the journey took the party of travellers through an uninhabited area of endless dips and rises over rocky terrain. Other than the fruit they had bought in the morning, they had not eaten a good meal for almost two days. By now Shana's stomach burned with hunger. Another steep hill loomed before them – an impossible hill – and still no sign of civilisation. After climbing steadily for an endless time, they reached the summit and were rewarded by a magnificent sight. A host of peaks and valleys tumbled down towards a great bald plain, hundreds of feet below. The afternoon sun formed indigo patterns in the crumpled hills and highlighted a large town overflowing the slopes of a plateau. The travellers pressed on eagerly, spurred on by their empty stomachs.

When they reached the well on the outskirts of the town, the Rabbi sat down and sent the rest of them on into the town to buy food. Dust and sweat had etched grimy streaks down his cheeks, and his shoulders sagged beneath the thin cloth of his robe. He looked thoroughly spent. He often slipped away in the night when the others were sleeping, to spend time in prayer, so perhaps he was seeking some precious solitude now to refresh himself.

The town was a close-knit, rough-edged community of Samaritan farmers. The travellers approached tentatively, mindful of the hostility that seethed between Jew and Samaritan. However, it soon became apparent that they were being received with passive indifference so they proceeded to the market. The food merchants did not engage in the Jewish custom of haggling over prices but quietly stated their non-negotiable terms and handed over the goods with a dismissive nod. Their manner, proud but not arrogant, commanded respect in a matter-of-fact way.

When the entourage returned with their purchases, they were surprised to find the Rabbi talking to a Samaritan woman, who must have gone to fetch water. She left her water jar at the well and started running back towards the town in a state of great excitement, calling out to them breathlessly, "That man is a prophet. He has just told me everything about myself! I'm going to fetch my friends; please don't leave before we come back."

The group sat down around the well to eat, hungrily tearing chunks off the bread and passing it around. The Rabbi declined the offer, even though the disciples urged him.

"I have food to eat that you know nothing about," he said, leaving them mystified once again. "My food is to do the will of him who sent me." He did not explain, but by now Shana had come to expect that, if she listened with her heart, ambiguous statements such as these would often become meaningful later on.

Before long a group of Samaritan women came hurrying

down the trail, chattering excitedly. Some stepped forward, staring curiously at the Rabbi and asking questions. Others hung back at first, uncertain in the presence of so many Jews, but soon let down their guard when a lively discussion struck up about their differing views on the correct place to worship. The Rabbi listened politely and then concluded the matter by saying, "God is Spirit, and true worshipers must worship in spirit and in truth."

A silence ensued while each of them assimilated this new paradigm, until the woman who had first come to the well changed the subject.

"Will you stay with us tonight?" she begged. "We have space for all of you. Come and meet our families so you can tell them also the things you have told us."

The Rabbi arose, slung his bag over his shoulder, and gestured with a smile that the woman lead the way. The rest of them followed, incredulous that they were about to be taken right into the homes of Samaritans with whom they would never eat, but no one dared object. Their arrival in town, led by the parade of women, drew some hostile glances from the townsfolk, but curiosity soon overcame their antagonism and collected a following of onlookers. The Rabbi stopped in the town square and began to teach them. He addressed these people in a different way to that which Shana had heard before, and told them plainly who he was and why he had come.

"Listen carefully," he said, "God loves you all so much that he has sent his Son so that you might have everlasting life."

"How can that be?" they asked.

"That which is born of the flesh is flesh. That which is born of the Spirit is spirit. Whoever believes in me will live, even though he dies."

"Are you the Messiah who was to come?" they asked.

"I am he," he said.

A baffled silence followed but no sign of the opposition he so often provoked. He picked up his bag again, indicating to the women that he had finished teaching and was ready to receive their hospitality. After a spirited discussion among the women in their strange dialect, the self-appointed leader assigned varying numbers of guests to each hostess. Shana, Ruth, Abigail, and Joanna were led by a thin, bare-footed woman with a tatty skirt wrapped around her bony hips, to a humble clay-brick house. She fussed around them nervously, with a train of fascinated children hindering her every move. Joanna made it clear by her manner that hob-knobbing with the Samaritans was offensive to her and treated her hostess with brittle politeness. She took it upon herself to order everyone around and commissioned Shana and Ruth to go out and gather wood for the fire while she and Abigail went to fetch more water from the well. Her condescending attitude towards Shana caused her to retreat into her shell whenever she was around.

"Don't take Joanna too seriously," said Ruth on the way, "she has a good heart but has a hard life. Her husband is excessively fond of women, and working at the palace gives him many opportunities to indulge his fancies."

"Why does he allow his wife the freedom to take long trips like this?"

"I think he is only too pleased when she's out of his way! He gives her everything she wants, I guess to make up for his misconduct." Ruth snapped a dry branch with her foot and added it the pile. "Joanna was sick at heart, wasting away in deep despair, and a friend of hers called the Rabbi to visit her.

He delivered her instantly of a spirit of heaviness, and in gratitude she decided to use her free time and money to support him on his travels." Ruth's mouth turned down in an ironic smile, "I don't think she knew quite what she was letting herself in for though."

Shana giggled but her defences began to dissolve in sympathy for the unfortunate woman.

"I sense she disapproves of our friendship," she said.

Ruth sighed. "I've been neglecting her. Perhaps she feels I don't need her anymore now that I have you."

"I've neglected Abigail too, but she seems to be genuinely happy for me to have found a friend."

"A wounded heart is a needy heart," said Ruth simply, and Shana felt humbled by her compassion and perception – of all people she should understand how haughtiness could so often disguise disintegrating self-confidence.

After they had gathered sizeable loads of wood, they sat down on the grass for a while to enjoy the cool breeze. Shana still hadn't told Ruth about herself and wondered whether it would change the way she viewed her. There was such division in who she was now, it was like she had three separate identities: first the girl who grew up in the Judean farmlands – a simple girl, prone to discontent but following her family traditions and more or less successfully managing the unruly parts of her nature; then Shana the woman – winsome, vivacious, free as a newly emerged butterfly; and now that same woman defiled and broken, with destroyed dreams and no future.

"Do you ever worry about the future?" Shana asked.

Ruth looked out over the hills thoughtfully. "I carry my husband, Yoav, in my heart every day. I hear his voice and see his face and long for him and miss him every moment. I can't think about the future. It seems impossible that life just keeps going on without him."

Shana looked over at her friend, aware again of the burden of grief she carried – so patiently that it had been easy to forget.

"We were hoping to begin a family very soon," Ruth went on. "We were so much looking forward to it, and Mama too." She smiled faintly at the memory and her lip trembled. Shana searched for something to say but found nothing adequate. Ruth let out a long breath and examined the ground in front of her. "The worst part is the long stretch of time ahead of me that it will take before this sadness fades. Sometimes I don't know how I will get through it."

Shana put her arm around her friend's shoulder. "The Rabbi will help you," she said desperately. "Can't we go to him and ask him? He never turns anyone away. Many of the women have spoken of the healing he has done in their lives."

"I know I could but somehow I feel that to ask for this pain to go away would dishonour Yoav, as though he wasn't worth suffering for."

"But if it was the other way round, and it was he who was left behind, would you really want him to suffer so much if he didn't need to? What do you think he would say to you right now if he could?"

Ruth compressed her lips and said nothing, perhaps considering what Shana had said.

They arrived back at the house, where Joanna was in the courtyard, stabbing at the dwindling fire and talking in a voice too loud and too bright that grated the nerves.

"I'm so glad you're back," she said looking at Ruth with an accusing smile. "The fire has almost gone out." She attacked the pile of sticks reproachfully, tossing one after another onto the fire in rapid succession. The tense undercurrent made Shana nervous. Ruth set the cooking pot back on the flames and began to stir the stew with a large wooden spoon, apparently unaffected by the atmosphere. The aroma of lentils with some unfamiliar herb emerged in a curl of steam. Shana had the uncomfortable feeling that she was required to get busy and went inside to look for something to help with.

The house, filled with unusual objects and ornaments, had an exotic flavour. A colourful tapestry curtained off one section of the room and, though faded and frayed along the edges, added a sumptuous note to the furnishings; several oil lamps set on a low wall cast a dim yellow light onto a collection of chipped clay jugs crowded on a shelf, together with a stack of engraved bowls; and some strange ornaments on the window sills suggested a foreign origin, probably collected from Egyptian traders en route to Galilee in search of fine linen.

The children crowded around Shana and stared up at her with enraptured faces, pulling at the sleeves of her garment and reaching up trying to touch her hair. She sat down on the floor, taking the youngest one onto her lap, while the children pressed in close against her knees. Without speaking, she picked up a length of rough-spun wool lying on the floor and began to twist it into shapes between her fingers. The children watched, fascinated, and their mother threw her a grateful smile. Just then the man of the house appeared in the doorway and stopped in surprise at finding his house full of strange women. His wife laughed gaily and beckoned him in, so he put down his bag of tools and yielded to her affectionate welcome.

"We have special guests," she said, helping him untie his

sandals. "These are friends of the Jewish Messiah, who has come to visit our town. Are we not fortunate? Tomorrow he will speak to us again and tell us more about himself."

Her husband frowned but, emboldened by the reinforcement of all the women, she continued. "It is said he does miracles too," she said, teasing his interest. "You have heard of him before, have you not?"

He was forced to grunt and nod but refused to be drawn into the conversation and turned his attention instead to his children, whose giggles had grown bolder around Shana. Soon the room was filled with pleasant sounds and smells, and even he let down his guard and began to laugh at his children's antics.

The meal was a little strained as the two cultures covertly clashed. Joanna picked at the food as though it were poisonous, saying she didn't feel well, which was probably true under the circumstances. Shana was glad when it was over and she could escape into the sleeping nook behind the hanging rug.

There was not much space; Joanna staked a spot next to the wall, leaving Shana squeezed between Abigail and Ruth. The floor was uneven, and the thick mat smelled mouldy. She lay awake, tense and uncomfortable, oppressed by the close proximity of her companions, and tried to distance herself from the maddening regularity of deep breathing all around her. A faint sniff came from Ruth's direction, and Shana wondered whether her friend was privately weeping. She stared into the darkness, trying to imagine she was back at home lying next to Beth. The open grasslands of the Judean hill country called to her from an impossible distance, and for a while, she was transported back to their beloved spaces, with the dust beneath her running feet and the wind on her laughing face.

Hot tears seeped into the roots of her hair. She lay still and silent beneath the crushing pressure on her chest, swamped in blackness. Abigail turned over in her sleep and unconsciously threw an arm over her. The soft weight of it brought a measure of comfort, and Shana slipped into a restless sleep and dreamed that she was pinned beneath a rock, surrounded by steadily advancing flames from which she could not escape.

"Good morning, ladies!" called a loud voice through the door. It was early. The farmer had already gone out to his fields, and the women were shifting around, drowsily tidying up the house. The lady of the house threw the door open. It was Simon, the big fisherman, with a load of linen under his arm. "Wash day!" he called brightly. "We're staying here again tonight and it's about time we got cleaned up. We'll be in Galilee tomorrow."

Abigail took the load from him, saying with a mock bow, "Your humble servant. Was everyone comfortable last night?"

"Yes. Most of us men slept on the roofs. It was a bit cold but we were given plenty of rugs. More than half the town was waiting outside the house this morning. Not much work going on here today, these people are all ears. The Master loves it of course and he's out there now in the square. We'll see you all there later, I'm sure." He strode off like a giant bear. Shana liked Simon best out of all the Twelve. He was a breath of fresh air, a comical character with a frizzy beard and an explosion of curly hair, who always made people laugh.

When they arrived at the well with the washing, the other women were already congregated with buckets and scrub boards. The Samaritan women had come out in full force in support of their new sisters. Garments were spread out to dry over every bush, and the sun co-operated by turning up its heat in a cloudless sky. Shana plunged a mud-stained garment into a basin and began to scrub it against a rock, worn smooth by centuries of laundering. The sunlight and birdsong, together with the rhythmic movements of performing a communal task, brought a satisfying sense of well-being. The women dipped and straightened in unison, heads bobbing up and down, arms working back and forth, in a vigorous, choreographed dance accompanied by the musical score of speech and laughter. The Samaritans began to sing together, verse after verse of pulsing, energising song that spiralled upwards in joyful crescendos, lifting Shana high above her troubles. This one glorious today, floating freely on the river of time, unfettered by past or future, was full and complete.

CHAPTER 18

GALILEE. THE NAME RESOUNDED like a musical note in
the song of Israel. Protected by a wall of mountains that
harnessed the rain clouds and sent them on the winds to
water the crops, Galilee was blessed with more than its share
of the country's rainfall, and wheat and flax, grapes and olives
flourished in its milder climate. Now in the dry season, a
patchwork of golden fields flowed between the gentle hills,
with spiky nodding heads of wheat poised for harvest.

The women walked directly behind the Rabbi now, the
twelve disciples having stepped aside to assist with an
overturned donkey-cart. After a while, they stopped in some
shade to wait for them. Shana had not yet had a chance to get
this close to the Rabbi, other than on the brief occasions
when she had been so overcome with her own distress that
she had barely looked at him. Buffered by the crowds that
always surrounded him, she had been happy to remain on the
fringes and observe him from a safe distance. Yet always
there was an insistent desire to draw closer, if she could only

overcome her shyness.

"How beautiful he is," murmured Ruth, tender with reverent adoration. Shana watched him chatting and laughing with a group of women. He was not beautiful, neither in feature nor form, but his face shone with such radiant joy that one could not look at him without being impassioned with love for life. He was close enough for her to hear him answering the questions of those who pushed their way to the front. Mary was one of them. Shana envied her boldness and the way she could be so natural and relaxed in his presence. Suddenly Mary swung around and searched the group behind her until she caught Shana's eye, and then beckoned her forward. Shana's heart began to pound but she could not refuse, so she squeezed past the women in front of her and slid into the space on the far side of Mary.

"Master, this is Shushana. You do not know her yet by name, I don't think." Mary thrust Shana forward, who stood mute and stricken with embarrassment.

"Shushana," he said, stroking the word with his rich voice and giving her his full attention, "a graceful lily, just like your name. How do you like Galilee?"

"It – it's the jewel of Israel," she blurted out, saying the first thing that came into her head, her cheeks aflame. "It's a more gentle land than Judea and . . . and the flowers are magnificent."

"You are one who appreciates beauty," he said, "and our Father delights to share it with you." He stepped off the path to pick a tall lily growing between some rocks and held it out to her. "Do you see this lily? It grows among the thorns and has a lovely fragrance. When crushed, its juices can be applied to wounds to relieve pain. This is the meaning of your name – Shushana."

Shana took the lily from him and gazed at it as if it were something of immeasurable value. Six delicate, pure white petals curled out to display the bold yellow stamens, and a sweet scent of honey surrounded it. She knew it was a personal gift from the Master that would never be shared with anyone else, and she was Shushana, a beautiful lily in his eyes. Sweet happiness poured over her, baptised her through and through. She held the cool petals against her lips and breathed their fragrance deep, deep into her soul.

Just then a sharp elbow edged her out of the way as Joanna now claimed her place, and Shana fell behind again, quite contented. The whole world was bathed in an ethereal light that radiated through each separate detail – each blade of grass, each leaf, each tiny hidden flower, all blending together into one splendid creation of which she was a part. Surely this was a glimpse of heaven where peace flowed like a river forevermore.

When the Twelve returned, they pressed on again for the last part of their journey. Shana was walking dreamily behind the others when she noticed that Joanna had stepped off the path up ahead and was waiting for her to catch up. Her expression did not look friendly. As she fell in beside Shana, she said icily, "You might be blissfully unaware of it but do you see what you did to my foot?" She held up her foot briefly to show a reddened bruise on the bridge and limped on in an exaggerated fashion.

"What happened? Did I step on you?" cried Shana in alarm. "I really didn't mean to; I am so sorry."

"Yes, in your haste to curry favour with the Master. I guess that is what is meant by riding roughshod over people."

"But Mary –"

"Have you never learnt to respect others, particularly your

elders?" Joanna said in a venomous whisper. "Do you think I haven't noticed the way you constantly disregard me and try to draw attention to yourself?"

Shocked tears sprang to Shana's eyes, "I – I really don't know what you mean."

"Yes you do. I've seen your coy smiles and the way you widen your eyes and look all bewildered to get people to respond to you. You're not bewildered at all; you are perfectly aware of what you do, and it's about time someone told you for your own sake!"

Her attack was vicious and Shana was in tears now, all the gladness gone from her heart. Perhaps she did unconsciously use her natural charm to attract attention, but it hurt so much to be despised.

"Stop crying! Are you hoping to get sympathy now?"

With that, Joanna disappeared into the background, and Shana walked on alone, fighting to swallow her tears lest someone should notice. She felt like a small child again, being severely punished for something she had done in complete innocence. The lump in her throat felt like a burning coal. She still held the lily in her hand, but it had wilted and its head drooped pathetically. She crushed it against her cheek releasing a strong scent of honey. As she breathed it deep into her lungs she began to grow calmer, until suddenly a hot anger took hold of her.

"How dare she accuse me like that!" she thought. "What a nasty, horrible woman she is!" She began to rehearse exactly what she was going to say to her as soon as she got a chance, just to show her she was not going to be intimidated by her. If only she had said something at the time, instead of shrinking back like a frightened field mouse. For a start, she would get Mary to inform Joanna that it was she who had called her forward to meet the Master. She even considered asking him to speak to Joanna himself and remind her of what he had taught them about treating others the way you want them to treat you!

She walked on with her head down, glaring at the pathway, while a host of slicing retorts boiled up in her mind. She hardly noticed the sparkling waters of the Sea of Galilee in the distance, with the lovely sweep of forested hills leading down to its shores, and the brilliant white birds overhead, flying in perfect formation.

Gradually the raging turmoil subsided, leaving Shana with a dull pain like a stone in the pit of her stomach. She joined in the conversation with the others, who had missed her and waited for her to catch up, but all the time the sick dejection persisted. Joanna ignored her and was full of fun and laughter – celebrating her victory, thought Shana with an ugly twist in her stomach.

As the afternoon wore on, so did the ache of hurt and anger, as well as the uncomfortable realisation of how utterly incongruous it was to be following the Master – the Prince of Peace as he was titled in scripture – and be consumed by this noxious resentment for another of his followers. Then an unexpected idea occurred to Shana, to do something completely out of the ordinary and take a step to obey the Master's teachings herself, even if she had to do so in cold blood. Before she could change her mind, she impulsively whispered to Joanna that she would like to speak to her and instead of delivering her prepared verbal missile she simply said, "I'm really sorry. I did not realise what I was doing. I will try to be more sensitive in future."

The look of surprise on Joanna's face made it almost worth it. "Thank you," she said quietly. "We will say no more about it."

In an instant, Shana felt released. It was a curiously powerful feeling, and all her animosity towards Joanna dissipated like mist, along with her fear of her. She slipped her arm around Joanna's waist and gave her a squeeze, shocked at her own boldness, and to her surprise Joanna responded with a hug in return. And Shana saw a little tear sparkling at the corner of her eye.

Galilee was a whirl of people everywhere they went. There were local folk who had been waiting for the Rabbi's return, and others who had made their way from Jerusalem or across the Jordan and from every village and town, walking, running, shouting and pushing, some carrying awkward home-made stretchers bearing loved-ones, some limping and leaning on sticks. Whether crippled in body or crippled in mind, the desperate masses of broken humanity streamed to the healer who never turned anyone away. And all the time Shana hugged to herself her own priceless gift of his acceptance and approval.

One afternoon, Shana and the other women were sitting beneath a tree, keeping out of the way of hordes of people toiling up a steep path in search of the Rabbi.

"Watch out!" yelled a sweating, red-faced man carrying a young boy on his back. "Make way, make way!"

"Wait your turn, Mister!" said another.

"Let the sick come through. You people who don't need healing, you're just in the way. Move over!" The man fought his way towards the front, inch by inch, with his little boy clinging onto his neck. One of the boy's legs dangled uselessly against his father's back. Seeing the man's determination, Shana left her companions and tagged along behind him, hoping to see a miracle.

Higher up, the Rabbi came into view, standing on a flat rock addressing a large group seated around him on the slopes. He looked up when he saw the commotion and beckoned the man to come forward. Shana dropped to the ground to watch.

With sweat streaming down his face, the man deposited his son in an untidy heap at the Rabbi's feet. The Rabbi squatted down and spoke to the boy for a while, then took him by the hands and pulled him upright. His leg twisted awkwardly from his hip. The Rabbi looked up towards the sky and prayed. What Shana saw next stunned her almost to the point of disbelief; the wasted leg straightened up and thickened, right before her eyes! The boy cried out and almost fell, but the Rabbi caught his hands and led him forward one step at a time until the realisation that he could walk unaided sank into his consciousness. After an astonished pause, the crowd erupted in a wild uproar, jumping to their feet, cheering and exclaiming to one another. Shana wept with amazement. No one could deny that God was among them.

Though every miracle was exciting, the most wonderful of all was the healing of a man born blind. The look on the man's face when the first images of shapes and colours gained access to his brain was something Shana would never forget. He was so overwhelmed with wonder, he could not speak. It would surely be quite some time before he would be able to interpret the mass of new information flooding his mind.

Life in Galilee was more relaxed than elsewhere in Israel. The Galileans grew up out of the very soil they dwelt on, rooted in the natural beauty and abundance of their region. They were earthy, uncomplicated, generous in nature and warm of heart, and treated visitors as members of their own families. Shana felt very much at home among them and loved the eventful journeys between the towns and villages, each day a new adventure.

One evening in Nazareth, she found an opportunity at last to tell Ruth her story. The whole group had taken an afternoon walk to the top of the hill that overlooked the town. Ruth pointed out her own hometown built on another hill not far away. It was a glorious evening with the sinking sun setting the stage for a magnificent sunset, and they all sat down on rocks to watch the pageant. Shana and Ruth sat in quiet companionship a little apart from the others, sharing the constantly transforming scene before them. The mountains in the east gradually faded to a translucent mauve smudge on the horizon, and to the west, shades of pink and orange developed along radial arms of cloud, the colours intensifying as the light melted away. Then faint stars appeared one by one, in the fading blue infinity and sprinkled their reflection on the lamp-lit town below.

Shana searched for an opening line, forming half sentences in her head. In spite of the trust which had developed between them, she still feared that her disclosure would be deplorable enough to Ruth to affect their friendship. She twisted a lock of hair round and round her finger, a habit of hers when she was particularly nervous.

"I need to tell you about myself," she blurted out at last.

"I'm listening, my friend."

"Ruth, you are so pure and good, and yet great suffering has come upon you through no fault of your own. But it is not the same for me; I have suffered through my own actions and caused others to suffer too."

Ruth listened without comment, and Shana held nothing back. She sensed no judgment in her friend, who, at the end of her confession, asked only one question.

"Did the Master forgive you?"

"Yes."

"Then you are forgiven."

A full yellow moon mounted the sky and sailed upwards, beaming victoriously, and fixed its approving eye on the two young women sitting arm in arm in restful silence.

CHAPTER 19

JOANNA HAD DECIDED it was time to return home. The group would be passing Tiberias later that day, where she would rejoin her husband in their residence in Herod's palace grounds. Dear Joanna. Shana had grown fond of her, once she had seen beneath her spiky veneer, and pitied her now for having to face the difficulties of her home life again.

Joanna walked forward with courage and dignity, head held high. Lately, a more gentle composure had replaced the clenched stiffness of her jaw, and her expression had lost much of its sharpness. She stopped at the crossroads where the road turned off into the city. The Rabbi was waiting for her. He took her hands in his and spoke his parting words, and then the women embraced her one by one, strengthening her with love and encouragement, assuring her that they would surely meet again. When she stooped to press her cheek against Shana's, there was nothing but mutual warmth between them. And then she was gone, a tall proud figure swallowed up into the busy confusion of Tiberias.

In Cana, while staying at the home of two sisters, Shana first became ill. She woke up one morning with a heaving stomach, feeling dreadful. She could not face food and was grateful there was to be no travelling that day. By midday she felt a little better, but the next morning, nausea overcame her again. She ran out to the back of the house with her hand over her mouth and retched and retched until she felt completely turned inside out. She sank down onto a rock, quivering all over and gasping for breath, her skin prickling. Abigail, who had followed her out, stood next to her with her hand on her back to steady her. Neither of them spoke. What Shana had already begun to suspect in the last couple of weeks, and Abigail had feared all along, had come to pass, and they both knew there was no cure for this kind of sickness.

Later on, the Rabbi announced that they would be heading towards Capernaum the next day so Abigail arranged that Shana would stay behind with their hostesses, Nita and Ilana, until their return. Shana crawled back into bed in a state of dazed shock. Though it should have been an obvious possibility, somehow Shana had rejected the idea so completely that she'd convinced herself that this would never happen – surely not on top of all her other troubles!

When the news was announced, Nita and Ilana assumed that Shana was betrothed and generously absolved her of any disgrace by turning all their enthusiasm towards the coming event.

"Your fiancé will be so happy when he hears, dear. As soon as you are well enough you must be on your way to give him your news," said Ilana.

"I'm sure no one will mind celebrating your wedding

early," added Nita, her eyes crinkling.

Shana did not reply. Their innocent words stabbed her cruelly, but the women would assume that her unhappiness was due to the discomfort of her condition.

After Abigail and Ruth left, the sisters fussed around her incessantly, suffocating her with kindness until she wanted to run screaming out of the house and get as far away as possible. But even that unreasonable thought brought on a fresh wave of fear. She had nowhere, nowhere on earth to run to. She lay on her bed in the darkened room, sick in stomach and sick in heart, unable and unwilling to eat, though the sisters coaxed her anxiously 'for her little one's sake'. To Shana, this life in her womb was nothing more than a sickness, and she wished she could vomit it out of her. Perhaps by starving herself, she could starve it to death, and they could both die together.

For two long weeks, she lay inert, suspended in a grey limbo, her mind dormant, her body limp, swamped in a thick cloud of nothingness. A doctor came and ordered her to take some broth, and the sisters fretted around a bubbling pot, adding every herb for healing they could think of and holding the liquid to her lips, their eyes round and pleading. Whenever a small trickle slid down her throat, they would let out their breath in relief and rejoice in their small victories.

Then one morning, Shana opened her eyes and lay staring up at the reeds of the ceiling. Her thoughts drifted without effort or direction, hooking onto anything her eyes rested upon. Her gaze ran up and down the knobby lines, stopping at each little knot and bend. A shaft of sunlight danced on the bed covers and flickered on the white-washed walls, making leaf shapes on the plaster. One arm cushioned her head and the other lay on her stomach, rising and falling with her breathing. She no longer felt nauseous. After a while, she became conscious of her hand resting on her stomach, and an image flashed onto the screen of her mind – a tiny curled shape lying just beneath her hand. And it was alive!

She stopped breathing and lay absolutely still. Everything in her focused on that dark secret place inside her, the place where another life, separate to hers, was stirring and striving for a chance to live. Some elemental instinct for survival shuddered to life and began to pump its lifeblood into her veins. She sucked in great breaths of air, as though to transmit life to the little one she had been denying. An overwhelming urge to protect rose up within her – even if it meant giving her life, even if it meant . . . keeping her life.

No one could have been happier than Nita and Ilana to see Shana up and about again. They gloated over her like two proud parents, crowing and congratulating themselves on their nursing achievements. Their maternal crooning made Shana feel even more like a very, very young girl.

"Have you thought of names yet?" asked Nita, eager to offer her suggestions. "How about Ariel? That can be a name for a boy or a girl, and it's such a pretty name. It means 'lion of God'. I do think names are so important, don't you?"

"Very!" said Shana, remembering her conversation with the Rabbi.

"But you'll have to see what your fiancé suggests," said Ilana, who always corrected her sister. They were so kind and rotund and pernickety, like two puffed up hens, and so maddeningly sweet and overbearing that Shana found their company an ordeal and could hardly wait for her friends' return. When they came back at last, she still had to endure another two days of crawling irritation, and the resulting remorse for her mean spirit, before she could escape their kind hospitality.

"We're moving on in the morning down to Nain. Are you well enough to come with us?" asked Abigail.

"I've never felt better," said Shana quickly, and it was true. Her increased vigour produced a wonderful sense of well-being that made it easy to believe everything was going to be alright. She awakened each day with a sense of wonder, as though all of creation rejoiced with her in the budding life she nurtured in her womb. She wondered at her new ability to compartmentalise her life into daily portions, discarding both past and future. Abigail did not press her to plan ahead right now, knowing that this season of contentedness must be allowed to run its course while the tender new life took root.

Two more weeks dissolved in this sky-blue timelessness before the seal of her denial was broken. One morning, back in Nazareth again, Shana noticed her swelling waistline for the first time and was forced to acknowledge the fact that she would no longer be able to continue travelling with the Rabbi. "I don't know what to do," she wailed, slumped on her mattress.

"Have you thought about where you can go?" asked Abigail gently.

Shana's forehead tightened. "I cannot return home," she cried. "Not in this condition! And obviously I would not be welcome in Aunt Ada's home. I have nowhere to go . . . except perhaps to my Aunt Deborah, but I'd hate to do that!" she said with emotion.

"For what reason?" asked Abigail.

"She loves me so much and thinks so well of me, as do all my cousins there. It would dishonour my family to expose my . . . my disgrace in that small town. I cannot do that to her!" Shana hid her face in her hands.

Abigail put her hand on Shana's hunched shoulder. "Not your disgrace, dear girl, do not say that any longer. To call it a mistake, although a serious one, is sufficient. Many of us transgress without any outward evidence. Because your transgression can be seen by all, does not make it worse than any other."

"Listen, my friend, I have an idea," said Ruth, who had been standing by helplessly. "My hometown is only an hour's walk from Nazareth, and I have felt for a while that it's time I returned home. I want you to come with me. My father-in-law is a generous man. He has a large house with many rooms and I'm certain he won't turn you away. You can stay with us until we can come up with another solution."

Hope stirred as Ruth went on. "Your company will help me so much. I have been very lonely there without Yoav."

Shana inhaled deeply and blew out her breath. "How kind you both are," she said, weak with relief.

A few days later, the three women stood interlocked in each other's arms at the crossroads that would divide their lives. Abigail had insisted that Shana take a pouch of money with her, saying she would surely need it. "I will often be at my room in Jerusalem," she said, "but if you need a place to stay and I am not there, you can get the key from the baker at the central market. We will see each other again."

"We surely will; we will not say goodbye. God be with you," said Shana, shedding a tear onto Abigail's shoulder.

The Rabbi joined them and began to pray, placing his hand lightly on Shana's stomach, though he had not been told of her condition. "Father, bless your daughter and this child within her. May your will be done in their lives and your hand of guidance and protection be upon them both wherever they go."

He took a small piece of torn parchment from his belt and handed it to Shana. It had some letters scratched on it.

"These words are for you," he said. "Receive them at the opportune time that God will show you."

CHAPTER 20

THE ANCIENT CITY of Sepphoris was everything Nazareth was not – grand, opulent, an architectural masterpiece. As the two friends zig-zagged through the maze of paved streets, Ruth pointed out the homes of various members of her extended family, including the goldsmith's shop belonging to her father-in-law where her husband had spent his days fashioning jewellery – every landmark weighted with bitter-sweet memories. Shana could see that her friend's return home was re-opening wounds that had just begun to heal. Both girls kept up an appearance of gay nonchalance while suffering their own private agonies. Shana's nervousness mounted with every step; oh how she missed Abigail's fortress of support.

"There it is now," cried Ruth, pointing to a tall white building surrounded by towering cypresses. Shana shrank even more; it was grander than she had ever imagined.

"You will love my mother-in-law, Marian, and she will love you too. Yoav's sister, Tara, will also be there."

"What if they don't want me?" whispered Shana.

"Stop worrying!" scolded Ruth with a smile. "Come on, you're dragging your feet. We want to get settled before Shabbat, and the sun is sinking fast."

They climbed the wide, curved steps leading to a richly embellished, carved wooden door. Ruth knocked and called out, "Marian, Tara, it's me. Where are you?"

The sound of running feet could be heard from within, and the door swung open to present a slightly-built young girl wearing an apron. Her face lit up instantly.

"Lila, how good to see you," said Ruth, handing their bags to her. "My friend Shushana will be staying with us. Will you please prepare the room next to mine for her." The girl nodded to Shana and scurried off as a woman appeared.

"Marian!" cried Ruth.

"What a wonderful surprise!" the woman exclaimed, cupping Ruth's face with her hands and gazing at her with obvious affection. "You look like a new person; your travels have done you the world of good. Come in and tell me all about it." She turned curiously to Shana.

"This is my very good friend Shushana," said Ruth. "I've invited her to stay with us for a while, if that's alright with you."

"With pleasure! Please come in and share our home." Marian ushered them into an expansive ante-room which led to several other rooms. "Where are you from and where are you headed?" she asked kindly.

"I come from a small village near Hebron," Shana began uncertainly.

"We've been travelling together for the past couple of months," put in Ruth quickly, "but let's have something to drink and we can tell you all about it. It's been a most exciting time."

"Daniel and I have missed you," said Marian, transferring her attention back to Ruth. "You're such a great comfort to us; he will be very happy to see you."

The kitchen was a large separate room with a wooden table and chairs in the centre, and shelves crowded with earthenware pots and bowls lining the walls. A fire burned in a small oven on a raised hearth. This room was more modest than the first, and Shana felt more at home here. She had never before been inside a house of this size or grandeur and felt uncertain of whether she needed to alter her behaviour accordingly. She watched Marian adding herbs and honey to a pot of boiling water while Ruth began to tell the story of the past months, encouraging Shana to add details to her account. They sat at the table and drank the tea, sweet and refreshing, which gave Shana time to take in her new surroundings.

Marian was an elegant, good-looking woman with a placid, confident manner. Her face, too, wore shadows of her recent loss, but she seemed to bear her grief with an attitude of brave resignation, referring often to Yoav during their conversation. Shana wondered how Ruth was going to explain her predicament and tensed every time there was a pause in the conversation, dreading another question directed her way.

Lila came in and announced that her room was ready.

"Come, let us settle Shana in," said Marian, rising. Shana followed the two women into a small separate room with a real wooden bed along one wall, made up with soft blankets. A carved chest with a domed lid stood at the end of the bed, which Ruth said was for her to store her things in. There was a patterned rug on the floor, and a rich tapestry hung on the wall opposite the bed. Light flooded in through a low window which looked out onto a garden. In the corner, a tall spouted jug stood next to an earthenware basin.

Shana gasped and stared. "It's beautiful!" she exclaimed. "I have never seen such a lovely room."

Marian smiled at her with genuine delight. "It's a simple room, but I think you will be comfortable. Make yourself at home. Ruth will show you the bathroom."

"Bathroom?" Shana's surprise betrayed her peasant roots, and she wished she had contained herself, but the women laughed kindly, enjoying her naivety. Ruth put her arm around Shana's waist and led her to a small room which held a circular stone bath and a row of water jars. Three high slits in the wall let in the light.

"You stay in here and have a wash," whispered Ruth, passing Shana a towel, "and I'll explain your circumstances to Marian. She will understand." Shana blanched. If only the truth did not have to sound so terribly immoral as though she was a shameless whore. If only the past could be left behind and not continually rubbed in her face and exposed for everyone to gape at and judge and wonder. How she longed to be able to run away and hide her swelling belly from staring accusing eyes. But she would be forced to proclaim her terrible mistake again and again to everyone she met. She badly wanted to cry but did not dare reveal her vulnerability to Marian, so she splashed her face with cold water and concentrated on taking even breaths to quell the rising panic.

There was a light knock on the door. "Come out, Shana, it's alright, Marian wants to speak to you."

Shakily, she followed her friend back to the ante-room. Marian put her hands on Shana's trembling shoulders. "My dear, you are very welcome to stay here. You must not be anxious about anything. We will be glad to help you. Such a thing could happen to any of us, given the wrong set of circumstances, and now we must all make the best of it."

Marian's kindness touched Shana in a raw and tender place, triggering the tears she had struggled so valiantly to restrain. She felt small and foolish but allowed herself to be held against Marian's solid shoulder and patted on the back with her steady, sensible hand.

The worst was over. The tension began to subside, and Shana hung onto the cherished thought of being able to close a door behind her and be alone for the first time since starting out on this journey from Jerusalem.

Just then the front door burst open and a tall, strikingly attractive girl swept in, charging the atmosphere with a highly-strung energy.

"Ruthie," she purred in a resonant, affected tone. "How splendid to see you again. And you've brought a guest." Her head inclined provocatively and her smile was wide and gracious. Long lashes fanned her immaculate cheeks and her slender hands gestured gracefully. Everything about her was studied, smooth and perfect. She had all the self-assurance Shana had always wished for, which made her feel miserably diminished and insecure by comparison. Again, there was the wearying necessity to pretend, to act a part in order to hide her vulnerability behind a mask.

Shana's voice rang hollow and artificial in the large tiled room. "I'm Shana," she said, taking a step forward. "You must be Tara. Ruth has told me about you."

"Good things, I hope."

Shana's cheeks blazed. "Oh yes," she said ineffectively, and then Ruth rescued her by distracting Tara with a flood of questions. She felt desperately tired. It was an effort to keep upright, and the small of her back ached, sending a draining weakness down behind her knees. Ruth seemed remote, now that she had been reclaimed by her family, and Shana felt like an outsider.

"How long are you with us?" Tara asked.

"I–I'm not sure," Shana stammered, disintegrating under the girl's direct gaze.

"You're very pale, my friend," Ruth interrupted. "You must be worn out; let us not keep you up any longer." She slipped her hand through Shana's arm and directed her towards her room. "Shabbat is almost upon us. I will bring you something to eat here; there is no need for you to come to the table, and tomorrow you can rest. I will explain to Father that you are not very well. He will meet you when we return from synagogue."

Ruth sat on the edge of the bed while Shana nibbled some bread with cheese and olives. Ruth, too, looked tired and strained, having suffered on behalf of her friend as well as her own sorrow. She pressed a kiss onto Shana's forehead and went out, closing the door behind her.

The room instantly flooded with stillness, granting Shana the solitude she craved. She carefully put her few belongings into the chest – her extra tunic, her cloak and her purse, along with the precious piece of parchment the Rabbi had given her, and the gold ring from Rafael, which she was determined to keep safe until she could return it to him. She blew out the lamp and sank back against the cushions like one rescued from drowning, and abandoned herself to the silent space. If only she could rest in this amniotic comfort and stillness forever.

Around midday, the front door crashed open, and the house resounded with the clamour of men's voices in hearty discussion about the Sabbath message. Shana quailed. In her initial gratitude for having somewhere to run to, she had not taken into account that it would mean exposing herself to a whole new community, where every innocent question would present a dilemma. During the night, she had tried to invent some sort of fake identity she could live by in order to save everyone embarrassment. In the morning, she suggested to Ruth that she could masquerade as a woman whose husband had abandoned her. Both she and Marian agreed that it could not do any harm and would avoid the inevitable gossip. They decided that the story would suffice for Tara and her father also. Shana hated deceit, the mask did not fit her well but she was compelled to wear it. So she got up, dressed in one of Ruth's clean robes, and went out to meet Ruth's father-in-law in her new guise – not as a wrongdoer but as one who had been wronged; not as one who would be judged but as one who would be pitied instead.

Father Daniel was a stern man with a permanent frown fixed on his forehead. He viewed Shana with a piercing gaze from beneath his brows, which made her wonder if he immediately saw through her subterfuge. Yet he was not intimidating, and she found she could meet his eyes without flinching. He absent-mindedly grunted his consent to her staying and dismissed her by turning his attention to some scrolls in front of him.

The women set about preparing the table for the second Sabbath meal. Shana helped carry the laden dishes from the kitchen and set them down on the white cloth. The men who had accompanied Father Daniel from the synagogue settled themselves on couches around the table, still engrossed in their debate, while the women stood back to wait on them. Shana watched with keen interest.

Father Daniel blessed the bread and recited a prayer in his deep gravelly voice, then passed around the cup of wine. He was everything Shana imagined a father should be – kind yet commanding immediate respect, and possessing a reassuring air of quiet control. Grey whiskers sprang from his creased face, and the thin seam of his lips parted occasionally to emit extraordinary braying guffaws of contagious laughter. But more often, he was silent and serious and appeared to be mulling over a dark inner conflict, his brows pulled down over his eyes and his bony fingers twitching nervously. He listened attentively to the others and weighed up what they said before he spoke. When he did interject, the conversation would stop immediately to make way for his comment. He spoke unhurriedly, delivering his opinion with the authority of a final word, and those who disagreed did so respectfully.

Two of the men were teachers of the law. They were discussing Roman interference in Jewish affairs, and at times the discussion grew quite heated.

"There cannot be justice as long as we Jews curtsy to Roman authority!" Father Daniel said vehemently.

"There cannot be peace unless we do!" objected another.

"The more they get away with impinging on the Sanhedrin the more control we will hand to them, as well as to those they commission to rule over us. Herod Antipas is no better than his father, both have murdered our sons!" Father Daniel's face twisted with dark anger. This bitter remark was bound to ignite a vengeful reaction by calling to mind the monstrous event, thirty years prior, when the Jews' baby sons had been mercilessly slaughtered because of Herod's jealous insanity over talk of a king being born in Bethlehem. Daniel's own son's murder must surely cut into his heart with a blade as sharp as the sword that had ended his son's young life.

The atmosphere in the room became torrid with emotion. The men reclined stiffly against the cushions, their dishes pushed back now, restraining themselves until the women cleared the platters and left them to their wine and their outrage.

The four women ate their meal in the kitchen. Shana could see that Marian was disturbed by the discussion, and Ruth saddened by the callous mention of her beloved husband's death. Only Tara chatted happily, oblivious to the strained emotions around her.

"Their schemes can only lead to disaster," said Marian with quiet anger, abruptly changing the subject. "I fear I will lose my husband too if he does not come to his senses. He channels all the pain of his loss into this festering rage, which gives him strength to go on, using it as a weapon to avert his grief. It is very dangerous." She turned to Shana and spoke seriously. "Never speak to anyone about anything you have heard, nor mention the names of Daniel's visitors if you should ever be asked. The safest thing is to remain completely ignorant and innocent of all their affairs."

"You have my assurance. But I . . . don't understand—"

"It's better that way," said Marian.

The next day, Ruth showed Shana around the town, introducing her to many of the women they passed and nodding cordially to the men. A great number of them had family connections of one sort or another with the house of Abishai, who was Yoav's grandfather. Shana's role as a rejected wife and mother-to-be was met with such warm sympathy that she felt ashamed to betray their kindness but consoled herself with the thought that if they knew the truth, their attitude may well have been quite the opposite.

Sepphoris, situated on the crossroads of one of the main trade routes between the Jordan and the wealthy northern regions, was a thriving and prosperous town. Most of the houses were bigger than those Shana was accustomed to, though Ruth's home still stood out as one of the grandest. The lifestyle was completely foreign to her. With most of the domestic tasks done by servants, an unlimited number of leisure hours stretched before her like a vast empty space. It soon became apparent that much time was to be spent visiting – by no means her favourite pastime, especially when she felt so alien to the culture and lived in constant fear of answering questions in a way that might uncover her pretence.

Beyond the city wall, planted fields sloped down into a forested valley. Shana longed to escape and go wandering freely through the woodlands but she was trapped, firstly by social constraints, and secondly by possible danger: the leopard and lynx lurked in the nearby hills, and probably scorpions and vipers too. She had to be content with gazing at it from the upstairs windows of stately houses while she sat with her hands folded in her lap, smiling politely. Though extremely thankful for this temporary shelter, she deemed that no prison could ever be more restricting, and her soul suffocated, stifled by sitting still and good manners and correctness while she marked time, second by long second, until her body could be free of this parasitic organism that held her captive.

"Shana, tidy yourself up. We've been invited by Tara to join a group of her friends who are taking embroidery classes. I'm so excited, I've always wanted to learn embroidery," cried Ruth, "and perhaps it will help you to stop fidgeting," she said, pinching her friend's arm playfully.

Embroidery lessons turned out to be a saving grace, and to Shana's surprise she discovered an aptitude for it. Ten or twelve women met weekly in the spacious home of a potter's wife, who was a skilful needlewoman. Shana took great pleasure in watching her transform simple, well-made garments into exclusive articles of clothing for the wealthy by the clever application of embroidery. She loved to see the tiny stitches form intricate geometric shapes, converting an ordinary tunic into one fit for a princess. She especially loved the work on wedding veils, using fine silk and cotton thread dyed in soft colours. From that time on, Shana was almost never without her practice cloth and needle, blood-stained and grubby though it was with her determined efforts to master the skill.

The day of the class became the day she most looked forward to each week. The women were kind and, in view of her unfortunate circumstances, sensitively avoided asking her direct questions. Tara always came along, but it was clear that her participation was far more inclined towards gossip than the craft. Her beauty and intelligence gave her a prominent position in the group, and she often led the conversation, selecting precise words to cleverly direct the discussion along avenues of her curiosity. Shana was content to let her shine while she took refuge in her shadow where she could safely enjoy the pleasant ebb and flow of chatter.

It was clear from the beginning that Tara had taken a strong dislike to Shana, who she evidently considered beneath her social status, and often when Shana and Ruth giggled together over some private comment, her sideways glances were shot with spiteful jealousy. Shana detested her phoney 'niceness', full of sweet, patronising smiles and flowery, flattering words. She hated even more the way the women responded to her in an affected, obsequious manner, crowing in high sing-song voices. It was like a too sweet pudding, and she found it sickening.

The one thing that always kept her going – her reward for a day of enduring much that was disagreeable to her – was the thought of her private little room. What a sublime pleasure it was to finally close the door and wrap the seclusion around herself like a soft shawl, to escape the questions, the fear of exposure, the cloying politeness and correctness that were the tools of survival in this stringent society, and to submerge herself in the silence and her own uninterrupted meditation. She would dream of her life in Judea, with its stark simplicity and sweeping vistas, wind racing through the rocky hills and the great high places connecting earth and sky, and vow that if she could only go back there, she would never be discontented again.

The sun slanting in through the window woke her from wistful dreams where she had been searching for someone or something, but she couldn't remember what it was she was looking for. She opened her eyes reluctantly, hating to leave whatever it was unfound. Already she had to brace herself to face the day – another day but one day less to carry the awkward weight of her stomach, which threw her balance backwards and made her walk with her feet turned out. The creature growing inside her was now making its presence known. She could feel it squirming and struggling and imagined it to be as impatient to be liberated from its confinement as she was.

There was a knock on the door. "Are you up? It's late," called Ruth. "Tara and I are waiting for you to come with us to the market. Are you coming?"

"Don't wait; I'll stay here. I'll be alright."

Receding footsteps. Relief. A few hours free.

Shana got dressed slowly, then helped herself to some bread and cheese and went to sit outside on the front steps in the sun. Lila was inside sweeping, and Marian must have gone with the others. There were not many people about, perhaps because it was market day, and it was pleasant to soak in the warm rays and watch the yellowing leaves of the tall planes float in gentle spirals to the ground.

Some distance away, the clipped staccato sound of horses' hooves striking the cobbled street could be heard. Shana listened curiously; it was coming closer, and she thought it might be some illustrious person in a horse-drawn carriage. When she heard the horses turn into the street in front of her, she stood up and tried to focus, shading her eyes from the bright morning sun. A shadow fell across her, and the horses halted. Against the glare, she could make out the shape of Roman helmets and two riders in red jackets, a sight that struck immediate fear in her heart. Roman troops were not often seen in Galilee, other than in the camp at Tiberias. It was too late to dash inside.

"Do you live here?" asked one of the soldiers in Aramaic. Shana's heart pounded; she was not sure whether it was safer to answer him or to keep silent.

"Where is your husband?"

She turned to mount the steps and tripped on the hem of her robe, giving the impression that she was scrabbling to get away.

"Wait. You have not answered my question."

"It is forbidden for Jewish women to speak to strangers on the streets," she said. "Forgive me, I must go."

The soldier laughed, his handsome features as hard as sculptured stone He saw her fear. "Yes, but it is also against the law not to answer to the authorities who guard your peace. Who lives here?"

"F–father Daniel," she stammered.

"He has many visitors, does he not?"

"Sometimes."

"They often come late at night, I believe."

"I don't know; I have not been here very long. Please, I must go now," she pleaded.

"The synagogue ruler, is he one of them?"

Shana felt herself blushing; she knew he was one of the regular visitors. "I don't know. I don't know anything about them and it's none of my business." She ran up the last two steps and clutched at the door latch. The soldier laughed again, the derisory laugh of a conqueror, as though he had got the answers he was looking for. She stumbled inside and bolted the door as the clatter of hooves faded away. How foolish of her to have displayed herself like live bait. Anyway, they had gone.

The truth was that the men from the synagogue, some of them Pharisees, came often, and recently it had been very late at night when she heard their muffled voices in the back room. Marian would look tired and troubled in the morning, and Ruth too seemed anxious, but neither of them mentioned the reason for it.

A few hours later, Shana heard someone at the door. She froze, half expecting a battalion of soldiers to burst in, but it was only Father Daniel coming home early for lunch. He went into the front room, and Shana knocked timidly on the door.

"What is it?" He always sounded a little impatient. Shana crept in, and his fierce expression softened as soon as he saw who it was.

"I–I just thought I should tell you that some Roman soldiers came this morning asking questions about you," she said timidly. Was it fear she saw momentarily widening his eyes before the bristled brows concealed them again?

"What did you tell them?" he asked gruffly, clenching his jaw so that his mouth disappeared completely.

"N–nothing. They wanted to know whether the synagogue ruler came here and whether anyone visited late at night. I told them I did not know."

"Well done, girl," he said, and then lifted one brow to expose a pale, piercing eye, which he fixed upon her.

"There is no need to mention this to the others," he said.

CHAPTER 21

A T THE NEXT EMBROIDERY CLASS, Shana was happily engrossed in stitching a row of gold leaves onto an offcut of red silk when, without warning, Tara launched a malicious attack on her. She waited until the initial pleasantries were over and there was a lull in the conversation, and then spoke in sugared tones, "So tell us more about yourself, Shana. We've all been itching to get to know you better, but you say so little. You seem so mysterious and interesting."

Shana went cold. She knew Tara's astute perception immediately picked up the nervous flutter of her eyelids, confirming she had located her weak spot. A reply was required, and they all waited kindly, except Tara.

"There's not much to tell," Shana began haltingly. "My life has been very ordinary really. I grew up in Halhul in the highlands of Judea, and . . ." her cheeks were on fire and she blundered on, "and my father arranged a marriage but—"

"I'm sure Shana doesn't want to talk about that," said

Ruth quickly.

"You have spent some time in the vicinity of Jerusalem too, I believe." Tara's words slipped like a blade between Shana's ribs. Her heart began to pound. How much did she know?

"Yes, I've stayed with my aunt a couple of times," she said in what she hoped was a nonchalant way.

"And a cousin too?"

O, God help me, she knows! "Y—yes, and his wife."

"What is his name again? I believe I may have met him once when the family were in Jerusalem for Passover, and my uncle brought him home to talk business."

"Haziel."

"That's right, Haziel. A fine man, and good looking too, don't you think?"

"I suppose so," Shana said faintly, swallowing to moisten her dry throat. Her fingers gripped the needle and cloth in an effort to control the trembling of her hands, all the time feeling Tara's sharp eyes boring into her.

Ruth again attempted to divert the conversation onto safer ground. "Tell us about the way of life in your village, Shana. How is it different to the way we live here?" she asked.

"Far simpler," Shana managed. "The community lives by the land, and not many are wealthy."

"Will you go back?" asked Tara, trying to regain the advantage. "Why did your father not take you in at such a time as this?" The knife twisted and several women looked up, shocked at the directness of Tara's interrogation. They must have seen Shana's white face and wondered. The silence grew uncomfortable. Shana looked down at her hands.

"You must not upset her over this, Tara," Ruth reprimanded gently. Tara's face flushed with jealous anger at

Ruth's defence of her friend, but she said nothing more. Thankfully, she did not walk home with them after the session but stayed behind to visit with one of the women.

As soon as Shana was alone with Ruth, she burst into tears. "She knows everything, Ruth, and she hates me. How does she know about Haziel?"

"Don't upset yourself. I don't believe she knows him at all. She is very clever, and I think that was just a ploy to find out more about something she has heard."

"Who could have told her I was in Jerusalem?"

"Our country is very small, as you know. Perhaps someone from here who knows your aunt and family mentioned you had stayed with them. A trader maybe? Tara must have thought it strange that you were living with them during the time you said you were married, and got suspicious."

"I was betrothed, not married," said Shana, getting confused. What had she told Tara? She was no good at this subtle twisting of facts to make people assume things.

The girls walked in silence for a while, considering the implications of this new state of affairs.

"If the truth gets out, I will no longer be able to stay here. It will cause great embarrassment to your family," said Shana.

"That's exactly why I don't think Tara will make known whatever she has managed to find out. I think she is only trying to scare you. The last thing she wants is a scandal concerning her and her family's name. Try not to worry anymore about it."

"Ruth, what's happening? Look!" cried Shana. The house was in view, and a cluster of people was gathered outside the door. Something must be wrong! The girls quickened their pace and then broke into a run when they saw Marian in the centre of the group. When they reached the house, Marian came forward to meet them, looking distraught. "A Roman official was murdered last night near here. They have taken Daniel away, and also some of his associates." She delivered the report dispassionately. Her composure was terrifying.

"Where have they taken him?" cried Ruth, gasping for breath.

"I don't know. Some of the men have gone to try and find out," said Marian faintly.

"Come inside and sit down," said Ruth, taking Marian's arm. The huddle of anxious women parted to let them through, asking if there was anything they could do and promising to come back later.

There was nothing anyone could do but wait for more information.

When Tara heard the news, she went hysterical. "No. No!" she shrieked. "Not Papa too. I can't bear it. I can't . . . bear any more." She burst out crying, holding nothing back, expressing noisily what both her mother and Ruth were feeling but could not release. Shana looked on in helpless shock. She thought of the two soldiers with their impassive expressions and frighteningly dominating presence, their shining swords so readily within reach of their gloved hands. Had they come back with Herod's police and ordered Father Daniel to be dragged out of his workplace and hustled off like a criminal? And a criminal perhaps he was. She recalled his dark, brooding rage whenever the Romans were mentioned, his threats of revenge . . .

Some neighbours came in and stood around, wringing their hands. Tara went to her room and called for Lila to wait on her with blankets and towels and warmed water. The sound of her wretchedness echoed through the house as she wailed like a child, "Papa. Papa."

Later in the afternoon, news came. Father Daniel was in prison in Tiberias under Herod's guard, awaiting trial, together with the others they had taken. He had been numbered among the Zealots, and there was little chance of his release.

Marian was seated at the kitchen table when they told her. She put her head on her arms and remained in rigid silence for a long, long time. Ruth stood next to her, weeping quietly. Tara gripped the edge of the table and doubled over with a succession of stricken cries.

Suddenly she whirled around and shrieked at Shana. "It's your fault. You have caused this by informing on my father. Not only are you an adulteress, you're a liar, a spy, and now a murderer too!" Her voice reached a crescendo, sending currents of shock through the room. Shana stood as still as stone. Marian sat up and looked from one to another in horrified disbelief.

"What do you mean, Tara, what do you mean a spy?" she said.

"Lila heard her talking to the Roman soldiers the other day when we were out. No wonder she stayed behind. It is she who has caused my father to be taken!" She pointed her finger at Shana, crazed with anguish.

"I did not tell them anything," Shana protested, shrinking back against the wall.

All eyes were upon her. Ruth looked at her questioningly, Marian stared with shocked suspicion, and Tara glared in hateful accusation.

Shana began to cry, "I did not. I did not."

"Why were you talking to them?" asked Marian quietly.

"They passed by when I was sitting outside. I did not want

to talk to them, but they kept questioning me. I didn't tell them anything . . ."

"She's a liar. Can't you see? She already lied about who she is. They must have paid her for the information; there was money stashed in her room. Lila and I found it in the chest when we got suspicious that she is not who she said she is. She obviously needs money to take care of her bastard baby and will stop at nothing to get it."

"That's not true," wailed Shana through her hands. She looked at Ruth pleadingly. "Surely you know it's not true?" Ruth looked away, and suddenly Shana knew it was no good. The anguish they were all experiencing, together with the jumble of half-truths and lies, was too much for any of them to distinguish what was true right now. Shana was not even certain herself whether something in her replies or her manner could have aroused the soldiers' suspicion.

"Get out, you brat!" hissed Tara. "Mama, tell her to leave. She cannot be trusted; she has brought enough trouble on this family."

No one came to her defence, not even Ruth. Shana stood quietly with her hands hanging at her sides. "I will leave tomorrow morning. I am as sorry as you are about Father Daniel. I love him too; I would never intentionally have caused this to happen."

She left the room, left them to their grief and suspicion and unspeakable heartache. She stood by her window looking out into the garden, now glowing gold in the evening sun. The baby, compressed between her ribs, began to kick repeatedly in objection to the stress shot into its veins. Shana put her hands on her stomach to feel the tiny limbs moving just beneath her skin. A strong emotion came over her, a powerful desire to shield this little creature from the harsh realities of the world it would soon be born into: a world full of hate, anguish, fear and pain; men turning against their own kind; lives tormented, cut short, destroyed. What choice did this baby have about its future, whether it would be happy or filled with sorrow, blessed or cursed? She thought of the prayer of blessing the Rabbi had prayed. Perhaps that would give it a better chance.

Another picture flashed into her mind of a place the Rabbi often spoke about, a very different world of green pastures and quiet streams, and peace that flowed from every man's heart of love. The Rabbi called it the kingdom of God, where his reign of righteousness would bring an end to sorrow. And he had come to bring it into being.

She sat down on the edge of her bed, listening to the air flowing in and out of her lungs and the throbbing of life-blood in her ears, not thinking, not feeling. The light ebbed away and darkness infiltrated, little by little, until its strange granulated substance filled the room. Much later Ruth came in and sat down beside her in the leaden gloom.

After as while she said, "I'm so very sorry you have to go. I believe implicitly that whatever happened was not your fault, but Marian and Tara's distress is so hard to bear, on top of what they have already suffered over Yoav, that they can only think you are to blame right now."

"I told Father Daniel about the soldier's questions, and he said I should not mention it to anyone else; he did not want you to worry. But now it looks as though I'm guilty of–"

"I believe you, and the others will in time," said Ruth, putting her hand on Shana's. "Will you go to your aunt? You mentioned she lives in Galilee not far from here."

"Yes, I will have to. Thank you, Ruth, for everything. I am so sorry it has turned out this way."

"Remember what the Teacher taught us, that we need never be afraid if we trust in God. We cannot do anything for Father Daniel, but we can ask God to take care of him and believe that he will. Please send me news whenever you can and let me know how you are. I will miss you terribly. You're a good friend and you have helped me more than you will ever know."

CHAPTER 22

SHANA PULLED HER CLOAK around her and shivered as the morning mist wrapped her in a damp shroud. She had not said goodbye but crept out while it was still dark, instructing Lila to pass on her farewell thanks. The journey to Aunt Deborah's home was only a five-hour walk, but Shana had hired a donkey to take the strain off her heavy body. By the time the sun had sent its first pink probes into the sky, the small caravan had already left the town behind, together with another closed chapter of her life.

The fields were covered in gossamer veils, which shimmered and steamed like boiling lakes of silver. With the warm sun on her face and the song of the lark in her ears, Shana decided to suspend her troubles during this short transition between past and future. She had prayed for Father Daniel and for herself as Ruth suggested and, having made up her mind to simply believe that all would be well, she felt as free as a child to relish the beauty of this new day. It was so long since she had been able to escape the stuffy confines of the town that it was like being released from captivity; her soul could breathe again. She looked forward to seeing her aunt and uncle, though dreaded the initial meeting, but felt confident that they would take her in. And perhaps there would be news of her family. And . . . of Haziel!

Deborah's let out a spontaneous cry of pleasure at the sight of her niece, but her surprise quickly turned to puzzlement. "I did not receive any news of your marriage. How strange. Where is Rafael?"

"I'm not married, Aunt. M–may I come in and explain?"

"Of course, dear. You're not in any trouble are you?"

Shana told the story in a few blunt sentences, just as she should have done at Ruth's house, leaving people to their own opinions and judgments. Deborah listened without comment and then got up and hugged Shana. "Well, this is the way things are, and that's what we have to deal with. You are very welcome to stay with us. Dania is married now, so there is extra space. We will all help you to work out a plan for your future, but right now there is a little one to prepare for, and that is the most important thing."

Shana loved her for her sound practicality. Then, tight with anxiety, she asked the question that had remained like a knot in her heart ever since she had left Jerusalem. "Is Haziel alright?"

"I've not heard otherwise and I surely would have if anything was wrong. I've had no news of your family for several months now, but we must let them know you are here with us and safe. They will be most anxious about you. Do they know about the baby?"

"No."

"This little one is a member of our family, no matter the circumstances of its birth. I am certain your father will come around to agreeing that you can return and bring up your child in the family home."

Shana shuddered. Apart from wanting to spare her mother this added blow, she could think of nothing worse than bringing up her child under her father's iron rule. Her future was something she would rather lock away for the time being; today had enough troubles of its own.

"Now, you sit down here and rest while I go down to Uncle Ethan's shop and tell him and Ivan everything you have told me," said Deborah, immediately taking command. Shana slumped down with relief and lay back against the cushions. It was a long time since someone had taken care of her.

Ivan came back with his mother and greeted Shana with tender reserve, averting his eyes from her swollen body in an effort to spare her embarrassment, and blushing to the tips of his ears. He was a little taller now and his shoulders had broadened, but still no substance filled his bony frame. Seeing his confusion, Shana got up, took his hands and placed them on her stomach. "Feel here, Ivan. Can you feel the baby moving? Isn't it amazing?"

He flushed again, and she saw the worshipful fondness still in his eyes, in spite of the adjustment he must have made to his high ideal of her. This was a great comfort because from now on she would have to hold her head high before those who might judge her. If only she could be more like Mary, who did not care at all what others thought of her, for being unaffected by others' opinions renders them powerless over you. Instead, she felt like a leper, with her protruding stomach going before her proclaiming: 'Unclean. Unclean.'

Uncle Ethan was more direct. "Well, my dear, you certainly have made a mess of your life since we last saw you." Shana hung her head and twisted her fingers into knots behind her back.

"Why did you not come to us in the first place?" he asked.

"I – I was ashamed."

"However," he went on kindly, "what is done is done. You are healthy and strong and you will have a healthy child of Israel, so we will worry about it no more. Welcome to our home; may you be happy here. Deborah will be glad of your company now that Dania has gone."

Shana relaxed under her uncle's paternal guardianship. He was like a father to her, better than a father, and she felt safe with him.

"There is something else worrying me, Uncle."

"Sit down over here," he said, patting a stool next to him. "What is it?"

"While I was staying at my friend's house in Sepphoris, a terrible thing happened. Her father-in-law, Daniel, was put in prison in Tiberias for his suspected involvement with the Zealots. His life is in danger, and the family think I was the cause of his arrest. That is why I had to leave."

"Go on."

"Some Roman soldiers questioned me one day when I was at home alone and, although I didn't say much, something must have confirmed their suspicions about him. Father Daniel and his associates were all arrested after the murder of a Roman official. The family think I was a spy and received money for my services. I would never do a thing like that, never ever! I love Father Daniel and am so afraid for him . . ." She broke off, screwing up her face in distress.

Ethan covered Shana's small hand with his – large, rough and work-worn, and utterly comforting. "Do you think he is associated with the Zealots?"

"It didn't occur to me at the time, but yes, quite possibly."

Ethan was thoughtful for a while and then said, "There is nothing you can do. What happened was very unlikely to be all your doing, if at all. He would have been sniffed out eventually anyway; otherwise they would not have been around there asking questions. Those men who get involved with the Zealots know full well that they lay their lives on the line. But there is always a chance of him getting out if he was not guilty of the murder. Now put it aside and don't let it upset you. It is bad for the baby. And meanwhile, there is plenty of work to be done."

Shana filled her lungs with air and sighed as a great weight fell off her shoulders. Ethan got up, and she followed him out of the room into the courtyard, where her aunt was busy grinding corn. She rolled up her sleeves, knelt down beside her, and immersed herself in the wonderful therapy of work. She poured some corn into the funnel and watched the mill transforming the hard grains into fine flour. Afterwards would come the kneading – adding a little oil and a little water until the substance separated itself from the fingers and formed a springy, elastic dough which would be pressed into a glossy roll ready for the coals. There were herbs to cut from the garden, juicy and aromatic and infused with medicinal properties. Later the fire would be lit. They would stir the greens into the pot with the lentils and onions and wait for the bubbles to appear, shiny with oil, to dance upon the surface. The family would sit together and talk, warmed as much by the fire as by the company of dear ones so closely connected. There was much, so very much to be thankful for.

The orderly little household was like an island in the turbulent waters of Shana's life, where she could shelter, cocooned and content. Daily tasks which had always frustrated her before, now became her lifeline. She yielded herself to each one, taking pleasure in the strength of her arms and the actions her hands performed. An acute awareness developed of the world around her: voices, movements, sounds; colours and textures defined by the shifting light; the breeze stirring the dust around her toes. Today was encapsulated and complete. And tomorrow would be another today.

Father Daniel often came to mind in vivid detail – the intense energy of his presence, his astute perception and fearsome sense of justice – it seemed impossible that anyone would dare hold him captive. One day, Ivan announced that he was taking a trip to Tiberias to buy fish, which he sometimes sold at the market, and Shana seized her opportunity to ask him if he would make some enquiries.

"My friend's husband, Chuza, manages Herod's household so it should not be difficult to find Joanna and deliver a message from me. Give her my greetings and then tell her what I have told you. She is very fond of Ruth and will want to help in any way she can."

"I will see what I can do," Ivan promised.

"Will you be staying in Tiberias a day or two until she can find out about Father Daniel?"

"Sometimes the weather is not favourable for a good catch, so I spend a few days there with my fisherman friend," said Ivan. "And if the weather is favourable, I often spend a few days anyway," he added with a laugh.

Would knowing be better than not knowing? It depended on the outcome of course, but if it were negative, would she rather not know? Waiting for Ivan's return pitched Shana into a frenzy of agitation. Days that had slid by effortlessly, now dispensed slow seconds one by one as though reluctant to part with them. After a week, she began to fear she might have put Ivan in danger too of being associated with the Zealots. But surely an enquiry after a friend or loved one would not elicit suspicion? She did not understand the politics of the Roman occupation. It seemed to her that no one really did, especially as Herod took sides, sometimes for, and sometimes against the Jews. Certainly it made the man on the street insecure. There was so much injustice, but any outcry was dangerous and brought bloodshed and further injustice. As a result, revenge and anger boiled beneath the surface, masked by a thin veneer of peace, which was sustained by the invincible hope of the Jews in the promises of their God to redeem Israel from all her enemies.

At the sound of Ivan's voice at the door, Shana let out an involuntary cry and dropped the spindle of thread she was spinning.

"I have good news!" he sang out triumphantly. "Your friend has been released."

Shana buried her face in her hands and sobbed with relief.

"Another man was found guilty of the murder, so the other suspects got away with severe beatings and strong warnings but their lives intact."

She leapt up and flung her arms around her cousin's neck. "Thank you, thank you, thank you!" she cried, as though it was all his doing.

Ivan squirmed with embarrassment and did not stop smiling for days. Neither did Shana until the dark thought occurred to her that Father Daniel would not stop his conspiring schemes. He would stop at nothing to avenge his son's murder and to revolt against the oppression of his people. He would be watched carefully and would never really be free again.

News filtered back from Halhul on the intricate person-to-person network of friends, family, and business associates who were woven together to form the fabric of Palestine. Deborah's message had reached Shana's family through a friend's husband on a trip to Jerusalem, who had relayed her news via a wool merchant, who traded with Haziel and lived near Shana's family in Halhul. He had returned now with a reply.

Deborah met him at the courtyard gate to hear the report. Shana saw her face crumple and a bolt of fear shot through her. Bad news! Sick with apprehension, she waited until the man left, and ran outside.

"Aunt Ada is dead," said Deborah, dazed. "She has been ill for a long time on and off, as you know, and the illness finally got the better of her."

Two completely opposite emotions impacted Shana at the same time – grief for her beloved aunt, and relief that the news did not concern her mother.

Shana led her aunt to a bench and they sat close together in silence, gripping onto each other's hands as they shared their sorrow. Dead. It was just a word. Nothing had changed around them, and yet the whole world had changed because Aunt Ada was no longer in it.

After a long while, Deborah wiped her eyes on her apron and made an effort to speak. "Your Mama was delighted to hear you are with us and that you are well. She sends all her love and said to tell you that Beth is growing up into a lovely young woman and keeps herself happy by believing all the time that she will see you before long. Your father is fine but having trouble with his back, so he struggles to do the heavy work."

"Did you tell them about the baby?"

"No. I thought it would only cause your mother to fret, and she will know soon enough when you return home. They will all be too delighted with the new child to bother about anything else, and your father is unlikely to turn you out with his own grandchild."

Shana's stomach crimped at the thought of having to face him. After a pause she blurted out, "Did they mention Rafael?"

"Nothing was said."

A stab of disappointment thrust deep as she realised afresh how disconnected his life was now from hers. He had always been part of her existence, even when they had gone their separate ways for long periods of time. He had been more than a brother and more than a friend; he would have been her lover. But now she was nothing to him, or worse. How she could ever live in the same community as him again: pass him on the streets, see him with his wife and children, and be treated as a stranger? She would have to walk on by with her child's hand in hers, a perpetual reminder to him of her betrayal.

It was nearing her final months now. She began to brood again as fears for her future invaded her thoughts. She tried to visualise herself as a mother but was unable to summon any such picture to mind. It sometimes felt as though the child she carried did not belong to her, as though she was just a vessel that incubated another life for a period of time.

And then one night, shifting uncomfortably on her mattress, a thought came to her which impressed itself upon her with such clarity and certainty that it immediately became an unarguable fact: this child was not her own at all. This child belonged to Judith!

The realisation settled itself upon her with a peace that defied understanding; it remained only to work out the practicalities. She spent the rest of the night in the grip of cyclic thoughts, weighing up the possible outcomes and consequences of her returning to Judea to present her bizarre gift, either still packaged within her body or upon her breast. These two streams of thought argued back and forth, and she had reached no conclusion by dawn, so she decided to discuss the matter with her aunt and uncle and consider their wise counsel.

"Bless you, my dear. What a wonderful solution. Judith has longed for a child for so many years, she will surely be overjoyed," cried her sweet-natured aunt, who always saw the best side of life and fully expected things to go just right. "She will want to take her new baby in her arms as soon as it is born so that it will know its mother from the start."

Ethan disagreed. "I don't think it would be a good idea to stay with them after all that has happened, which means you will need to wean the child first. You can stay here with us until then."

Deborah looked disappointed. "By that time, it will be like handing over someone else's child," she argued. "Those first weeks and months are so precious with one's infant. There is no reason to deprive Judith of that joy."

Shana's thoughts now turned to Judith – her dear, patient face, always shadowed with the weight of longing she carried in her heart. Then she visualised Judith's expression of radiant wonder as her arms were filled at last, and she knew what she must do.

"I think you are right, Aunt Deborah. I must go to Judea as soon as possible so that Judith can share the birth of her child. I know of a place I can stay in Jerusalem until the birth. Afterwards, I will nurse Judith's baby until such time as they don't need me anymore."

CHAPTER 23

S HANA'S JOURNEY back to Judea was long and tiring with
many stops. The guide had been reluctant to let her join
the caravan, even travelling on a donkey, and had he known
just how pregnant she was, he would definitely have refused
her. But Shana carried the unborn child in a compact bulge
just below her ribs and felt so strong and healthy that she
knew she could manage the trip without endangering the
child. Even so, by the time they reached Jerusalem she ached
all over.

As she climbed the hill to the village, so endearingly
familiar and now so empty of Aunt Ada, a medley of
emotions coursed through her. It had rained during the day,
and brilliant white clouds swam on the surface of the puddles
in the afternoon sunlight, cheering her a little. She hurried up
the path, queasy with apprehension, keeping her head bowed
and her veil gathered around her face so she would not be
recognised. It was important to arrive before Haziel got back
from his shop.

She could see Judith in the courtyard, bent over a smoking fire. When she got to the entrance, she called her name softly. Judith spun around and gaped, taking in Shana's condition. Her mouth fell open, and a mixture of shocked surprise, bewilderment, and pain crossed her face as she understood the implication. Before she could speak, Shana went up to her, took her hands, and held them against her bulging stomach.

"Judith," she said, looking into her eyes, "this child belongs to you."

Judith stared back, not comprehending. "What . . . what are you saying?"

"I mean," said Shana slowly, "that in a little over a month's time, you will have Haziel's baby — if that is what you want."

Tears sprung to Judith's eyes. She stood with her shaking hands still on Shana's stomach, struggling with her emotions, and then broke down and wept. At that moment, the baby shifted against their hands, and something amazing — supernatural — took place: Shana sensed that the ownership of the child had been transferred to Judith, and she knew Judith felt it too.

It was a wildly joyous moment. Suddenly the muddle of powerful emotions erupted, and both women began to laugh. They laughed and laughed and laughed, holding onto one another and rocking with mirth until tears streamed down their faces. They laughed until they could laugh no more and stood panting and sobbing, and then doubled up again with fresh convulsions of laughter.

It was upon this scene that Haziel entered the courtyard.

Exhilaration from this explosive release, together with the completely perplexed expression on Haziel's face, triggered another wave of hilarity, which both women tried to quell with snorts of suppressed giggles. Any apprehension Shana had about the first meeting with Haziel dissolved in the ridiculousness of the situation.

Judith went towards Haziel with her arms wide and face shining. "Look, Shana has brought us a baby! Our own baby."

She began to laugh and cry again, and Haziel looked annoyed to cover up his embarrassment.

"Listen, my husband," Judith went on, "whatever has happened before no longer matters anymore. It has turned out to be a blessing. Don't you see? Only God can turn things around for the good, even our mistakes. And this child has your blood in its veins." She threw her arms around him, though he remained unyielding and severe. He glanced over her shoulder in Shana's direction, and Shana noticed an ugly scar that snaked up from his neck and across his cheek. And in his eyes she detected a distinct blaze of recrimination.

His attitude withered her at first but later made her strong with indignation. She was glad of the anger for it gave her a measure of power over him while at the same time establishing an invisible barrier between them.

Shana left them alone then – Judith to relish her joy, and Haziel to come to terms with this strange turn of events. She hurried back over the hill to Jerusalem, hoping she might find Abigail at her room. She had given Judith the address and told her to visit her there so they could plan for the coming event.

Abigail was not there and the steps remained unswept, so she collected the key from the bakery and let herself in. The musty smell of the room intimated that it had been closed up for a while, probably since they were last there together.

Shana bolted the door behind her, lit a lamp, and dropped down onto the couch beneath the window. The thick stone walls kept the room icy cold and muted the outside noise, giving it the secluded air of a cellar. Some half-finished handwork still lay over the stool as a comforting token of Abigail's presence.

Shana sat for a long time re-living the events of the day, going over them in detail in her mind and often laughing out loud at the absurd spectacle she and Judith must have presented to Haziel. She reflected on all that had happened since she was last in Jerusalem: the people she had met, the places she had seen and everything she had learnt. There had been joy and there had been pain, some hard times as well as times of contentment. It had been a rich experience of life, and through it all she had sensed the guiding hand of a shepherd. Could it be the great Jehovah watching over her?

However, the next weeks could prove to be the hardest of all. There would be the virtual imprisonment of these four walls around her, the aloneness, and worse, the torturous idleness. She picked up Abigail's unfinished embroidery. How thankful she was to have learnt the craft during the time with Ruth, as now it would give her something to do and perhaps fetch a little money after the baby was born. There was not much left of the money Abigail had given her.

Shana had never lived alone before. As much as she loved solitude, it only had value in a social context; otherwise it quickly became loneliness. She went out to the market daily to buy food and to fill her water jars. She bought colourful yarn and began some handwork. Judith came often to spend an hour or two with her. She loved to sit with her hand on Shana's stomach while they chatted, exclaiming each time she felt a movement, and it gave Shana pleasure to see the fresh rosiness in her cheeks and the mounting excitement shining in her eyes.

A new intimacy that developed between them which made it possible for them to openly discuss everything that had happened. Judith told Shana that Haziel had spent a week in prison while the council decided his fate. The scene at the temple courts had excited much interest, and when the story leaked out that Haziel was involved, the council were placed in a difficult position. They were afraid of the Rabbi's present popularity, and imposing a harsh sentence would be in direct opposition to his public demonstration of mercy. Finally, Haziel had been given a severe flogging – not so much, Haziel thought, as a penalty for his transgression, as to silence his subversive talk. Aunt Ada had been devastated by the whole thing and took to her bed again. It had been a tough time for their family.

However, as Judith pointed out, the Jews were a forgiving people and once punishment was duly administered they generally considered a wrongdoer absolved of his misdeeds and easily forgot about it. Likewise, after many shared tears, Judith's forgiveness was complete, and they were able to lay the matter to rest.

As the confinement time drew near, the women began to discuss the practicalities of the birth. Haziel agreed that Shana should move into their outside room so that Judith could attend to her needs during the event, and so Shana could nurse the baby for the first few months.

"How will the neighbours receive me?" asked Shana anxiously.

"They have accepted Haziel, so they will accept you. Only the Pharisees no longer greet him in the streets, and he doesn't care about them anyway."

"They will look down on me."

"Perhaps so, but do you care?"

Shana thought about it and then said with resolve, "No. What I most care about right now is your happiness." And she realised with joy that it was absolutely true.

CHAPTER 24

SETTLED INTO Judith and Haziel's home again, Shana awaited the birth with mounting trepidation. With each passing day, she grew more uncomfortable, which made her irritable and impatient. Her fear of undergoing the inevitable birth process was usurped only by her desire to get it all over with.

The day came suddenly, it seemed. The midwife examined her, confined her to her room, and went on standby. Judith stayed with her, beside herself with anxiety and excitement. Haziel paced around outside, sneaking surreptitious glances towards the open door of the room where Shana lay moaning with discomfit. When her groans grew louder, he disappeared, the midwife was summoned, and the long labour began.

Caught in a cycle of crushing spasms, Shana twisted and turned. "Mama! Mama!" she cried. Cast adrift on an ocean, she was tossed from wave to wave so that she could not come up for air. Tides of pain ebbed and mounted, each time reaching levels beyond what she thought she could endure. If only she could stop awhile to rest.

Just before dawn, with a final cry, her body released the babe, which shone and squirmed in the lamplight, making mewing, gasping sounds. It was a little girl.

Shana collapsed against the pillows; it was all over! The midwife scooped up the little creature and, after washing and salting the tiny body, wrapped it tightly in a cloth and laid it in Judith's waiting arms. The wrinkled face screwed up and turned puce as it began to cry – short, breathy little wails, pressed from tiny lungs. The tender glow on Judith's face when she looked down at the babe would be forever imprinted on Shana's mind - mother and child lit up in the soft light like a scene from a celestial kingdom. Euphoria beyond anything she had ever experienced suffused Shana through and through. She felt like a queen, the happiest and most blessed of all women.

When the warm bundle was placed on her breast, her entire being was given into the milk that flowed as her strength passed into another life. It seemed to her at that moment, that everything she had suffered, or might suffer in the future, was worth this glorious event – this giving of life to another.

Later, Judith called Haziel in and put the baby in his arms. He held the bundle awkwardly with his arms braced in front of him and stared down at the pinched face and delicate pink head with its covering of dark fluff, and two coal-black eyes locked sightlessly onto his. A look of bewildered amazement crossed his face, followed by a palpable flicker of paternal pride. Never had Shana seen him so tender and disarmed. He did not look at her but smiled bashfully at Judith, returned the baby to her, and hurriedly left the room. He failed to acknowledge Shana at all.

Before the birth, Shana had agreed that Judith would take over all the nurture and care of the baby from the start and bring her to Shana only for her feeds so that a natural bond could develop between mother and child. It had seemed a perfectly feasible arrangement, but now that the baby was born, everything was different.

Shana sat up in her bed and waited, her ears tuned to pick up the sound she was straining to hear. She watched the leaves scuttle fretfully back and forth in the courtyard in the cold afternoon wind, plaited and unplaited the tassels of her bedcover and shifted uncomfortably. At last a muffled sigh came through the wall, followed by a few hiccoughing wails and the sound of Judith's footsteps hurrying across the room. Then a series of shuffles and bumps. Whatever was taking Judith so long?

The baby's cries became urgent, echoing her own silent protest, and she had to suppress the urge to get up and run to fetch her herself. When Judith finally came in, Shana reached greedily for the howling bundle, its tight little fists flailing in indignation, and Judith went out again. The howling stopped as the baby began to suckle, making soft gurgling sounds in its throat. Shana stroked the downy head and examined the exquisite little hands with their tiny shell-tipped fingers, her heart brimming with a love she had never known before. For that half hour of perfect bliss, the child was hers alone.

But then came the parting. Judith's approaching footsteps brought a sinking sense of dismay. Shana clutched the sleeping babe more tightly to her chest, consumed by a fierce possessiveness, but she was forced to relinquish her and watch Judith's eager pleasure as she hugged the child to her own bosom and tiptoed out, tossing a happy smile in Shana's direction.

An overwhelming sense of loss overcame her. It frightened her because she had never expected to want her baby, certainly not with such savage intensity, and now she could not imagine ever being able to separate from her. It was unthinkable to renege on her decision to allow Judith and Haziel to adopt the child, so she knew she had no choice but to endure whatever suffering this would cause her.

She lived for the feed times that punctuated her long days, wishing with all her heart that she could be involved with all the little tasks required in looking after the infant. She lay alone in her room, nursing her torn body and listening to the parade of visitors who came to croon over the baby and bring gifts to Judith. More than once, she overheard comments about how much the child resembled Haziel, but her own name was hardly mentioned – not surprising under the circumstances, but still it hurt and made her feel terribly empty and alone, used and abandoned, wrung out and discarded like a shrivelled grape skin.

One day, after a crowd of cheery women had visited Judith, each taking a turn to hold the baby and coo and comment, admire and advise, Judith finally brought the infant in for her feed. The time passed too quickly before Judith was back again to take her away. The house fell silent. Shana could hear the careful sounds of Judith's movements as she crept around in the next room so as not to wake the baby. An ugly emotion began to writhe in her gut and gradually take root. She felt poisoned by it and tried to dismiss it, but it became a seething sinkhole, pulling her down into its bitter spiral. She hated Judith with a dark rage that grew in intensity the more she thought about it. She hated her for her happiness, for the power she held over her and her child, she hated her for her indifference to her struggles and her pain.

Angry tears stung her eyes. She threw the blanket over her head and howled silently into her pillow, longing to be with the Master again, to gaze upon his kind face and feed her soul with his words. Only he could rescue her from this dark pit of malice and hate.

Later, Judith came to bring her some broth and, seeing her swollen eyes, asked, "Are you alright?"

"I'm fine," Shana mumbled, frowning over her soup. Judith sat down and patted Shana's arm. Her touch sent tingles of irritation through her, but she did not pull away.

"It's normal to feel blue after a birth, Shana. It will lift in a short while, and you'll be yourself again."

Shana kept her eyes down. "How would she know?" she thought viciously.

Judith looked at her helplessly and then at the sound of a small cry next door, she leapt to her feet and hurried out. Again the vitriolic rage blazed up. Shana hated herself as much as she hated Judith, and everyone else besides.

Help arrived the following week in the beloved form of Abigail, who had returned from Galilee and got news of Shana's whereabouts from the baker. When Shana caught sight of her puffing up the pathway, she squealed with delight and ran out to meet her. "Thank God you've come," she cried, wrapping her thin arms around Abigail's neck and sagging against her with relief.

"You're very pale, my child. Where is the baby?" asked Abigail.

"Is the Master here?" Shana interrupted.

"No, he's still in Galilee, but Mary is with me. I came back to take care of some business. Now where is the babe and why are you back here again?"

The whole story came out in a rush. When Abigail heard the wonderful conclusion, she could wait no longer to see the child so Shana took her into the house to meet Judith.

"What a beauty," exclaimed Abigail, reaching eagerly for the baby. She cradled her in her grandmotherly arms, murmuring endearments with heartfelt delight, and Judith beamed with pride. Shana stood aside, seething with silent rage.

Later, when Judith said she was going out for an hour and taking the baby with her, Shana at last poured out her tormented heart. "I don't understand the way I feel, Abigail. Why am I so angry and hateful?"

"My dear, the emotion you are experiencing has a very common name," Abigail said gently. "It's called jealousy."

The word struck Shana like a blow. "Jealousy! I've never been a jealous person."

"Possessiveness over one's newborn is naturally very strong at first. You don't really hate Judith at all. You hate having to give up your child to her when all your instincts cry out to nurture her yourself. Don't be too hard on yourself over this; it will diminish over time."

"I'm so unhappy," sobbed Shana, collapsing onto a stool and burying her face in her hands.

Abigail sat down next to her and stroked her hair. "There, there," she said. "Everything is going to be alright."

Those magic words! It was amazing how much they always helped. Abigail prayed quietly until the turmoil of the past few weeks drained away and peace prevailed over her emotions. That evening, Shana found that when she had to part with the baby after her night feed, she could do so without a struggle.

During the next week, Shana began to feel restless. She longed to escape the stifling confines of her room, breathe fresh air into her lungs again, take up some work and get involved in the activities of the household. She needed to think about her future. But even as she considered these things, a bleakness seemed to blanket her soul. Nothing seemed to matter very much anymore. Everything required such monumental effort – and to what purpose?

CHAPTER 25

THE CHILD WAS NAMED Juanita because she was a gift from God, the answer to the cry of Judith's heart. She was an adorable, responsive little girl, who delighted everyone who came to see her. The black curl on her forehead was Haziel's signature written on her dainty face, and one slight dimple, which twinkled only when she smiled, bore witness to the child's birth mother. Judith took on motherhood as easily as if she had been born to it. She flourished with new vigour and soon learnt how to carry out her duties with the baby tucked under one arm. Haziel remained on the sidelines, appearing and disappearing as usual, but his pleasure was evident in the way his eyes filled with proud amazement whenever he looked at his daughter.

He acknowledged Shana now, without animosity but without warmth, and treated her courteously like a stranger. It was best that way. Shana moved about quietly on the periphery like a shadow, listless and dispirited; she felt, sometimes, like a very old woman. Her days, regimented as they were by feeding times, dictated that she could not go far from the house.

She threw herself into the weaving and the chores, working feverishly in an effort to keep her dejection at bay, and often wandered aimlessly on the nearby hills. The winter months passed – grey, colourless days that matched the season in her heart. She was neither happy nor particularly unhappy, but her days were flat and empty.

The highlight of her life was when Abigail visited. Recently she had brought Mary with her, who was like a draught of new wine, though she caused some scandal in the village, which Haziel was quick to mention. Shana defended her hotly. "I doubt that even one of them equals Mary's goodness. It counts for nothing what they think of her, or of me for that matter." She tossed her head defiantly and a spark flickered to life in her spirit again.

Her friends brought news that the Rabbi had arrived in Jerusalem again for the Passover, which was two weeks hence. His appearance had caused quite a stir, Mary told her. Crowds from all parts of Israel welcomed him like a king, but at the same time, opposing parties of Pharisees and teachers of the law hounded him relentlessly in the hope of finding evidence to use against him. Jerusalem, packed to the hilt with more than the usual influx of pilgrims for the Feast, was buzzing like a hive of agitated bees.

Shana desperately wanted to see the Master again – just one glance of his eyes or touch of his hand would revive her slumbering soul – but how could she leave the house for long enough to find him among the multitudes?

One fine spring morning, Shana went out to gather the wild mushrooms that had pushed up in the night through the moist, sun-warmed earth. Her body had begun to reshape itself and she could feel the curve of her hips again as she walked. The field was a canvas of brilliant green scattered with yellow and white daisies and crimson poppies with heads raised jubilantly to the sky. The sun soaked into her, thawing the icicles around her heart, and a part of her former self began to awaken as from a long hibernation, the part of her that embraced life in spite of its hardships and forever reached upwards to the light. The whole world belonged to her, and she belonged to it, and everything was going to be alright.

When she returned with her harvest of mushrooms, Abigail was waiting for her. "The Rabbi is in the next village," she called out. "He spent the night with his friends Mary and Martha. If we hurry we might be able to catch him before he returns to the city."

Shana flew into the house and deposited the mushrooms onto the table. Judith automatically put her finger to her lips, glancing towards the baby, who lay curled like a half-opened bud in the little cot Haziel had made. Shana scurried out with a quick wave, leaving a small whirlwind behind her.

When they arrived at Martha's house in Bethany, some of the Twelve greeted them warmly and ushered them into a spacious room where the Rabbi was reclining at a table, surrounded by a large company of people. He nodded at Shana in pleased recognition, sending a thrill of happiness through her, and continued his teaching. He was speaking gravely about disturbing future events and what he referred to as 'the end of the age'.

"Many will come in my name, claiming, 'I am he'. False messiahs and false prophets will appear and perform signs and wonders. Watch out that none of you are deceived.

"You will hear about wars – nation rising against nation,

and kingdom against kingdom. Do not be alarmed. There will be earthquakes in various places, famines, and fatal diseases These are the beginning of birth pains. Such things must happen, but the end is still to come. First the good news of the kingdom of God will be told to the whole world, but everyone will hate you because of me, and there will come times of unequalled distress."

He paused and looked around at them all before delivering a strange declaration. "Then the Son of Man will come in his Father's glory."

After a shocked silence, one of them asked, "W-when will this take place?"

"No one knows the day or the hour, but only the Father. The day will come unexpectedly like a trap. Be careful that your hearts are not saturated with anxieties, drunkenness, and the endless pursuit of pleasure, for the Son of Man will come on a day when you least expect him, and each person will stand before his judgement seat. That day will bring about the destruction of the heavens and earth by fire; all wickedness and those who do evil will be weeded out of the kingdom. But when the new heaven and new earth is revealed, you who have followed me will reign with me."

They glanced sideways at one another to see if anyone understood what he was talking about.

"Do not let your hearts be troubled," he said, more gently. "Trust in God, and trust also in me. I'm going to prepare a place for you in my Father's house. You know the way to where I am going."

"No, we don't, Lord," one of the Twelve said. "We don't even know where you are going."

The Rabbi looked weary – wearier than Shana had ever seen him, yet light still glowed on his countenance.

"I am the way, the truth, and the life. No one comes to the Father except through me."

"What is the Father like?" asked Mary.

"If you know me, you know my Father as well. I am in the Father and the Father is in me."

Could God really be like this beautiful man? He was so perfect in every way, embodying power and humility, wisdom and strength, meekness and gentleness, together with the fearsome authority of a king. Everything about him was wholesome and warm, yet commanding. He pulsed with passion for life and love for his fellow men, with all the vital emotions of joy, sorrow, anger, and tenderness. They had seen him blaze with zeal for the house of God and weep for his beloved Jerusalem, longing to draw her under the protection of his wings.

Shana's love for him was pure and devoted. She had come to believe, as did all his disciples, that he was the Messiah — the anointed one spoken of by the prophets of old, who had come to reconcile man to God.

"I am going away," he said, "and where I am going you cannot come, but I will come back again."

He was going away? The listeners shifted uneasily and waited for an explanation. But he only said, "The Father will send the Spirit of truth to be with you forever, and he will explain everything to you."

He rose to his feet and looked around at them with an expression of infinite tenderness. "My peace I leave with you. Do not be troubled or afraid."

He touched Shana's shoulder lightly as he passed by. Everything in her wanted to run after him, hold onto his robes, and stop him leaving — she guessed they all felt that way, but they had to let him go. They watched him making his way down the path towards Jerusalem until he was out of sight.

Back at home, preparations for the Feast were in full swing. Judith attacked the spring-cleaning of the house with dedication, removing every trace of yeast. No shelf or corner escaped the thorough sweep of her hand, for, as she kept repeating, this was symbolic of the cleansing of God's people from sin. From the 14th day of Nissan when the moon would be full, no yeast would remain in the home for the duration of the Feast.

Haziel had already purchased a lamb, which was waiting in the stall until the day of sacrifice. Shana tried to close her ears to its pitiful cries. She hated to think of the thousands upon thousands of such lambs that would have their throats cut and blood poured out as a sacrificial offering. From the time of the Israelites' deliverance from slavery in Egypt, the blood of lambs had been placed on their doorposts as a sign so that the angel of death would pass over them. Year after year, these sacrifices created a powerful reminder of God's covenant with them, and that man could only be absolved from sin and death by the blood of a substitute. Hence it was a joyful celebration, but one which always saddened Shana until the poor innocent lambs had fulfilled their purpose.

With Judith's family coming, as always, to share the Passover meal, there was much preparation to be done. Haziel constructed a temporary table large enough to accommodate all the guests, Shana was sent back and forth to the market to buy ingredients for the various dishes, while Judith washed the rugs and swept continually. In the midst of it all, the baby gurgled with delight at the diversion.

Judith's family arrived. They had already accepted Shana

back into the family because of the joy she had brought into Judith's life, and soon the house was filled with laughter and warmth and the mutual energy generating from fellowship with close relatives. The men went off early to Jerusalem to present their lambs at the temple. It would be a long wait until their return. Tens of thousands would be queuing before the sacrificers, while the blood flowed in rivers down the gutters into the Kidron Valley.

At midday, Shana went outside to fetch some water. It was growing strangely dark. She blinked, feeling slightly dizzy as if the blood was draining from her head and interfering with her vision. It seemed as though a great black shadow had blotted out the light of the sun and night had fallen in the middle of the day. She rubbed her eyes and ran inside, bewildered, thinking she had perhaps been mistaken about the time. The other women were lighting the lamps, equally puzzled and alarmed by this sudden onset of night. There were sounds of running feet and shouting as the villagers scurried indoors. An ominous hush fell upon the village. Even the absence of the incessant bleating of the lamb left a quiet as silent as death.

They waited anxiously for a time, but when nothing seemed to be happening, the women cautiously resumed their activities by lamplight. About three tense hours passed. Suddenly an eerie rumble rocked the ground beneath them, like underground thunder. There were muffled screams from the nearby houses, and Judith snatched the baby to her chest, who howled with fright. Could this be the end the Rabbi had spoken about? The family clung together and waited, but after a while, everything became very still, and then the light slowly returned. They surmised that it must have been a freak weather condition, which thankfully appeared to have passed.

Haziel returned with the other men, breathless and agitated, carrying the slaughtered lambs, which they prepared and laid upon the waiting coals. They spoke excitedly about the complete chaos in the city, further exacerbated by the unusual darkness. They mentioned that the prophet from Nazareth had caused a huge upheaval which threatened to turn into a full-scale riot, and had been arrested. Shana's blood ran cold.

"Where have they taken him?" she whispered

"Why do you worry?" said Haziel. "He's always managed to get himself out of trouble before, and he's certainly caused enough of it. It seems that no one can make up their minds about him: first they applaud him and hang on his every word, and now they're crying for his blood!"

"Where is he now?"

"The last I heard, he'd been handed over to Pilate. Herod tried to pass him off because he couldn't find any reason to accuse him. They were at it all night, so we heard, trying to find a good enough excuse to sentence him."

"Sentence him?" Shana could barely breathe.

"For once the Pharisees and Sadducees are united on something. They all want him dead." He spoke carelessly, each word stabbing her like a sharpened arrow. Did he have no heart at all?

Realising the effect this was having on her, Haziel's tone softened a little. "It's not that bad. You know how excitable people get at these feasts, you can barely move on the streets, but by now most of them will be more interested in their meal than in trying to change the world. They will probably keep him locked up until after Passover and then release him when things have quietened down. One thing in his favour is that those religious men are very afraid of popular opinion. It can too easily turn against them."

Shana felt a little comforted. She wanted to believe what Haziel had said, and he was right, the Rabbi had slipped through their fingers before and could do so again. Furthermore, hadn't the multitudes cheered and welcomed him just days before, when he rode into Jerusalem on a donkey? He was at the height of his popularity.

Yet the recollection of the Rabbi saying he was going away niggled at the back of her mind like the persistent bleating of a Passover lamb.

A pale full moon appeared on the horizon. The meal commenced, but Shana's heart was not in it. She wished she could be with the Master's followers, who would share her concern. The rest of the family entered into the spirit of the celebration with their customary merriment, but she could not participate.

After the meal, they relaxed against the cushions and chatted drowsily. Across the table from Shana, Judith reclined against Haziel's chest, cuddling the sleeping baby in her arms, presenting a sublime picture, illuminated in the candlelight, of a perfect family surrounded by love and happiness. There was a painful tug at her heart, seeing the baby – her baby – belonging so completely to someone else, while she herself remained on the outside of the circle, as lonely and barren as a desert.

Yet she rejoiced, even in the sweet, sacrificial pain of her loss, because she knew that by giving them this priceless gift, she had brought about their happiness.

Chapter 26

T HE DAY FOLLOWING THE FEAST was a special Sabbath.
Shana awoke long before dawn, gripped by an urgent
desire to be with the Master's followers, who she knew would
be congregated now in Jerusalem. The baby would only wake
up in about an hour's time but would probably not object to
an early breakfast. She washed and dressed and crept into the
house to fetch Juanita from her cot. After the feed, she
deposited her next to Judith, who opened her eyes but did
not have time to ask questions before Shana disappeared into
the morning mist.

Though the city was further than a permitted Sabbath
journey, Shana had no qualms about breaking what she
considered a petty law. She was only concerned about being
seen, but it was unlikely anyone would notice her among the
makeshift shelters which crowded the hills during the Feast.
She hurried through the olive grove and down the hill to the
stream, ducking between the trees at the base of the Mount
of Olives just as the first golden light quivered on the top

leaves. From there it was easy to slip through the city gates and merge with the thousands of pilgrims camping along every street. She went to Abigail's room first, but when no one came to the door she ran to where the disciples often assembled at the home of one of their brothers.

Even before she knocked on the door, she heard the sound of wailing coming from within. The door opened and Simon Peter stood before her like an apparition. There was a ghostly pallor to his skin, and his hair stood out in a tangled mess, but it was his eyes, frozen in a wild stare of shocked anguish, that frightened Shana the most.

Mary, who sat slumped on the floor with her face in her hands, staggered to her feet when she saw Shana. She took a few unsteady steps and clutched onto Shana as though she could not remain standing without her support.

"They killed him," she said in a strangled voice. "Crucified him!"

The word sliced clean through Shana's soul.

Crucified? No, surely not him! Never, never!

"They beat him and abused him so badly he was barely recognisable as a man. I saw him. I was there." An edge of hysteria came into Mary's voice as she fought to survive the unspeakable horror she had witnessed. She broke down and cried like a traumatised child while Shana held onto her, suspended temporarily in the disbelief that comes before the truth sinks in.

"He was so good, so very good, the only truly good person that has ever lived," sobbed Mary. "I loved him so much . . ."

Shana looked out from within her sheltered place and surveyed the scene around her. She saw Mary the Master's mother leaning on Joanna's shoulder, quietly weeping. Abigail sat hunched over her grief with her head on her knees. The men stood around, desolate, with shoulders slumped, and the women rocked in one another's arms, grey-faced with exhaustion and sorrow. Judas was missing.

Eventually John, one of the Twelve, stood up, wiped his face on his shawl, and addressed them as persuasively as he could. "Brothers and sisters, listen now. The Master warned us about this before he died. He knew what was going to happen and he did not try to stop it. He told us he was going to his Father but would come back again. We have to believe that he told us the truth." His voice wavered, but he went on. "He said that now would be our time of grief, but that joy would come, and then we will understand what this is all about."

Mary the Master's mother looked up and confirmed her agreement with a nod, but her sorrow was for her son – her boy.

They remained quiet, strengthened by John's words, each trying in his own way to make sense of everything the Master had told them. It was evident that a mighty confrontation had taken place between darkness and light. And darkness, it appeared, had extinguished the light.

Shana's body reminded her it was time for Juanita's feed.

"We'll all be staying here for a while," her friends told her, with diluted smiles showing bravely through their tears.

Since leaving home that morning, the whole world had changed. The light, too harsh, stripped the colour out of everything. Bushes beside the path crouched stricken, a grainy black tinge darkening the surfaces of the leaves. Each man she passed appeared hideously inhuman as though charged with evil power and capable of unthinkable cruelty. Shana's stomach twisted into a tight aching knot. She walked with unconscious mechanical movements as though her spirit had dislocated from her body.

At home, Judith tried to coax her to speak, but she could not. She treated her for shock with honeyed water and wrapped a blanket around her. Haziel came in with the news that had already spread throughout the village. Hearing the facts pronounced in such a matter-of-fact way gave the story a crushing finality. Shana went to sit outside and leaned with her back against the wall, staring dry-eyed and unseeing into the vacant sky. It seemed impossible that the sun would still shine on a world as barbaric as this.

Eventually, the insistent chirp of a little bird nearby captured her attention and brought to mind the Master's words, "Not even a sparrow falls to the ground without the Father knowing. Do not be afraid." Gradually a string of disconnected phrases began to penetrate her consciousness, starting as a trickle and becoming a flowing stream. The words lifted her up and carried her upon the water. "I am the good shepherd; I lay down my life of my own accord for the sheep, no one takes it from me. I give my life as a ransom for many. I came to give you life to the full, everlasting life. Peace I leave with you; do not let your heart be troubled." It was as if the Master was still speaking.

An impossible peace washed over her. Her limbs grew heavy and relaxed, and she yawned. All she wanted to do was sleep and sleep and never wake up.

That night, sleep saturated her whole being, took her away for a long, long time, and in the morning, gently deposited her back on earth, enfolded in a soporific stupor. Judith brought the baby to her, and Shana dozed even while feeding, and then drifted back into the velvet cocoon again.

The sun was already staring insistently through her open door when she was awakened by the sound of running feet.

"Shana, wake up, wake up, something amazing has happened!"

Mary burst in, exclaiming, "He's alive! The Master is alive! I saw him. It's just as he said it would be. Get up and come with me quickly. The others wouldn't believe me, but I knew you would. I'm so happy I could fly. He's alive! Hurry. Hurry!"

Shana was already on her feet, tugging her robe over her head. "How? Where?"

"I went to the tomb this morning. The stone had moved. I was afraid that his body might have been stolen, but the grave cloths were there. And then I saw him! It was misty; at first I thought he was the gardener, but then he spoke to me. He said I was to go and tell the others. I'm so happy, I'm so happy." Overwhelmed with joy, she laughed and wept at the same time. "I had to share it with someone who would believe me. You do believe me, don't you?" she implored.

"It's written all over you," said Shana, regarding Mary's enraptured face. "We have all seen miracles the Master has done; he has even raised the dead. Why should we not believe he can overcome death? Yes I do believe, with all my heart!"

They flew over the two miles to the city. The door of the house stood open and sounds of great rejoicing came from within. Peter, who had just returned from the tomb and seen for himself, was shouting with exuberant outbursts of joy. Everyone was on their feet, talking at once, hugging each other, overcome with inexpressible gladness. Peter began to dance around the room in such a comical fashion that he had the whole room in an uproar. The enormous leap from the depths of despair to such dizzy heights of joy had made him a little crazy. After a while, he dropped panting to the floor and sat hugging his knees, drawing laughing breaths and wiping his eyes until he eventually quietened down and grew thoughtful.

A discussion began, as threads of understanding weaved together to explain this momentous event. One by one, they each recalled the Master's words – words that at the time had been incomprehensible, but in the light of what had happened, now made sense. They came to understand with growing wonder that their beloved Master, Yeshua, had willingly offered his own body as a substitute, at the very hour of the lamb sacrifice, to make atonement for sin that separated mankind from a holy God. By his own blood, like the sign on the doorposts, the angel of death would pass by those who believed, and they would be saved.

"I am the resurrection and the life. Whoever believes in me, even though he dies, he will live, for I will raise him up on the last day . . ."

Darkness had not triumphed over light at all; life had conquered death!

The days following were a whirlwind of dashing back and forth to the city between feeding times in a frenzy of excitement. The Master appeared to two more of the disciples and again one evening, to the whole group, but he never stayed for very long. His followers cleaved together, their fellowship filling the void left by his absence. Almost every day there was another revelation about what he had taught them previously. Shana marvelled at the way the pieces came together. God was no longer a distant deity but made known to them personally by the man they knew so well, who had made a new covenant between God and man for the forgiveness of sins. He had not come to be their earthly king, as many expected, but to be their heavenly king, who would establish through them his kingdom of righteousness and peace on earth – the kingdom of God – beginning like a tiny mustard seed and growing and growing into a mighty spreading tree which would draw many into its shelter. What joy this wonderful news would bring to all the world as it reverberated outwards, touching individual lives until it spread to every nation, like yeast that would in time work its way through the whole dough.

But what none of them could foresee was the depths of degradation into which the world would still plunge before this would come about.

CHAPTER 27

THE BABY FRETTED constantly. Her formerly cheerful, placid nature had changed to petulant discontent. Shana no longer enjoyed the feed times. The child would suckle for a while and then break off and scream, her face turning scarlet with rage, fists punching the air, body rigid. Judith was tense with anxiety and kept saying the child was too thin. The doctor confirmed what Shana had already begun to suspect – her breast milk was drying up.

"You need to rest more, slow down, relax. Give more focus to the child and that will stimulate the natural response of the body. And drink a lot of water," he said.

Judith frowned every time Shana took off again for the city, and sharp conflict developed between them. She resented Shana spending so much time away from home, and both she and Haziel strongly disapproved of her allegiance with the group they referred to as 'the radicals', believing them to be deluded. They refused to listen to her explanations. Shana found it perplexing that their hearts were so closed. It made her weep to think of the terrible suffering the Master had endured on their behalf, only to have it all waved away with a disapproving flick of the hand.

"Please consider the baby, Shana, she needs you," Judith implored reproachfully. "Spend some time with her."

"She only needs me for food," snapped Shana, "and how can I produce it for her if I'm feeling frustrated and imprisoned in the house all the time. I need to be happy in order to function, and right now my friends are all I have."

"You don't have to go to extremes all the time," said Judith crossly. "Just get your priorities right."

"Exactly!" said Shana, sweeping out of the house in a huff and escaping to the city again.

One day, after Shana had been complaining about Judith's insensitivity, Abigail sat her down and gave her a serious talking to. "Didn't the Master teach us that to follow him is to follow the way of love?" she said. "He demonstrated to us that we should serve one another, care for each other, and do for others as we would want them to do for us. My dear, you are being very selfish."

Her words cut deep. Shana had never thought of herself as selfish before. It was only later that night, lying awake in her bed, feeling miserable, that she was able to see how much she really only thought of herself and what suited her. It was a night of tears, peering into a place inside herself she had not seen before, and it was ugly.

The next morning she offered to stay with the baby so that Judith could accompany Haziel to the market. It was a long morning. She grew fidgety and quickly bored and had to keep forcing her attention back to the child, who cried every time she stopped rocking her. When at last Juanita fell asleep in her arms, she sat looking at the little face still streaked with tears. She wondered about the child's future and all that awaited her in life and then began to think about her own future. She could not stay here forever, nor did she want to, but the thought of returning home filled her with dread. Darkness began to close in on her again. She sighed wearily. Was there to be no end to this struggle for survival which stole away her small islands of happiness and reawakened the insidious fear that reduced her again to a defenceless child?

Her friends would soon be leaving for Galilee and she could not go with them. A desperate loneliness engulfed her. In this huge, busy world, full of people all interconnected with one another, she was an outcast, belonging nowhere. Panic clutched at her throat. The baby woke up and began to yell. Shana paced back and forth like a caged animal, rocking her too violently, shocked at the anger that overtook her.

"God, help me," she whispered over and over again.

After an age, Judith returned. Juanita had eventually gone to sleep again, and Shana forced a bright smile, hoping it would seem that all was well. "How was the market? Were sales good?"

"Yes, fine." Judith looked uneasy. "There is news from your family. I–I'm sorry to have to tell you that your father is very ill. Your mother is calling for you urgently."

The world came to an abrupt standstill. Trembling began in her stomach and spread throughout her whole body. Judith took the baby from her and laid her in the cot. "My friend Leah said she will be able take care of the feeding so that you will be able to go," she said.

Shana pictured Leah, full-breasted and robust, who lived nearby and had a two-year-old boy, not yet weaned. It was the obvious answer. An irrational pang of jealousy was quickly overpowered by a sense of doom. Life was again taking her where she did not want to go, forcing her to face what she did not want to face. But even as the ground was disappearing under her feet, she felt a strengthening within, enabling her to do what she had to do.

The next day, she kissed her child goodbye – her daughter who was not her own – and left her behind, feeling as though something had been torn violently out of her heart.

She spent the night in Jerusalem, where her friends gathered around her and prayed, reassuring her that she was in God's hands and the Master was always with her. Shana drew courage from Mary's unshakeable conviction that he was as much alive as he had been before, only more so by his Spirit. Mary too had no idea of what her future held but it did not bother her for, having put her trust fully in God, she had a wonderful capacity to live for the moment and expect the best. Abigail had decided to remain in Jerusalem with the fellowship of believers, which was rapidly expanding. It was comforting to know she would not be too far away.

Mary and Abigail accompanied Shana to the departure point early in the morning. Mary held her tightly and wept unashamedly, while Abigail remained strong and stoic. Their love went with her as she passed through the city gates with the caravan of donkeys and lifted her eyes to the hills.

The journey was another transition between two lives, two worlds. With every passing mile that distanced her from Juanita, Shana missed her more. She yearned to cuddle her giggling little body into her neck and stroke her petal cheek, to feel her curls against her skin and breathe in the baby sweetness of her scent. This throbbing sense of loss would remain for a long, long time, but gradually the thread connecting them would grow thinner, the ache less acute.

As the caravan approached Halhul, Shana turned her attention towards what lay ahead. It was a year since she had last seen her family. So much had happened in that year, so much had changed. She thought of Beth, who then had stood on the tiptoes of ripening womanhood. By now, maturity would have filled out her bones and enhanced her deer-like gracefulness. Shana brightened a little; Beth was the one bright star on her horizon. She longed to see her mother too, but her eagerness was tainted with apprehension about how their relationship might have been affected by the sorrow she had caused.

Then her father. How ill was he – ill enough not to be able to cast her out?

And Rafael? The thought of seeing him terrified her.

As the travellers crested the final peak and began the descent to the village, Shana felt as though she had plummeted over the edge of a cliff where there was no going back. The top of the synagogue showed above the village houses, and she could see the rooftop terrace of her family home, where a line of washing fluttered like flags of welcome. It all looked unchanged, just as she had left it, but she was returning disguised as who she was before, and this time without any sense of belonging.

The first person she encountered on her way to her father's house was a friend of Zippora's. She had hoped not to have to face anyone so soon, especially not someone so fond of gossip, and by the girl's expression of spiteful pleasure, it was evident that her reappearance was going to fuel some interesting conjecture in the village.

"How nice to see you! Where ever have you been for such a long time?" the girl asked with a quick glance at Shana's stomach.

"Helping family with their business. I've come home because my father is ill. I–I haven't seen him yet; I'm on my way there now," Shana stammered, hoping she would be sensitive enough to let her pass without further interrogation. Though she held her head high, inwardly she was crumbling.

"Yes, I heard so. You've put on a little weight at last. It suits you."

Shana blushed. She pushed past the girl, feeling her inquisitive scrutiny prickling all over her body. "I must go; my mother will be waiting."

Already she felt exposed, stripped of her dignity. This was certainly not going to be easy!

It was dark inside the house. She did not see her mother at first, who was sitting in the doorway looking out. She pulled Shana into a grasping embrace, with a cautionary finger held to her lips. A lamp flickered next to a raised bed at the back of the room. Shana gasped. A crumpled form lay beneath the blankets, and the pallid shape of her father's face, with mouth slack and eyes closed, floated independently in the pool of darkness. The whole room was filled with the rattle of his breathing – the slow drag of air into watery lungs, gurgling like gravel in a drain . . . a pause . . . the air rushing out, and then heaved in again. At each interval it seemed the noise would cease and the labouring body give up the struggle to cling onto the life that was leaking away. It was clear he was dying.

Shana stood next to her mother, holding her hand. Dark shadows lay in the pouches beneath Milcah's eyes, betraying the weariness of one who had endured beyond capacity. The room was cold. A dank, sickly odour hung in the air, the odour of breath from dying lungs. Shana crept a little closer, struggling to take in the fact that this helpless, lifeless form was her father – the man who had intimidated her, shamed her, towered over her and ruled her with a rod of iron – now lying as helpless as a child, powerless against the forces that robbed him of his strength.

Unexpectedly, compassion overcame her, the urge to comfort him, tell him it was alright. She knelt by his bed and very gently touched his arm. His eyes flew open. She was shocked by the startling intensity of his gaze, even through the opaque film that covered the diluted blue of his irises. The stiff, curling hairs of his brows projected over his eyes, making him look so fierce that she almost ran out, but she made herself sit quietly and stroke his arm lightly. He relaxed, still looking at her, and tried to speak, but the rasping in his throat made his words unintelligible. He made an enormous effort to make himself understood and he fell back exhausted after each word, to gather the last vestiges of his strength to try again.

"I'm g–glad y–you've c–c–c come," he managed to say at last, before disappearing again into the twilight world where his body was no longer quite attached to his will. Those few faltering words were a gift greater than any fortune he could have pressed into his daughter's hand. She knew it was the closest he would ever get to saying that he loved her, and she accepted his offering with a generous surge of reciprocating affection.

"I love you, Father," she whispered. It no longer mattered how much he had hurt her, because in that moment she saw clearly that he had not known what he was doing.

One eye flickered open, she knew he had heard, and then he was swamped again in the surging tides of his breath. She tiptoed out of the house into the last light of dusk, where her mother sat slumped on the bench.

"I'm so glad you're here," said her mother, echoing her father's words. "Beth will be back soon. She's gone to buy some meat to make soup for your father. It will give him strength. How are you, my dear?" Her perfunctory question required no answer.

"How long has Father been like this?" asked Shana.

"He was never the same after you left. Not ill but lacking energy and not much appetite. I think he was more upset about driving you away than he would admit. He started losing weight and was often unwell, and then took a sudden turn about two weeks ago. I'm so glad you're home. I've missed you and worried about you every day. It's been a very difficult year."

The sound of voices and approaching footsteps announced Beth's return; there was somebody with her. Shana ran to meet her, and the sisters fell into each other's arms, trying to subdue their joyous exclamations. The other figure, a man, stepped forward in the darkness.

"Hello, Shana."

Rafael!

An unidentifiable mixture of emotions rushed through her. He could surely hear the pounding of her heart, her quickening breath. She fought to regain her composure and managed a weak greeting before he took command of the situation by turning their attention towards her father.

"We must hurry to get some broth to him to give him strength. The doctor is on his way. I will make a fire."

They set about the tasks briskly, united in a common purpose, which gave Shana a chance to recover. She was grateful that the dreaded reunion with Rafael had already taken place, and that present circumstances precluded the necessity for small talk or polite questions. Beth and Rafael worked together, quickly laying the logs in the small hearth inside the house while Shana filled the lamps with oil and Milcah busied herself with preparations for the meal.

Shana watched her sister as she bustled about. She was taller and had filled out considerably. Her voice, discussing practicalities, had a low, musical timbre that caressed the ear. Soon the fire blazed, lighting up Beth's face as she bent over the stove. Shana stood transfixed – she was beautiful! Her auburn hair flamed around her face, and such delicate luminous skin smoothed over her slender nose and the soft contours of her cheeks. Her mouth, a small pink bud set sweetly above the mound of her dimpled chin, was gentle and composed. Beth, sensing her gaze, looked up and smiled. The glow upon her countenance was more lucid than the firelight could create; it was a radiance that emanated from a hidden place in her heart.

Shana looked from her to the tall man prodding at the fire beside her and it struck her like a bolt of lightning!

It made sense, of course; she was surprised she hadn't thought of it before. It was the perfect solution to her father's thwarted plan.

From the top of her head and down through her feet, it felt as though all the essence of her being drained out and she had started to crystallise into a shell – a shell which would look like her on the outside, but inside of which she would be absent. She had had no idea what to expect on her return, but whatever it might have been, it certainly wasn't this!

Out of some dungeon in her soul, she accessed a fragment of reserved strength, the kind that is only available when one's very life is threatened, and with that strength she continued to chop the herbs and stir them into the pot, using words when necessary, even managing a little levity, so that no one would suspect the crisis that raged within her. Gradually she began to realise what this would mean – a lifetime spent living in the shadow of what could have been, and never being able to escape from the cruel reality of it without losing her sister too.

Shana held her father's head up so that her mother could dribble a little soup between his lips. He growled at Shana to leave him alone. She was terrified of his displeasure, uncertain what to do. His angry expression flickering in the lamplight made him look grotesque, beast-like. Even in his weakness he still had the power to make her feel like a frightened child, who desperately wanted to please him but did not know how.

The doctor came, took his feeble pulse, and told them that the best they could do was stay by his side and give him small sips of soup or water whenever he would allow them. They took up a shared vigil. Every few minutes, the dying man demanded attention, petulantly as though they had neglected him. He would take a sip of broth and seem satisfied but within minutes would be straining to call for attention. The rattling of his breath never ceased.

Shana was again overtaken with compassion. Under the taut yellow-grey skin, mottled with brown and red marks, resided a helpless man, clinging to the last shreds of his life and terribly afraid of letting go. And he was her father.

After Rafael left, Shana and Beth took turns to keep watch at the bedside through the night, insisting that their mother should sleep though it was difficult to sleep at all, listening to those rattling breaths. In the early hours of the morning, it was Shana who sat beside him in the semi-darkness, being sucked into the black heaving tides that even now washed across the shores of an unknown place. "God be with you,

Father," she whispered, her touch light on his arm, "The peace of Yeshua be upon you."

Suddenly he drew up his legs, bones cracking like dry twigs, and strained to sit up. He appeared to be trying to reach for something. He flung his head back and his eyes were wide, staring upwards as though seeing something in the semi-darkness. With a shock Shana realised that the room had gone silent, the tides had stilled. He sank back and closed his eyes, and then after a long pause, he drew another slow breath and was quiet. He breathed peacefully, almost imperceptibly, as in a deep sleep, but after a time, Shana saw that the rising and falling of his chest had ceased. She sat beside him for a long while, her hand still on his arm. His hands were folded on his chest, his face peaceful.

Eventually she got up and as she did so, she accidentally kicked over a jar of water next to the bed. She froze in tense readiness for the swift clout of an angry reprimand, but there was only silence. In a flash it dawned on her that never again could he make her feel small and incompetent; all his tyrannical power was gone forever.

She went to wake up her mother.

The gathering of the whole village for the funeral made it easier for Shana to face the community again the first time. The grilling she might have been subjected to was inappropriate in the circumstances so had to be reduced to polite enquiries. She had no idea how much was known about her situation. Many of the villagers were genuinely pleased to see her, many warm and welcoming, and it was wonderful to see her friend, Kyla, again, who had married during the past year and proudly displayed the small mound pushing out the front of her robe. She would tell her everything in due course.

Since Hassim had only one brother, from whom he had long been alienated, Rafael took on the formalities of the ceremony, and his quiet, confident manner brought a reassuring normality to the atmosphere that calmed them all. He was gently courteous towards Shana, showing neither a hint of resentment nor any indication of having known her or cared for her in any special way. He was a family friend and that was all. It was like having entire sections torn out of the story of her life. Nothing she had ever experienced before, hurt the way this did. Fortunately the occasion did not require of her a happy face, and it must have appeared to others that she really grieved for her father. In truth it was a relief that he had gone.

A crowd of family friends accompanied them back to the house, bringing gifts of fruit and wine. They stayed until late afternoon, filling the gloomy house with new life. Milcah borrowed energy from their support, but after they had left, she fell down exhausted onto the bed where her husband had lain, and sobbed until the number of her tears was complete. Then she got up, splashed water on her face, put on her apron and set about her tasks. That night, she slept without waking until morning.

The women took everything out of the house and cleaned it from top to bottom. They cleaned away the smell of death, washed illness out of the blankets, and swept the silent gloom out of the door. Then they put everything back, arranging it in a different way. There was the freshness of a new beginning. Once or twice during a lull in the activity, Shana noticed her mother lift the edge of her apron to wipe away a tear but mostly she was light-hearted, delighting in the company of her beloved daughters.

That evening, they sat around the table longer than they

had ever been able to before, letting the fire burn down with their sleepy conversation. They reminisced kindly about the man who had made such a mark on all their lives. For the time being, they did not stray from general subjects; there would be time enough to review the past and consider the future. There was also no mention of Rafael, but every now and again, Shana caught an anxious glance from Beth's direction and knew she was suffering with the conflict between her own happiness and the pain which that same happiness might inflict upon her sister.

However, for the moment, Shana was consoled by the company of the two women she loved more than anyone else in the world. Tomorrow would come, but not yet.

CHAPTER 28

THE HEAT OF EARLY SUMMER, which curled the edges of the leaves and drained the green from the wheat fields, introduced the long season of dryness, which Shana always anticipated with a degree of melancholy. She and Beth lolled in the shade behind the house on the rough wooden bench made inexpertly by their father. The widow who lived nearby had invited Milcah to spend the day with her, hoping to offer her some comfort by way of diversion, and it was the first opportunity the sisters had had to talk in private. They chatted cautiously as Beth gently probed for details about the child Shana had left behind.

"When Mother and Father got your message from the wool merchant about the baby and heard that you planned to give up the child to Judith, they both wept –"

"Father wept?"

"He said he was proud of you for your decision; he seemed to think it redeemed you. Mother so much wanted to go to you, but Father wouldn't let her. He said you must stand on your own feet. I was very worried about you . . ."

"Does Rafael know?"

"Yes, I told him. He said that you were brave and strong and would be alright."

The long silence that followed grew uncomfortable, with both of them reluctant to say the things that needed to be said. Beth snapped a twig into tiny pieces between her fingers and kept her head bowed. A curtain of red-gold hair partially hid her face, but Shana could see the crease dividing the pale line of her brows, and her mouth pulled taut into a small puckered shape that accentuated the scalloped curve of her upper lip.

"You've grown up a lot this past year," said Shana, "become very lovely."

Beth inclined her head briefly towards Shana with a bashful smile, the pink flush on her cheeks complementing her prettiness. Shana took a steadying breath and reached over to put her hand on Beth's shoulder. "You're in love, aren't you?"

Beth turned her flaming face away. She stared at her hands in her lap and said nothing, but tears glistened beneath her lashes.

"I know, Beth," said Shana. "It's Rafael, isn't it?"

Beth looked up, searching anxiously for her sister's response. "Do you mind, Shana? I . . . I could see all those years that you didn't really love him – not as a husband. I always knew you loved Haziel. And . . . and Father wanted it so much."

"How long have you loved him?"

Beth examined her twisting fingers. "I have always loved him," she confessed quietly.

A hundred pictures came flooding back – Beth running

out whenever Rafael came to visit, as excited as the child she was then; Beth dancing around him, always delighted to see him, waiting on him with clumsy girlishness. When she was younger, he used to pick her up and swing her around, and she would shriek with happiness and then hang on his arm and beg for more. She made little gifts for him: childish, crooked offerings made from twisted wool. Once or twice in later years, Shana had seen Beth staring wistfully after her and Rafael when they set off on a walk without her, but she had taken it for girlish yearning for her own romance.

How carelessly she had taken for granted those happy times when life lay sparkling in the palm of her hand, never once considering that it could all be taken away, never realising the gift that had been hers to cultivate. And now she knew with all her being that she could not deny the same opportunity to the sister she loved, no matter what the cost.

"I'm happy for you. You will make Rafael a wonderful wife, and I wish you every blessing," she said.

A look of such profound relief swept over Beth's face that it compensated in part for the foundation of pain she had unknowingly laid in her sister's heart.

"Are you pledged to him yet?" asked Shana.

"Not yet. Mother said I'm still too young, not in years, but in maturity. Rafael doesn't mind waiting. It's too soon in any case after . . ." she broke off, embarrassed.

Shana relieved her of her confusion by jumping to her feet and saying with a brightness she did not feel, "Come, let us make some herb tea. I have so much to tell you."

Shana coaxed the embers into a little flame, placed a pot of water on the metal rack, and watched the bark and lichen, shrivelling and weeping in the licking flames. Faced squarely with the greatest challenge of her life, a part of her she had never known before took over and continued to function on the surface, separate from the tempest that stormed beneath, as though she were divided into two halves. And with shaking hands, she was made the tea.

The sisters sat down side by side, sipping cups of the fragrant infusion, and Shana began to tell the story of the Nazarene carpenter, who had not only changed her life but the destiny of the whole world. She painted vivid pictures before Beth's fascinated eyes, reliving every detail as she did so. As she repeated the Rabbi's words to Beth, they flowed like ointment over her wounded heart, ministering strength to her. Beth listened with rapt attention, marvelling at Shana's account of the miracles she had seen, laughing at her descriptions of Peter, and weeping when she heard about Ruth's loss. Finally she listened, tense with apprehension, as Shana related the events of the final Passover.

"Crucified?" Beth's horror was as real as her own. "It's so atrociously inhuman! Why couldn't he use his power to escape?"

"He could have, but he knew he had come for that very purpose – to die for us. Oh Beth, he was so pure, so full of love for every person, he was willing to do whatever it took to rescue us from eternal separation from God. How I wish you could have known him too." Shana gazed into a distant place as she went on to describe the events that followed.

Later, as the afternoon sun turned the fields to gold, the story reached its conclusion. Somehow it had formed a bridge over which Shana could cross into this next phase of her life – a life that would be established on prepared ground: ground that had been ploughed, dug over and turned, that would remain fallow for a time during the season of dryness, while it gathered resources for the nurture of seeds to be sown when the time was ripe. It was not the season for striving; it was a time to simply endure.

There were things to be considered, decisions to be made. Rafael came by on the first day of the week to help the three women decipher the facts and figures of their estate. Hassin had kept all the details of their means to himself. Apart from what was left of the small bag of money he dispensed to his wife each week, they knew not whether there was more to be had, or from where, and Shana had very little left of what Abigail had given her. The women were familiar with the cultivation, sowing and harvesting of their two fields and had always tended the small flock of sheep. These things they could continue doing, which would bring enough money, together with their herb and vegetable garden, to sustain them. But it turned out that there was a sum of money owing, which Hassin had borrowed from a moneylender, known to be ruthless, for the purchase of an expensive ram. He had sold all the young males during the Passover, and then this prize ram had died – got itself caught in a hedge and attacked by wolves – so not only was the amount still owed, but they would need money to purchase another ram to keep their flock going. None of the women shied from hard work, but in this case hard work would not be enough.

"We will have to sell the chest," said Milcah sadly.

"Oh no, Mother!" exclaimed Beth. "There must be another way."

The chest was their mother's pride and joy. It crouched importantly in the centre of the room, an exquisitely carved piece with an intricate pattern of inlaid bone on the lid, which had been passed down from generation to generation in her family. It was the only thing of value they owned. They all regarded it forlornly, racking their brains for an alternative solution.

"What was Father going to do?" asked Shana. "He must have had a plan?"

"I don't know. He never discussed his business with me. I could see he was worried though," said Milcah with a sigh.

Beth did not contribute much. She sat purring serenely in Rafael's shade, without a worry in the world. It irked Shana because, as innocent as it was, Beth basked in the knowledge that whatever happened, Rafael would take care of her.

"I will go and talk to the moneylender and come to some arrangement with him. He must surely be reasonable in our circumstances," said Shana, and by this, she indicated that she would now be taking up the reins.

"Would you like me to come with you?" offered Rafael.

"No, I will go alone. He may be more sympathetic that way. I will request reasonable terms, and then we will just have to find ways of making the extra money."

After Rafael left, Shana announced her plan. "We will expand our garden so that the excess produce can be sold at the market. Mother, you have always enjoyed that work, haven't you?"

"When I had time, but there never seemed to be enough of it."

"When I was in Sepphoris, I learnt the skill of fine embroidery. While there is no market for that kind of thing here, I could embroider garments which could be sold in Jerusalem. I know I can do it, but it will mean selling a few sheep in order to purchase some good quality clothing to embroider."

"Oh, we couldn't do that," said Milcah quickly. "We can't possibly risk diminishing the flock before the lambing season and we have to use whatever money we can find to buy a ram."

"Why not borrow one?" asked Beth ingenuously.

"Old Pascal next door could let us run our sheep with his herd, but he's such a stingy old goat that I doubt he will agree," said Shana.

"Can you try him, Shana?" asked Milcah.

"How much does he know about me?"

"I'm not sure. It would soon be evident if he lets you into his house or not."

"Better Beth goes."

Beth paled in alarm. "Me? I'm terrified of him. I always hid away when he visited Father."

They sat in silence for a while. It was one thing having a plan but quite another to put it into practice.

"Tomorrow," said Shana firmly, "we will do what needs to be done and if our efforts fail, we will find another way." She got up. "Come, Beth, let us begin by digging another bed for the herbs. Mother, can we leave the chores to you?"

Action was the only thing that kept Shana from the snapping jaws that threatened to drag her down into the depths. She attacked the stony ground with vengeance, hacking into the hard surface to expose the softer ground beneath. Beth handled her spade dreamily as though it was a spoon, which infuriated Shana, who had to make up for her lack of effort by doubling her own. By nightfall, half the bed was dug. Shana's hands were sorely blistered, and her body ached from the unfamiliar demands made upon it, but an iron will smelted in the furnace beneath her ribs.

The next day, she marched off in the direction of the moneylender's shop, so set on her mission that it bothered her not the possible inferences in the greetings of folk from her former life.

The moneylender knew immediately why she had come and was not sympathetic, but her determination took him by surprise, and he found himself agreeing to a delay – a fairly extended one – on the return of his loan. He satisfied himself by charging high interest in return.

Beth squirmed and objected so much about approaching the farmer about the ram that Shana went herself and had the door slammed firmly in her face. Somehow she must acquire the clothing; it was the only way to make the money they needed. The Rabbi's words came back to her, "Ask whatever you wish in my name, and you will receive it." It seemed too simple, but he had said it. She figured that to ask for something 'in his name' must mean it needed to be endorsed by his will, as though he himself asked the Father on her behalf. He had often reassured them about God's willingness to supply for his children's needs, so it was a simple deduction that she could boldly request the things she required.

"Almighty Jehovah," she began. She pictured the Rabbi smiling at her bungling attempts to sound religious, so she put her request at his feet in straightforward words. "Fa . . . Father in heaven, I need fine clothing to embroider . . . and a ram." Then she added a line she had heard at synagogue, "Nothing is too difficult for you." She felt sure he had heard and would therefore supply.

Rafael came up with a solution. He would put down a deposit on the oak chest with some money he had set aside for leatherwork materials. Then when their money came in, they could buy it back from him. Shana knew it was his way of making them a loan without compromising their pride, but she also knew it would put his business at risk if for any reason they could not pay it back. However, she had to accept but was determined to return every shekel with interest. Rafael said the chest could remain in their keeping, but Milcah would not have it that way, so he was obliged to lift it onto his shoulder and carry it away, leaving behind a dark, unbleached patch on the floor.

There was an argument that evening about how the money would be best spent.

"A ram is the most important," insisted Milcah.

"If we buy a ram, there won't be enough money to purchase items to embroider," objected Shana.

"A ram will give us another ten or twelve sheep to sell, which will surely bring in a greater return than a few fancy robes."

"But only after six or seven months. We cannot wait that long."

"The robes might not sell immediately either," said Beth.

"Well, at least they can't die!" snapped Shana in exasperation.

Eventually, after a long day of tramping around all the farmers in the district, Shana came back with a compromise. They could hire a ram for a month, which would hopefully reap some results, and then with the rest of the money she could purchase a few robes and get started on the embroidery. She planned to send the finished articles to Abigail to sell at the market and then purchase more garments with the money.

Shana worked like a slave. By day she dug, weeded, and planted, and by night she sat in the light of a ring of lamps and worked meticulously with silk thread, fashioning intricate designs onto plain woven robes. Her blistered fingers struggled painfully at first, more than once leaving blood stains on her work, but gradually her skin toughened and her needle flicked in and out with skilful speed. It was good to have something to keep her busy, especially during the long evenings when her spirits would sink to a very low ebb.

Beth was learning the craft too to keep Shana company, and Rafael often came and sat with them while they worked. He continued to treat Shana with courteous respect, but gone was the easy congeniality between them. Sometimes Beth would place her hand possessively on Rafael's arm, unaware of the cutting pain her loving action caused her sister. For not a hint of it showed on Shana's serene face.

CHAPTER 29

A S THE WEEKS FLEW BY, inching closer to the date set for the first debt repayment. Shana redoubled her efforts. The work was agonisingly slow, and due to the pressure, she did not enjoy it. Late at night after the others had gone to bed, she had to force herself to go on, though her eyes struggled to focus, her back ached, and her limbs drooped with fatigue. She had to continually fight down the prickling irritation that crawled up and down her spine, along with the ever-present heartache. She was pressed to the limits of her endurance, both outwardly, where she had no choice but to demand that her body continue to function, and inwardly, where the furnace of her secret trial never let up its heat.

One evening, something happened that stoked up the fire even more. The three women were lounging on cushions around the table as usual. Shana was concentrating on her needlework, and Rafael, who had joined them for dinner, was leaning back against the wall, idly watching her fingers dart back and forth with the needle. Beth sat beside him, resting her head against his shoulder with her eyes closed, and Milcah dozed intermittently, her chin nodding on her chest. It was quiet in the room except for the soft popping sounds of the lamp flames licking the air, and the rustle of fabric on Shana's lap. Something caused Shana to look up and she caught Rafael's gaze upon her. He looked away hastily, but there was time enough for Shana to catch a glimpse into his soul; it was all she needed, for she knew him so well. The love in his eyes was plain. How different from the way Haziel had looked at her with lust burning in his eyes. And before Rafael had turned away, she saw, too, the sad longing and the resignation, and she knew he loved her still!

She gripped her embroidery, frowning over the needle and thread, and willed her trembling fingers to hold steady. The lamps were burning low, and Beth sighed, got up sleepily, and began to clear the bowls from the table. Taking the signal, Rafael bid them good night and went off into the darkness, leaving behind the comforting residue of his masculine presence.

During the hours of night, Shana re-examined her life. At first she rejoiced in the knowledge that the love she had so sorely missed was still hers, and her beloved was hers again for the taking. She knew she only had to shed her carefully guarded shell of indifference at an opportune time and allow him to see her heart, and he would know that he could have her back.

Immediately, a vivid scene played out before her, cutting short her dreamy imaginings – Beth, heartbroken, all her dreams in tatters and her sweet, innocent face burning with acid tears as she stepped into her suffering sister's shoes, while her sister wrenched her happiness out of her hands.

With a certainty as final as the last shudder of death, Shana knew she could not do it. In the early hours of the morning, lying staring into the darkness, Shana packed away every shred of hope for a future with Rafael in an iron box in her heart, locked it, and threw the key into a bottomless pit.

She got up, dressed, and went about her business. She laughed when Beth described a funny incident she had shared with Rafael, and smiled while Beth chatted animatedly about her plans for her future wedding and ideas for her new home and how many children she would like to have. Shana took up a piece of fine, white silk fabric and began to work on an exquisite embroidered veil that she would present to Beth for her wedding, each stitch representing a love she did not know she was capable of – a love willing to suffer long and lay down its life for another, just as the Master had taught.

When Rafael came around, she busied herself with other things so she would not be much in his company. She was careful to address him in a manner that was cool and distant so he would never know the response he had evoked in her heart, so that he would know she . . . did not love him. Yet there were times when, even with her strong resolve, a powerful temptation would blaze up – suggesting, enticing, insisting that she give way.

"He was yours to begin with," the voice would reason. "He belongs to you. Why should you deny his happiness as well as your own?"

"God, help me. I daren't go against your will."

"Beth loves so easily. She will soon attract another man, but you will never have another opportunity to marry."

Again and again, she was presented with beautiful visions of a future as Rafael's wife, visions which contrasted severely with the colourless desert-scape of her life as an unmarried woman, growing old alone, childless and unfulfilled. If anyone other than Beth had been involved, nothing would have stopped her grabbing her chance of happiness, but a cruel twist of fate had trapped her in this devastating predicament from which she could not escape.

One day, when she could endure her private suffering no longer, she permitted herself a few tears and cried out to God in desperation. Help came swiftly – so swiftly that it bore the signature of God upon it, for he sent her a messenger.

Nathan was an acquaintance of Rafael's, whom he had met at the rabbinical college – a learned man, wise beyond his years, whom Rafael very much admired. He was visiting from Jerusalem, and Rafael brought him around to hear what Shana had to say about the one many now referred to as the Messiah. He listened with piqued interest when she began to describe her personal association with the Master. Afterwards he asked many questions and argued a number of points but allowed her to counter his opinions, and then weighed up her explanations carefully. Unlike so many of the educated men Shana had met before, he possessed the priceless quality of humility. She found it easy to converse with him and was glad when she heard he had been elected as an elder of the small village synagogue and would be coming to live in the community to work as a teacher.

Milcah invited the two men to stay for dinner. The sisters were animated and charming in their company, and the little home rang with lively repartee, as well as more serious discussion. It was a pleasant respite from the journey of endurance Shana was being forced to travel.

Late in the evening, just as the men were preparing to leave, Shana shyly produced the precious piece of parchment she had treasured, given her by the Master.

"It's a reference to the writings of Zephaniah, who was a prophet from the royal line of Judah, the house of David, from which the one you call the Messiah is descended," said Nathan at once. "I am particularly interested in the prophetic writings, although I have not memorised much. I will look it up in the synagogue scrolls and let you know what it says."

Shana thrilled at the thought. She knew the Rabbi meant it as a personal message to her, but she had not yet had the opportunity to find out its meaning.

Two days later, Nathan came back alone. It had been a particularly difficult day for Shana, made all the more difficult by Beth's incessant, contented humming while she worked. She loved to see her sister happy and did not want it otherwise, but it accentuated the barren landscape of her own heart, which she had to keep so carefully hidden. It terrified her to think of having to live in this cheerful shell that imprisoned her screaming soul, for the rest of her life. It seemed to her that she was still suffering punishment for her past sin, even though she knew she had been forgiven.

Nathan had a round cheerful face, softened by a springy, neatly-combed ginger beard. His kind, laughing eyes crinkled when he grinned, giving him an appealing boyish appearance, although he was quite a few years older than Rafael. He was smiling now with pleasure at being able to bring Shana the interpretation of her message, which he had transcribed onto some parchment. They sat down together on the bench in the courtyard.

"This is a particularly beautiful piece of scripture," he began, in the educated manner of one who knows. "It is a prophecy for the people of Israel, spoken over six hundred years ago by the prophet Zephaniah, but you will understand what it means to you personally. This is what it says:

'Sing, O daughter of Zion,
Be glad and rejoice with all your heart,
The Lord, the King of Israel, has taken away your punishment,
He has turned back your enemy.
Never again will you fear any harm.
Do not fear, O Zion,
Do not let your hands hang limp.
The Lord your God is with you,
He is mighty to save.
He will take great delight in you.
He will quiet you with his love.
He will rejoice over you with singing.' "

Tears streamed down Shana's cheeks. There was no doubt about what the King of Israel had spoken to her at such a time as this. As these life-giving words penetrated deep into her heart, hope gave wings to her soul, breaking the chain which had held her captive for so long, and she began to rise up in spirit, set free from fear and the dark despondency that had plagued her throughout her life.

"W–will you teach it to me so that I can memorise it?"

"Certainly. And then you can tell me more about your Teacher and everything you can remember that he said." He took a square of cloth from his belt and passed it to her. "Here, dry your eyes and let's begin."

"May I ask you a question?"

"Go ahead."

"If God has forgiven me for everything I have done wrong and taken away my punishment, as this scripture confirms, why is there still so much difficulty in my life?"

He took his time to reply, leaning his chin on his fist and

crinkling his eyes in contemplation. "The scriptures say that God tests and disciplines those he loves. This is not the same as punishment; it is the training of a loving Father. Its purpose is to change you more into his likeness so that you are able to receive more of his blessings and ever-increasing joy. Try to see hardship, not as a bad thing, but as a gift."

Receiving Nathan's gentle wisdom brought the dawning of a new day. From that time on, Shana's spirit began to sing, even through her tears. She talked to her heavenly King the way she would speak to a close friend, pouring out the muddle of her feelings, longings and fears without fear of judgement. She confessed to him her struggle with the temptation to grab from life that which he had not given her and asked for strength to endure. A growing assurance came that God was with her always, even when she did not feel his presence. There were times of sweet intimacy when fountains of joy bubbled up inside her, but more often only a settled knowledge of his presence.

During the following weeks, Nathan visited often, sometimes together with Rafael and sometimes alone. He brought a measure of fun and laughter back into Shana's world with his playful zest for life. They would sit cross-legged around the table, Shana always with her sewing, while Beth fussed around helping Milcah prepare food, humming softly to herself and flourishing in Rafael's company. Nathan cross-questioned Shana constantly about the Master.

"You should have been a lawyer," she told him, and he laughed, saying that all truth needs to be tested. Sometimes he would go quiet for a while as though pondering something, and then an expression of budding amazement would come over his face and he would recite a section of the Writings, exclaiming how it lined up exactly with the events Shana described. He always went away frowning thoughtfully as if grappling with an inner conflict and kept coming back to ask more questions.

One evening, both he and Rafael arrived as the women were finishing their meal. They sat down and, discarding the usual small-talk, Nathan placed a scroll on the table and folded his hands as though about to make an announcement.

"I have been studying the writings of the Prophets and I believe that this rabbi you have been telling me about really could be the long awaited Messiah," he declared.

He went on to explain some of the passages of scripture he had found, and read out a few he had copied down onto the scroll. "Shana, your friends witnessed exactly what happened to this man when he was arrested and put to death. Listen to this, it is described in detail over 600 years ago by the prophet Isaiah and also in the Psalms, by men who could never have foreseen how this would take place: *'I offered my back to those who beat me, my cheeks to those who pulled out my beard; I did not hide my face from mocking and spitting. They pierce my hands and feet.'*

He paused to run his finger down the scroll in search of another text, quivering with eager intent. "You told me how badly they abused him before he was crucified; it happened exactly as it says here: *'Many were appalled at him, his appearance was so disfigured and his form marred beyond human likeness. He was led like a lamb to slaughter. The Lord makes his life an offering for sin.'*

"It is truly amazing how it fits together with our understanding of the sacrificial sin offering. Here it says: *'We all, like sheep, have gone astray, each of us has turned to his own way; and the Lord has laid on him the iniquity of us all. He was pierced for our transgressions and crushed for our iniquities; the punishment that brought us peace was laid upon him, and by his wounds, we are healed.'*

Nathan looked up in awe. "God promised Israel a deliverer – a redeemer. I believe he has come. He was the Passover lamb!"

Waves of excitement radiated from Shana's belly. As Nathan continued to explain his new understanding, Rafael listened respectfully with a guarded expression, adding a comment or an objection here and there. His nature was such that he would be more reticent to accept such radical ideas, yet he seemed to be open-minded and attentive. But the more evidence Nathan gathered to prove his theory, the more uncomfortable Rafael became. As a prominent leader in the village synagogue, he would know that to entertain ideas such as these would put him in danger of being cast out.

"I have to return to Jerusalem next week and would like to meet with those friends of yours," announced Nathan as he got up to leave. "Rafael will be accompanying me."

"How wonderful!" Shana exclaimed, delighted at the prospect of being able to receive first-hand news of her friends. "I will explain how to get to Abigail's house and she can introduce you to the others. And you can take my first completed garments to her to sell and ask her to send back any money she can make from them, even if she has to sell them to a retailer."

During the following week, Shana caught herself humming, too, while she went about her business.

CHAPTER 30

SHANA GREW INCREASINGLY anxious. The agreed date for the first repayment on the loan was only days away, and she had hoped the men would return before then with at least enough money to pacify the creditor, but there was no sign of them. Beth was worried too – it was unlike Rafael to stay away from his shop this long.

Late one afternoon, while Beth and Milcah were out collecting firewood, Shana returned exhausted from working in the field and found the money-lender at the door waiting for her.

"The p–payment is only due tomorrow," she stammered with a sinking heart, hating that he saw her fear.

"Tomorrow is the Sabbath. The payment is due today before sundown," he said forcefully.

Shana had been so intent on everything that needed to be done that she had forgotten it was almost the Sabbath and was still hoping for the men's timely return.

"If you cannot pay, you can bring me one of your sheep as

agreed. I'll wait here." His tone was non-negotiable. Not only would this rob them of precious stock, but it would amount to a double payment because the herd should be in lamb by now.

Shana thought quickly. "Just a moment, I have something I can give you as surety. I am certain I will have the money within a week."

She had been intending to return Rafael's ring to him, but as they were never alone, and she did not want to embarrass him in front of the others, an opportunity had not yet presented itself. She fetched it from her private box of belongings and held it out to the creditor, assuring herself that as soon as it was redeemed she would make a point of giving it back to Rafael. From the way the little man's eyes lit up when he saw it, Shana knew that the ring was more valuable than she thought. He reached for it greedily and hurried off, more than satisfied, and Shana had the distinct impression that he hoped she would not be able to make the payment. Watching him scuttling down the road with the symbol of her lost life clutched in his hand, it occurred to her how the true value of things so often only becomes apparent after they are gone.

A few days later, her friend, Kyla, waddled over to visit, like a ship in full sail with her enormous stomach protruding in front of her. She proudly displayed the little clothes she had made for her baby and brought news that the men were back at last. Beth was beside herself with excitement, unable to keep still or get down to her chores. Shana, too, was impatient to hear news of her friends and find out whether her garments had been sold. For the rest of the day, the two sisters kept peering down the street, trying to recognise approaching figures in the distance.

"That must be them," Beth said again, wrinkling her eyes, and again Shana dropped what she was doing to have a look.

"It can't be. Those two are the same height, and Rafael is much taller than Nathan."

It was only after dinner that the men's silhouettes finally appeared in the doorway, by which time the girls' excitement had turned to disappointment and they felt wilted and reproachful.

"News from yonder city, my ladies," rang Nathan's jovial voice, his warm presence immediately flooding the room. The girls revived at once and both spoke at the same time, asking a host of questions, while Milcah enticed the men to the table with the remains of the vegetable stew and her freshly baked bread. "I hope you have not already eaten," she said.

"Not enough to shy from your cooking," said Nathan. "We will need our strength to meet the demands your daughters place on us."

Milcah laughed merrily. She had quickly warmed to Nathan, who treated her like his own mother with his affectionate teasing. Extra lamps were lit, filling the room with a dancing radiance and the atmosphere of a celebration, and they all sat down. Shana noticed immediately that there was something different about Rafael. He smiled dazedly and seemed to glow with a mysterious light.

"Tell me, tell me!" she demanded. "What news of my friends?"

Rafael looked towards Nathan, who took his time to finish an oversized mouthful before wiping his beard and sitting back. "Splendid people!"

He got up and planted an irreverent kiss on top of Shana's head, which caused Milcah's mouth to drop open.

"Mary made me promise to pass that on to you," said

Nathan, "and she sent you this." He took a small bundle of cloth from inside his belt and handed it to Shana. She opened the drawstring and looked inside. It was a beautiful bangle of small coloured stones in twisted gold settings.

"She made it herself. She's working at the jeweller's shop on the street next to the market square. What a wonderful lady. And . . ." he said with a dramatic pause, "I have this!" He dropped another small bundle onto Shana's lap – her first payment! It may as well have been a fortune for what it was worth to her.

"Thank you, thank you," she cried, and forgetting herself entirely, jumped up to hug him, causing her mother's eyebrows to shoot towards her hairline.

Nathan sat down again, rosier than ever, and spreading out his hands on the table, he began to recount word for word everything he had been told. The Eleven had gone to Galilee and met with the Master on several occasions – there was no longer any doubt about him having risen from the dead. After that, he had shown himself to the disciples, who were waiting together in Jerusalem, and then disappeared from their sight for the last time. By speaking of him thus, Nathan pronounced his acknowledgement of the risen Lord.

He went on enthusiastically, "During the Feast of Pentecost, when all the disciples were together, they had a strange experience. The Spirit of God came down on them all, just as the prophet Yeshua promised, to empower them to continue the work he began on earth. He told them he would send his Spirit to all who believe."

"Something truly amazing must have happened!" Rafael burst out. "Peter and John were able to heal a crippled man. They were thrown into prison because of it. The priests and Sadducees are trying to quell this new movement, but the message is spreading like wildfire; there are already about five thousand believers, and in spite of all the opposition, the numbers are growing continually."

"It is undeniable," Nathan agreed. "After we heard Peter speak, we were both thoroughly convinced that what he said was true. I suppose you can now call us believers too."

"But–but they'll put you out of the synagogue!" Milcah cried.

A shadow passed over Rafael's face, but he said with finality, "I cannot deny the truth."

Beth looked aghast; she had been so proud of his position as a deacon. After a weighty silence, Shana turned to Nathan. "What about your commitment to the synagogue?"

"That will be up to the assembly. I could never continue to teach half the truth and omit what I now know to be true. What I have heard and come to believe, I am compelled to pass on, no matter what the cost. This world will never be the same again; what has happened here in our little land has the power to change the entire course of history." A new zeal burned in Nathan's eyes. He had no doubt about his mission now.

"There is still something I do not understand," said Beth. "Why did the Messiah have to die in that terrible way?"

Nathan replied. "God is holy, Beth, and not one of us have ever been able to keep the law perfectly. As such we are all condemned and cut off from the presence of God for all eternity. Only one man has ever been perfect, and for our sakes, he took on himself the full wrath of God against sin so that we could be reconciled to God."

"B–but I still sin," said Shana.

"Do you want to?"

"No."

"Well, it no longer has power over you, either to cut you off from God or to force you to do what you do not want to do. And do you know what the really good news is?"

"Tell us."

"The law could only ever change our outer behaviour, not our hearts, which is why it has never worked. But the Spirit of God living within us has power to change us from the inside out, little by little as we co-operate with him."

"Which is why lasting peace can never come by any political power," added Rafael. "But Isaiah prophesied that the Prince of Peace will reign in justice and righteousness forever. There is hope for this world!"

The little village was shaken at its roots. The synagogue assembly implored Nathan to discard his new beliefs, promising him greater benefits, but when they saw he was adamant, they turned against him with vengeance and expelled him from his teaching post. Rafael insisted that he was as much a Jew as ever and tried to convince them to embrace the fulfilment of the very scriptures they taught, but he was told to keep his ideas to himself, so he too gracefully bowed out.

Together the two men went from house to house, carefully explaining from the scriptures the truth that had become so clear to them. It was bound to cause conflict, especially among the hot-headed Judeans. When a small crowd gathered on the Sabbath, not at the synagogue but in the courtyard of Rafael's house, the whole town was divided. News of unrest travelled from Jerusalem also – vehement opposition from the ruling council against the Lord's followers, even to the point of threatening to put them to death, and the apostles had been jailed again. Terrified for

Rafael's safety, Beth implored him to keep quiet about what he believed 'for her sake'.

"What kind of man do you think he is, Beth?" said Shana sharply, after he had left. "Could you respect a man who did not have the courage of his convictions?"

"Things will settle down," reassured Milcah. "It's not a bad thing anyway that the council is having a good shaking up. Israel has been as much oppressed by their rule as by the Romans."

While conflict raged on in the city, out in the country the peasants soon set their differences aside to continue their ploughing, sowing and harvesting, faithfully regularising the heartbeat of the land. Eventually, Nathan diplomatically negotiated a rather uneasy compromise between the villagers' opposing beliefs. He, together with Rafael, became the leaders of a small group of believers, who gathered around them like an extended family, and it was conceded that this group could retain their Jewish customs and continue to attend synagogue on the Sabbath, but would meet separately afterwards to fellowship with one another. Under Nathan's inspired teaching and Rafael's exposition, they grew in understanding of the new covenant established through Yeshua for the forgiveness of sins. Shana, too, was often called upon to tell them first-hand about the man now known as their Lord.

And so life in the village regained its harmony, only in a very different key.

The close community of believers provided great comfort to Shana, and she was delighted when Kyla and her husband joined them, attracted by the change in her.

"You're so different, Shana. You've become so strong and steady, I can hardly believe you're the same person," said

Kyla.

"I don't think I am the same person anymore," Shana replied, for it was true. The months of enduring all kinds of hardship, both physical and emotional, learning to trust the Lord in all things, had built a steel framework of faith and character into her life that supported her, as well as others around her. But no one suspected that deep down she still bore the secret residue of her loss and loneliness.

One night after the others had gone to bed, she went up to the rooftop terrace to pray. The moon, almost full, flooded the village with liquid yellow light. Gazing up into the faintly spangled sky, she recalled the many times she and Rafael had sat here together, pointing out the constellations to one another and making up some of their own. A great surge of longing for him welled up again. It felt as though she had lost a limb or a chunk out of her heart, which had left a huge hollow space behind. She wondered if they could ever resume their friendship once he and Beth were married but thought it unlikely. The ache in her heart became overwhelming, and she gave herself up to the luxury of weeping to ease the pressure.

A slight movement disturbed her, and a hand touched her shoulder. It was Beth, silver as a spirit in the moonlight, her long hair wafting out to one side in the breeze. "What is it, my sister?" she asked, tears of empathy sparkling on her lashes. "Are you missing your child?"

"No. Not a lot. I got used to not thinking of her as mine."

"Then what is it?" she asked.

"I'm alright, really. Just thinking about everything that has happened," said Shana, wishing she had let Beth believe that her sorrow was for her child.

Beth sat down next to her and put an arm around her

shoulders. They sat in silence for a long time, something passing between them that could not be translated into words. After a while, dew came down in a fine mist and drenched their hair, so they went downstairs and crawled side by side under the covers like they used to when they were children.

Beth was quiet the next day. Shana was afraid that she was upset over seeing her unhappiness. She attempted to reassure her that it was just a passing mood and, to prove it, acted bright and chatty, even singing while she worked. But Beth remained withdrawn, detached, and preoccupied.

Another day passed and Beth's strange melancholy remained. Shana tried in vain to cheer her up and could see that she made an effort to respond but with difficulty. In the afternoon, Beth went out and did not return until evening. Her eyes were red from crying.

"I have something to tell you," she whispered to Shana. "Can we go for a walk?"

They went down the path that led towards the Big Tree. Shana had not gone back there since the last time she had been with Rafael. She turned off onto a side path, wanting to avoid the site that held so many memories, and they came to a copse on the hillside. Beth leant back against a tree and took a deep shuddering breath. She blew it out, struggling to compose herself. Shana waited, a ball of fear tightening in her stomach – her sister's distress was her own distress.

"I've broken off with Rafael," said Beth at last.

"What?" cried Shana in genuine alarm. "Why? You have been so happy with him!"

"I cannot marry him," said Beth, grappling with her emotions. "I have seen . . . I–I have no doubt . . . he still loves you, Shana."

The two sisters stared at one another.

"Don't say anything, Shana. You know it's true. And I know you love him too. It could never be right for us to marry."

Shana opened her mouth but could not speak, completely overwhelmed by the depths of her sister's love – her generous, sacrificial love.

"I'll be alright, really I will," said Beth, fighting back tears. "I have a close friend now whose company I enjoy very much; he makes me laugh, so I won't be lonely."

"Who do you mean?"

"Nathan, of course!" Beth brightened, her voice still husky. "Isn't it wonderful that we can all be friends?"

Shana's head reeled. She steadied herself against a tree and waited for the tumultuous pounding of her heart to still. She wanted to say something but could not find the words.

"Come, let's go," said Beth. "Mother will be wondering where we are."

"Rafael will never trust me again," whispered Shana.

"He did not deny it when I asked him to tell me truthfully whether he still loved you. His silence was his reply. I told him that I already knew, had known it for a while, and would rather have him for a brother-in-law. Come on, let's go."

Two weeks went by. Rafael did not come around, although Nathan visited often, as high-spirited as ever. He did not mention anything, but it was evident he had heard the news by the way he took special care of Beth, teasing and taunting her until he made her laugh. Shana floundered in a pool of unanswered questions. Why did Rafael stay away? Was he suffering the effects of this double rejection, now having lost Beth too? Worse still, had both she and Beth now lost his friendship? The fact that she knew he still loved her did not mean he would ever want to be with her again, not after what had happened. She longed for him to come but dreaded seeing him and jumped each time she heard footsteps.

When it looked as though Rafael was never going to return, Shana surrendered her hopes and her fears, which left her numb but calm.

One morning early, Nathan came by and found Shana busy milking the goat.

"Rafael asked if you would meet him at a place he called the 'Big Tree'. He said you would know where he meant."

A jolt shot through her body and her heart palpitated wildly in her chest; the day of reckoning had come! Had he decided to tell her there was no chance of a future together, that it would be wiser for him not to visit anymore, or . . . ?

A deep calm came over her. She set the bucket aside and dried her hands slowly on her apron. She released the goat and went back to the house. The sun made rainbows in the dew on the grass, cool and wet between her bare toes. She fetched her headscarf, secured it carefully over her hair with a leather headband, and started down the path, her breath smoking on her lips. After a few steps, she turned back and went to fetch the ring, glad she had been able to redeem it in time, for she was determined to return it to Rafael now, whatever happened.

The path, now overgrown with disuse, led her forward, one light step at a time. The warmth of the sun rested against her cheek. She passed the rock they used as a target for their home-made slings, and there, still balancing on a tottering base, were the broken remains of a shepherd's hut in which they had played.

She entered the cool secrecy of the woods. The saffron scent of bruised crocuses rose from beneath her feet. She could see Rafael's tall figure through the trees, his back turned to her. He was standing very still, looking out over the field where they had romped as children. The heat of summer had turned the fields to brown, and the olive groves beyond were grey and faded. Everything was shrouded in a film of dust, thirsty for the first rain.

She went and stood beside him and looked out across the field with him. His strong frame was like a fortress, steady and secure. He turned to search her face – questioning, a little uncertain. There was still pain in his eyes. She slipped her hand into his and smiled shyly.

"I've missed you so much," he said.

"I have missed you too."

He closed his fingers around her hand, claiming possession of her again. "We belong together, Shana."

"I know," she said.

The old tree trunk had rotted in the middle and parted into two sections. In a powdery crack between the rotting wood, a sapling had pushed its way through from the damp earth and its tender leaves reached upwards towards the mottled sunlight.

An exquisite warmth spread throughout her whole being. One day the scars would fade and Rafael would trust her again. The part of him he still withheld from her – that tender damaged place inside – she would coax back, one day at a time, as she proved her love for him, and he would delight in her freely again. He would call her his beloved, and he would be her Rafael, which means 'our God heals'. She would stand by his side while he proclaimed the words of the King of Israel, the King of the whole earth, words that would resound through the years and echo down the centuries, to heal the nations.

In his heart, she had found her home.

"Blessed are those who have not seen me and yet have believed." JESUS

John 20:29

* * *

Thank you for sharing this journey with me. Your support in the form of a quick review on Amazon website or on Goodreads would be hugely appreciated.

The story of Shana and Rafael continues in
WOMAN OF METTLE
viewBook.at/WomanOfMettle

FREE BOOK BY THE SAME AUTHOR
THE WHITEWASHED TOMB
A biblical fiction novella
Get your copy at www.lindacaddick.com
or buy now at:
viewbook.at/TheWhitewashedTomb

Would you like to be notified about the next publication?
Email linda.inspirepub@gmail.com or visit
www.lindacaddick.com

BOOK CLUBS
Discussion questions can be seen at
www.lindacaddick.com/book-club-qs.html

ABOUT THE AUTHOR

LINDA CADDICK, the daughter of a pioneering farmer in Zimbabwe, spent her school years confined to boarding hostels, but during the holidays wandered freely on the farm, where she developed a lively imagination and a love for nature. Strongly attracted to Cape Town, South Africa, she went to live there at the first opportunity.

Her writing skills were developed during many years of producing descriptive editorial for a restaurant publication. After almost 20 years of city life, her dream of living in the country was realised when she and her husband, together with their two small children, bought a run-down caravan park in the Cape Winelands and turned it into a popular resort for church and family outings.

Linda's passion is to write inspirational novels which illustrate the truth of the gospel through true-to-life characters and stories that will appeal to all.

www.lindacaddick.com
www.Facebook.com/LindaCaddickAuthor
linda.inspirepub@gmail.com

NOTES

To find scriptures instantly, go to: www.biblegateway.com

CHARACTERS FROM THE BIBLE

Yeshua, the Rabbi, Teacher, the Master – Jesus. All quotations taken from scripture except conversation about Shushana's name in Chapter 18, and the prayer at end of Chapter 19.

Peter – one of the Twelve disciples.

Mary mother of Jesus

Mary Magdalene – often portrayed as a prostitute although the Bible does not state this, but to suit the narrative, this view is taken.

Joanna – mentioned in the Bible as the wife of Chuza, who was manager of Herod's household.

All other characters are entirely fictitious.

CHAPTER 2
Describing Judith - Proverbs 31:12

CHAPTER 3
Teaching in parables – Matthew 11:25, 13:34-35
Fishermen left their father to follow the Prophet – Matthew 4:21-22

CHAPTER 4
Pigs killed and madman healed – Luke 8:32-37
Many believe he is the Messiah – John 40-42
Prophecies concerning the Messiah – Matt. 21:6, Micah 5:2,4, Matt. 2:23,
    4:13-16, Isaiah 35:5,6
John, beheaded – Matt. 3:3, Isaiah 40:3 Matt. 14:6-12
Receive the kingdom like a child – Mark 10:15
Secrets of the kingdom, hearts calloused – Luke 8:9-10
Teaching in the boat – Matthew 13:2
Good shepherd, my sheep follow me – John 10:2-16
Eternal life – John 10:28
Thief comes only to steal . . . life to the full – John 10:10
Did not come to condemn the world, but to save it – John 3:16-18
Do not worry – Matthew 6:25,27,34
Seek first the kingdom – Matthew 6:33
Kingdom of God is within you – Luke 17:20-21
Woe to blind guides, hypocrites – Matthew 23:15-17, Matt. 23:24-26
Born of water and the Spirit – John 3:5
What good to gain the world and lose your soul? – Matthew 16:26

CHAPTER 10
Lazarus raised from the dead – John 11:1-44

CHAPTER 11
Healing on the Sabbath – Matthew 12:9-14

Upholds every letter of the law – Matthew 5:17
Trap him in his words – Matthew 22:15
Seek and question – Matthew 7:7-8

CHAPTER 12

Adulteress taken before Yeshua – John 8:2-11(The bible records this event as taking place during the Feast of Tabernacles, but due to the timeline of the story and to support the narrative, poetic licence has been taken to set it during the Passover Festival.)
Yeshua's family come to take charge of him – Mark 3:20-21

CHAPTER 13

Set free from mourning – Isaiah 61:3, Jer. 31:13
Women travelling with the Master – Luke 8:1-4
God is kind to the undeserving – Luke 6:35

CHAPTER 14

My dove in the clefts of the rock – Song of Songs 2:14

CHAPTER 15

Teaching and healing at the temple – Luke 21:37-38, Matt. 21:14
Joanna – Luke 8:3
Mary (Magdalene) – Luke 8:2
Kingdom of God, peace – Isaiah 2:3-4, 61:1-3, 9:6-7, Jeremiah 31:12
Law of love – John 13:34, Matthew 7:12
Spoke with such authority – Matthew 7:9
No one comes to the Father except through me – John 14:6

CHAPTER 16

Come to me all you who are weary – Matthew 11:28
Joanna, Mary – Luke 8:2,3
Only does what his Father commands – John 5:19
Man of sorrows, acquainted with grief – Isaiah 53:3
He has sent me to bind up the broken-hearted – Isaiah 61:1
In this world we all have many troubles – John 16:33
He has turned my mourning into dancing – Jeremiah 31:13
Knew her personally – John 1:47-48

CHAPTER 17

The Rabbi in a Samaritan town; Jesus the Messiah – John 4:4-42
God sent his son – John 3:16
Whoever believes in me will live – John 11:25

CHAPTER 18

He was not beautiful – Isaiah 53:2
Loving others as yourself – Luke 10:27
Treating others as you want them to treat you – Luke 6:31
Prince of Peace – Isaiah 9:6
Galilee a whirl of people, healing every sickness – Matt. 4:23-25

The lame walk, the blind see – Matthew 11:5
God did not send his Son to judge the world, but to save it – John 3:17
CHAPTER 20
Murdering our sons – Matt. 2:16-18
CHAPTER 21
The reign of God – Ps. 23, Isaiah 2:3-4, Isaiah 61:1-3, Isaiah 9:6-7, John 13:34, John 15:17, Matt. 7:12, Revelation 17:15-17, 22:3-5
Trust in God – John 14:1
CHAPTER 22
Simply believe – Mark 11:24
CHAPTER 23
God can turn things around for our good – Romans 8:28
The good shepherd – John 10:3-16
CHAPTER 25
Rabbi in Jerusalem for Passover – John 12:12
Vehemently opposing him, evidence against him – Matthew 26:3-5 &59, Mark 11:18, Mark 12:12
Visiting Mary and Martha – John 12:1
Rabbi describes end times – Luke 21:5-34, Matt. 24:37
Judgement – 2 Cor. 5:10
Destruction by fire – 1 John 4:17
New heaven and new earth – 2 Peter 3:10-13
Don't allow your hearts to be troubled. Trust in God – John 14:1
My Father's house has many rooms, you know the way – Jn. 14:2-4
I am the way and the truth and the life – John 14:6
If you know me you know my Father – John 14:9-11
Longing to draw mankind under the shelter of his wings – Luke 19:41-44, Matthew 23:37
I am going away, but coming back again – John 14:28
The Father will send the Spirit of truth – John 14:16-17
I am leaving my peace with you – John 14:27
Cleansing house of yeast – Exodus 12:19, 1 Corinthians 5:7
Blood on the doorposts – Exodus 12:22-23
Lamb sacrifice – Mark 14:12, Luke 22:7 2 Cor. 5:21
Onset of darkness – Matthew 27:45
Arrested – Matthew 26:57
Applauded him – John 12:13
Crying for his blood. Passed from Herod to Pilate – Luke 23:12-20
Slipped through their fingers – John 7:30
Rode into Jerusalem on a donkey – Matthew 21:6-10
CHAPTER 26
Weeping and wailing – John 16:20, Mark 16:10
"I saw him" – Luke 23:49
Beat him and abused him – Isaiah 52:14

Judas missing – John 13:18

The Master warned us before – Matt. 26:2, Mark 8:31, Luke 9:44-45, John 13:19, 13:33, 14:29, 16:7, 16:20-22, 16:27-28

Mary confirmed what he was saying – Luke 2:34

Confrontation between light and darkness – Jn. 1:4-5, 3:19, Luke 22:53

Not even a sparrow falls – Matthew 10:29-30

Good shepherd who lays his life down for the sheep – John 10:14-18

Peace I leave with you – Matthew 11:30

I come to give you life – John 10:10

"He's alive" – John 20:1, 11-18, Mark 16:9

"Others wouldn't believe" – Luke 24:11, Mark 16:10-11

"I went to the tomb" – John 20:1, 11-18

Peter had seen for himself – Luke 24:12

Inexpressible elation – John 16:20-22

Pay the penalty for sin – Isaiah 53:10-12

Whoever believes in me – John 11:25-26

Life had conquered death – Isaiah 25:8, Hosea 13:14

The Master had appeared to another two – Luke 24:13-32

New covenant – Matthew 26:28, Luke 22:20

Heavenly king – Luke 19:38, John 18:36, Revelation 19:16

Like a mustard seed – Matthew 13:31

Like yeast working its way through the dough – Matthew 13:33

Depths of degradation – Romans 1:21-31

CHAPTER 27

Love and serve one another – John 15:12

With them all by his Spirit – John 14: 16-17&23

CHAPTER 28

Why didn't he use his power to escape? – Matthew 26:52-54

He knew he had come for that purpose – John 18:11, Mk 8:31

Ask whatever you wish in my name – John 15:7

God's willingness to supply for needs - Matthew 6:28-32

CHAPTER 29

Sing, O daughter of Zion – Zephaniah 3:14-17

The chains broke off – Psalm 107:13-15, Isaiah 52:2

God tests and disciplines those He loves – Proverbs 3:11-12, Hebrews 12:11, James 1:2-4, James 1:12

Confessed to Him her struggles – 1 John 1:9

Times of sweet intimacy – Psalms 42:7-8, Isaiah 62:5b

Knowledge of His presence – Matthew 28:20

He had no beauty or majesty to attract us, man of sorrows, pierced for our transgressions, by his wounds we are healed – Isaiah 53:2-12

Many appalled, his appearance so disfigured – Isaiah 52:13-14

Led like a lamb to slaughter – Isaiah 53:7

CHAPTER 30
Yeshua appears to disciples – Mk. 16:14-19, Lk. 24:13-51, Jn. 20:19-29
Feast of Pentecost experience – Acts 2-4
Peter and John healed a crippled man – Acts 3:1-8
Thrown into prison – Acts 4:3
5000 believers – Acts 4:4
Power to change from the inside out – Romans 8:4, Philippians 2:13
Prince of peace reigning forever – Isaiah 9:6-7
To heal the nations - Revelation 22:1-3, Isaiah 2:4, 55:10-13

LINDA CADDICK

CPSIA information can be obtained
at www.ICGtesting.com
Printed in the USA
LVHW022016270220
648407LV00012B/1371